Books by T. A. Belshaw

Tracy's Hot Mail
Tracy's Celebrity Hot Mail
Out of Control
Unspoken
Murder at the Mill

www.trevorbelshaw.com

Edited by Maureen Vincent-Northam

Cover design by: J. D. Smith Design

http://www.jdsmith-design.com

ISBN: 978-1-8382204-5-7

The Legacy
By
T. A. Belshaw

Authors Reach 2021

www.authorsreach.co.uk

www.facebook.com/authorsreach

For my editor, Maureen Vincent-Northam who has
been with me from the start

Chapter 1

Jessica Griffiths opened the door of her little Toyota and climbed out onto the asphalt drive. She pushed the door shut and stepped slowly towards the front door of the old farmhouse. She hesitated on the step, holding the key tightly in her right hand. It was the first time she had been back to the house since Alice, her great grandmother, mentor and soul mate had died.

Taking a deep breath, Jess shoved the key into the yale, twisted it and pushed the door open. She stooped to pick up a small pile of mail, *mostly junk by the looks of it,* and stepped inside closing the door behind her.

The air seemed thick and clung like a shroud; the silence was absolute, even the bane of Alice's life, the big old clock on the wall, had stopped ticking. Her heels echoed eerily as they clicked across the solid timber floor. She turned towards the lounge and stood in the doorway for a moment as she remembered those last few moments she had spent with Alice. The chair she had died in was in the same place, the lion's foot coffee table was at the far end of the room where the paramedics had moved it to give them space to work. Her hospital style bed had been made; Gwen, her carer must have been back to see to that.

Jess dropped her bag on the floor, next to the chair she had sat in to listen to Alice relate the story of her troubled, abuse ridden past, the chair she had sat in to read the memoirs that Alice had asked her to bring down from the attic. There were more volumes up there when she felt ready to retrieve them, it wouldn't be today.

Jess slumped down and stared across at Alice's empty seat and her thoughts immediately returned to that dreadful day. She could see herself kneeling at Alice's side as the old woman stared fixedly at the big clock, she saw herself stroking the back of her hand, telling her that everything was going to be fine, that she shouldn't take any guilt with her as she passed over, that her actions had been totally justified. Alice had responded, moving the nail of her index finger against Jess's hand, letting her know that she had heard and had understood. Then she breathed her last.

The paramedics had arrived shortly after but there was nothing they could do. Jess stood in the kitchen with Gwen, while they performed a perfunctory assessment of her body before zipping it inside a bag and carrying it away. There would be no post mortem, Alice's ninety-nine-year-old body had finally given out, that's all there was to it.

When the emergency services had gone, Gwen made tea and she sat on the sofa with Jess, holding hands and sobbing until there were no tears left.

'Alice gave me a letter for you,' she said eventually. She walked through to the kitchen and returned with a white envelope in her hands. 'She said you weren't to have this until she had gone.'

Gwen picked up her coat, bent forward and gave Jess a kiss on the forehead. 'I'll leave you to read your letter in peace. I'll come back later to tidy things up.'

Jess turned the letter over in her hands and read the front of the envelope. *To Jessica.*

She waited until she heard Gwen close the front door before carefully easing it open. Inside, written in Alice's familiar, neat handwriting was a one-page letter, and a folded bank cheque.

My darling Jessica,

Well, that's it, my dear, I've moved on to wherever it is I've moved on to. Don't cry too much for me, I've lived a long, interesting life that has been full of love, lies, recriminations and revenge. It's been a good life, on the whole, made better by you being a big part of it. You already know all about my altercations with my daughters and granddaughter. I sometimes wonder if they were ever really part of me at all. Then I think of you and our remarkable similarities, you think like me, you act like me, you laugh at the things I laugh at, and you look, pretty much like I did at your age, had we been together in the same room back then, people would have taken us for twins.

I hope you won't feel too ill of me when you read the final chapters of my 1938 memoir, my dear. There was little else to be done and I'd do it again tomorrow, if I was forced to. I hope you understand why I did what I did.

Soon, you will be contacted by a firm of solicitors who are administering my affairs. You might remember their name from my old notebooks. You are the main beneficiary of my estate, but I have put conditions in place. I won't go into them here but please believe me, my love, they are there to protect you as much as the house and the money.

Regarding my funeral.

I'd like you to organise this Jessica as you are the only person I can trust to do as I ask. If you don't feel up to it, please let my solicitors know and they will arrange everything.

I'm not expecting great crowds to turn up to see me off, you'll be lucky to see half a dozen people if I'm honest and I don't really care anyway. I don't want a religious service, though I know they'll still sing a couple of hymns and the vicar will wax lyrical about the afterlife. I'd like to be cremated. I don't see the point in me taking up space on the earth when my consciousness has long left it. I'd be happy if you could sprinkle my ashes somewhere close to my mum and dad's graves though. If the powers that be won't let you do that, then just chuck them around what's left of the farm, though I'd appreciate it if you didn't dump me anywhere in the vicinity of the old milking parlour foundations.

I'm sure I only lasted as long as I did because of the love you showed me, Jessica. Our bond is sincere and secure and nothing, not even death, can break it. Please don't worry when your own end is in sight and you begin to see the misty light, emanating from the tunnel in your dreams. When you arrive, you'll find me waiting to take you inside. This I promise.

Goodbye, my darling. I wish you luck and happiness every day for the rest of your life. We both know it won't be like that, it never is, but I wish it for you nonetheless. I also hope that before too long you'll see what a louse Calvin is. Please be careful, Jessica, that man is dangerous.

I also wish you good luck in your future choice of men, though as you are pretty much a clone of me, I'm not going to hold what little breath is left inside of me. We can't really help ourselves, we are attracted to 'bad boys', they fascinate us, we have to know if we can tame them. Well, we can't. I finally gave up trying and I've no doubt that one day, you will too. Until then, just be as careful as you can, enjoy the fun times but don't allow the bad times to get out of hand. One slap is one slap too many. Don't fear being lonely, Jessica. Solitude has its benefits.

Sending you all my love from this life and the next (if there is one).

Your loving great grandmother,
Alice.

Jess read the letter twice before opening the envelope to slip it back inside. Stuck in the bottom of the envelope was a cheque for two thousand pounds,

made out to Gwen. On the back of the cheque Alice had
written a note.

*Don't dare refuse to take this money you silly,
wonderful woman. You deserve every penny,
and more. I don't know what I'd have done
without you. Love, Alice.*

Jess dragged the coffee table back to its usual spot,
laid the cheque in the centre and sat her empty mug on
top of it so that Gwen would easily find it when she
came back to clean up.
     She was about to leave when she remembered the,
as yet unread, 1939 memoir that Alice had slipped into
the drawer of her bedside cabinet. She pulled it out,
held it to her chest and spoke aloud.
     'I wonder what other secrets you have for me to
discover... what was it that Amy called you... Alice,
Hussy?'
     Jess dropped the letter and notebook into her bag
and left the house.

     The funeral passed off as well as could be expected.
The autumn weather was glorious and no one needed to
wear a top coat. As she walked into the crematorium
chapel, Jess thought back to Alice's memoir, where she
had described the day of her father's funeral...
     *It was the perfect day for a funeral, if you can have
such a thing. In the films and in books, a funeral is
always held in foul, wet, windy, weather, as though the
deceased was playing a final practical joke on the
mourners. My father, it seemed, had ordered wall to
wall sunshine for his funeral. This made me happy for
two reasons. One, I wouldn't have to stand around,
shivering while water dripped down my neck from the
branches of the old oak, and two, the blue sky gave me
the crazy idea that the sun was celebrating his
reunification with the love of his life. This thought*

cheered me, and I clung on to it all the way through the service.

'You ordered up some beautiful weather for your big day too, Nana. I hope you're reunified with your mum and dad now,' Jess whispered.

Alice was remarkably correct in her prediction of the number of people that would attend. There were six, including the man holding the service.

Gwen sat on the front row with Jess while Alice's daughters, Martha and Marjorie, sat at the back along with Jess's mum, Nicola who slipped in just as the service was getting underway.

They sang along to the same hymn that had been sung at Alice's father's funeral all those years before. Jesus Wants Me for a Sunbeam and All Things Bright and Beautiful, which Jess had chosen, knowing Alice wouldn't have minded. The funeral celebrant, conducting the service, kept God out of it in the main, but he did slip in a prayer for Alice after Jess read out the eulogy that she had written herself. She did hear Martha and Nicola splutter when she waxed lyrical about Alice's generosity.

At the end of the service, the curtains closed in front of the coffin and Jess whispered her final goodbye. She left the chapel with Gwen, to find Martha, Marjorie and her own mother waiting for her.

'Jessica, firstly I'd like to thank you for organising the funeral, though I think it should really have had a proper vicar leading it.' Martha looked around the empty car park. 'I thought there might be a few more here to see her off, but then again, she wasn't the most popular of people.'

'She outlived all those who would have wanted to be here, Grandma,' replied Jess.

'I suppose that's one way of looking at it,' Martha replied. 'Now, listen, Jessica. We need to have a talk about the future. I've had a letter from a firm of solicitors representing my mother and it seems there is something for both myself and Marjorie in her will. I have to admit I'm quite surprised by this news, but I sort of knew she'd see sense in the end.'

'She's seen sense,' echoed Marjorie, who had been under Martha's spell from the day she was born.

'I haven't seen a letter, but then again, I haven't been back to my flat since Nana died. There might be something waiting for me there.'

'There might not be, Jessica, don't be disappointed if there isn't, maybe my mother did the decent thing after all.' She narrowed her eyes and looked hard at Jess. 'Let me know if you do get one though. We can all go to the solicitor's together.'

With that she turned tail and strode purposefully across the car park to Nicola's battered old Ford. Marjorie trotted along behind.

'Don't forget. Let me know straight away if you receive a letter.' Martha slid into the back seat of the car and slammed the door behind her.

'Well, I'm surprised at that, Jessica,' Gwen looked puzzled, 'Alice always said that her daughters would never see a penny.'

'I don't mind, Gwen,' Jess replied. 'It's only money, though what my grandma would do with it at her age is anyone's guess.' She walked across to her Toyota and opened the passenger door for Gwen. 'I think she just likes to be in control of everything. She'll be thinking she's the head of the family now.'

'I just think it's sad to see families split over money.' Gwen slipped inside and shut the door behind her. She fastened her seatbelt as Jess climbed in alongside. 'When do you get her ashes and what are you going to do with them?' she asked.

'I should have them in a couple of days, Gwen. As for what I'll do...' she smiled and tapped the side of her nose. 'I've got a cunning plan,' she said.

Chapter 2

Jessica stepped through the lychgate and strode purposefully along the grey-slabbed path that divided the graves at the front of the Norman church. She nodded to an old couple who were sitting on one of the memorial benches that lined the path and made her way down the side of the church to the even larger collection of graves at the rear. She smiled as the warm October sun peeked out from behind a patchy cloud, it was a perfect day for a second funeral.

Jessica flicked her head so that her dark, shoulder length, chestnut curls fell away from her face, and strolled amongst the mostly, ancient gravestones until she reached a set of two, set side by side under a huge oak branch that hung over the stone boundary wall. Jessica looked over her shoulder to ensure she wasn't being watched, then knelt between the two graves and pulled an oblong, cedar box from inside the hessian bag she had carried carefully into the churchyard.

'Here we are, Nana,' she whispered, looking over her shoulder again. 'I won't tell if you don't.'

Jessica put her hand into the bag, pulled out a small, gardening trowel and dug a neat hole about a foot deep in the centre of the gap between the graves. She opened the box and took out a plastic bag containing the cremated remains of Alice Mollison, her great grandmother. Jessica took a metal nail file from her handbag, pierced the bag, then dragged the file across to open up one end. Picking up the bag carefully, she tipped the contents into the hole and laid the empty bag on top of the ashes.

'I hope you met your mum and dad again, Nana, but just in case you didn't, I'm putting you in here so that you're reunited, on earth at least.'

Jessica fished around in her bag until she found a silver locket that Alice had given her as an eighteenth birthday present. It contained what on a casual inspection, was two photographs of the same young woman, but if one was to look a little closer the differences, though slight, were distinctive.

'And here's the both of us together, forever, Nana.'

Jessica dropped the locket on top of the ashes and backfilled it with the trowel, then she stamped the newly dug earth down and stood for a few minutes thinking about Alice. Not the dreadful events in her life that she had described so vividly in her memoirs, but the happy times, the weekend sleepovers, the birthday surprises and the loving, sage advice that she had passed on.

'Bye Bye, Nana. Sleep softly,' she whispered as she stowed away the garden trowel and stepped away from the grave. 'I'll pop back now and again. I hope you're happy, wherever you are.'

Wiping away a tear, Jess retraced her steps and walked back through the lychgate, onto the main road. As she reached her little Toyota car, her phone rang. The number wasn't listed on her contacts.

'Hello.'

A deep male voice with an educated accent, replied.

'Hello. I'm trying to contact Ms Jessica Griffiths.'

'You've found her,' said Jess, wondering if she was about to receive a scam call.

'Ah, that's good,' said the man. 'My name is Bradley Wilson of Wilson and Beanney Associates. We are a firm of solicitors. We sent out a letter a couple of weeks ago but we haven't had a reply as yet. Your mobile number was listed as next of kin in the case file. I wonder if we could make an appointment?'

'I haven't been staying at my flat. I had a few problems... but the answer is, possibly, it depends what it's about.'

Bradley was quick to reassure her. 'The company I represent was given the task of administering your great grandmother's will. There is also a Family Protection Trust that she set up a couple of years ago. Mrs Alice Mollison was a relative of yours, I believe.'

'That's right, but it was Ms Mollison, she never married.'

'Ah, I see, but I do have the right person. Ms Mollison was your relative?'

'She was, I've just been at her graveside as it happens.'

'Oh, I'm so sorry to have disturbed you,' Bradley Wilson said, sounding as if he genuinely meant it.

'That's okay, I'm back on Main Street now,' replied Jessica.

'Thank goodness for that. I would have felt guilty all day.'

Jessica felt that she liked the man already. Suddenly a light flashed in her brain.

'Wilson. Beanney... Are you the same Wilson, Kendall and Beanney Solicitors that used to have a Godfrey Wilson as a partner?'

'He was my great grandfather,' said Bradley. Did you ever meet hi...? No, you can't have, you're far too young, Godfrey died about forty years ago.'

'Alice knew him very well,' replied Jess. 'It looks like she's been using your company's services for eighty years or so.'

'Now that's what I call a loyal client,' Bradley said with a laugh. 'So, how should we proceed? Could you spare a little time to go over the details this week?'

'I'm good all day tomorrow, and I'm okay again on Friday afternoon. I'm tied up the rest of the week.'

'Friday afternoon it is then. I look forward to meeting you, Ms Griffiths. Shall we say, two o'clock. Our offices are in...'

'I know where they are,' replied Jess. 'I drive past there most days.' Jess didn't mention the fact that she had parked up outside those offices whilst researching the novel she was about to write, using Alice's hand written memoirs as the source material.

'Fabulous. Until Friday then.'

The smooth-as-honey voice vanished, leaving Jess wondering why she felt so attracted to a man she had never met, what the heck a Family Protection Trust was, and how it would affect her life.

Chapter 3

'You have to go back to your flat sometime, Babes. You must be sick of wearing the same clothes.' Sam clicked 'like' on the Facebook post she'd been reading and looked across at her best friend.

'I know, Sam. I've been telling myself that all week. I know you want the place to yourself but what happened really freaked me out. I used to love my flat, but after that shenanigans with Calvin, well, it just wouldn't be the same now. It had a lovely atmosphere, but now he's spoiled it.'

Sam sat on the sofa next to Jessica and put her hand on hers.

'I'm not chucking you out, you silly mare. I just think it's something you need to do, even if it's just to get a car load of your clothes. You won't get away with t shirt and jeans at the Sapphire bar on Saturday. They won't let you in.'

'I'm not sure I'm going if I'm honest, Sam. It's not really my thing, and I don't like playing gooseberry, you know that.' Jess pulled a face.

'Don't be silly. Jamie won't mind, he likes you.' Sam patted her hand reassuringly.

'I'd still be the spare in a three,' Jess replied. She thought for a moment, then slapped both hands on her thighs and stood up. 'Come on, I'll get my big girl's pants on and I'll go back to the flat. There's a solicitor's letter I need to pick up anyway. I'm meeting him this afternoon.'

Sam got her keys from the mantle.

'No going back on it this time, lady. You need to get inside that place again to let the emotional phantoms out. You've nothing to fear. Calvin has long gone, we took his keys, remember.'

Jess pulled on her overcoat and wrapped a white, knitted scarf around her neck. The weather had taken a cold turn during the last week.

As she climbed into Sam's Volkswagen Golf, Jess's mind went back to the last time she had been in the flat. The day her once funny, loving partner, Calvin had attacked her and tried to strangle Sam. The day her world had fallen apart, the day she received that awful phone call telling her that her beloved Nana was dying. Together they had managed to fight the deranged Calvin off and had thrown him out of the flat. She had heard nothing from him since, although he almost certainly knew where she was staying. She found herself continually staring in the rear-view mirror when she was out in the car in case he was following her and, at night, when Sam had gone to bed, she'd turn out the lights and peek through a crack in the curtains to see if he was keeping her under surveillance. Calvin wasn't a man to give in when he thought he'd done nothing wrong, which was just about one hundred percent of the time.

It was a short drive across town. Sam pulled into the empty, double parking space, pulled on the handbrake and killed the engine. She turned her head to the left and gave Jess what she hoped was an encouraging smile.

'Come on, tiger, let's do this.'

Jess took a deep breath, undid her seatbelt and climbed out onto the tarmac. She looked nervously at the entrance to the flat, thought for a moment about getting back into the car, then summoned up all her courage and slammed the door behind her.

Sam clicked the lock button on her fob as if she had read Jess's mind. She waved the key at her best friend. 'Too late,' she said.

Jess took another deep breath, reached into her bag, pulled out the flat keys and stepped smartly across to the front door. She slipped the key into the lock, turned it and pushed the heavy wooden door open.

She jumped as Sam put her hand on her left shoulder.

'Shall I go first? He won't be in there, love. His car isn't here.'

'I know,' Jess replied. 'It isn't that...well, it is, but it's mainly that I was so happy here for so long. Until those last few weeks, I was the happiest I had been in my life. Bloody Calvin.'

'Try to remember the times before he moved in,' Sam suggested. 'The times I came around in the evenings and we'd get riotously drunk watching Dirty Dancing for the hundredth time.'

Jess bit her lip, put one foot on the doormat, then stepped back again. 'I can't...'

Sam slipped behind and gave Jess a two-armed push. She hurtled forwards and steadied herself at the foot of the stairs. 'That's cheating.' She laughed nervously.

Sam pointed towards the landing. 'Up, Missis,' she ordered.

Jess climbed the stairs slowly. When she reached the top step, she stuck her head into the flat and looked left and right. The place seemed to be as they had left it a few weeks before. She blew out her cheeks and stepped into the open lounge. Sam followed, reassuring words on her tongue.

The flat was spotless. Jess tried to remember when she had last cleaned. It would have been her that did it. Cleaning was women's work, as Calvin had often told her, and, he had insisted, it was her flat after all. Calvin was a stickler for cleanliness and didn't like even a single cushion to be out of place, but he drew the line at starting up the Dyson himself. He had once called Jess into the bathroom and showed her a smudge of dirt on the floor of the shower. She had had to clean it and rinse off the chemical spray before he would go in.

'Let's be fair, Jess, you wouldn't like to have athletes' foot, either.'

Jess, who had never suffered from the fungal infection, had said nothing and went back to making their lunch.

Jess wandered into the kitchen, filled the empty kettle and put it back on the stand. 'We may as well have a coffee while we're here.'

She reached into the cupboard and took out a jar of good-quality instant. Calvin's designer packet of Barista was in its place on the bottom shelf. On impulse she picked it up and shook it. *I'm sure that was almost used up,* she thought. She remembered Calvin complaining that he'd be running out soon and needed a top up when she did the weekly shop.

Puzzled, Jess walked through to the bedroom. The bed was made, but there was nothing of his in the bedside cabinet, nor anything in the built-in wardrobe. It was the same in the spare room.

Jess breathed a sigh of relief. Sam had helped her clear all his things out the morning after Nana had died. They had left his stuff outside on the parking bay as they had promised they would. She hoped he was there in time to pick it all up before the local lads spotted it. She hadn't hung around long enough to find out.

She tutted at herself for caring, and walked through to the bathroom. Just inside the door she stopped and sniffed. Tom Ford aftershave, there was no mistaking it. Calvin was the only man she had ever known that used it. It was just too expensive for most people. Jess couldn't even afford to buy it for him as a Christmas present.

'Blimey, that scent hangs around,' she said aloud.

Sam came into the bathroom and handed Jess a mug of coffee. She sipped her own and sniffed.

'Ugh. I have expensive tastes myself as you well know, but I never could understand why anyone would pay hundreds of pounds for that muck. It's awful.'

'You get used to it,' replied Jess. 'And, if you can still smell it weeks after you dabbed it on, then it might explain the cost.'

'Nothing lasts that long in the air,' said Sam suspiciously. 'Oh shit,' she said and pointed to the lavatory seat.

Jess groaned as she saw the envelope sitting on the closed, grey, lid.

'Shit,' she echoed. Turning on her heels, she hurried out into the lounge.

Sam found her sitting on the sofa with her head in her hands when she followed a few seconds later, the letter in her right hand. She put her coffee mug on the table and set next to Jess.

'Shall we burn it, shred it or dissolve it in hydrochloric acid?' she asked.

Jess sighed heavily and took the letter from her friend. On the front was the single word 'Jess' written in his elegant handwriting, it was surrounded by a drawing of a broken heart. With shaking hands, Jess tore it open and slid out a single page. She wiped a tear from her cheek and unfolded the letter.

My Darling, Jess

So, it has come to this.
Never, even in my worst nightmare did I think
I would have to write this letter. I thought we
were bonded together, solid, unbreakable. I
thought our love was a thing of pure beauty
and could never die.
I hope we can put this thing behind us and
start over. I have already forgiven you for
your over reaction and I hope you can forgive
me for any perceived failings. I didn't mean
this to happen, I honestly didn't. I like Sam
and I would never want to hurt her, but I was
forced into a corner by lies and jealousy and I
did what I tend to do when I find myself in
those circumstances, and tried to defend
myself as best I could. I was forced to do
similar things as a child, at home when my
father turned on me. It's not something I like
to shout about, but it kept me alive back then. I
suppose I don't know my own strength when

I'm cornered and in fear. I hope Sam is okay, please give her my best regards. I know I probably frightened her and I really regret that.

The thing is, Jess, I was going through a bad patch. I was struggling to find work, and you, my usual reliable rock, was spending all your time with your Nana. I can understand why you did that, but I felt lost and alone over that last couple of weeks. You were always there for me in the past, and I didn't know who I could turn to.

I ended up falling into Tania's trap. She had been trying to tempt me for weeks, cornering me after the classes I gave at Uni, following me into the café when I dropped in for coffee. I wouldn't normally have been so weak, but I was so lost, my darling, I just needed the company.

I'm not blaming you, or Nana, for it. Sometimes things can't be helped and this was one of those times. If Nana hadn't fallen ill when she did, none of this would ever have happened. It was just fate, trying to test us.

I haven't been in touch by phone or text because I thought I'd give you a chance to calm down. I know you were upset by the whole thing and your Nana's death won't have helped with that.

You may have news about her will by the way. There is a solicitor's letter with a few others, mainly junk mail and bills, in the drawer of the coffee table. I hope there are good tidings inside.

Don't forget your friends when you are rich. Ha Ha.

Speaking of money. I'm managing to survive by doing a bit of home tutoring and I've been sofa surfing for a while. I really could do with moving back in here, but the rent and utility bills are due and I don't have the funds to pay them. I don't know if you mean to keep the place on or whether you've moved in with Sam, permanently. Could we meet up here, or on neutral ground, to discuss things? I'm really getting a bit desperate now.

All my stuff is in a friend's garage and it's a right pain when I need something. When I say friend, he only put me up for a few nights. He said his girlfriend didn't feel right having sex, with me sleeping on the sofa. I snuck back in here for the odd night, though I only brought a bag with me, I didn't want to move all my stuff back before I knew we were going to be all right again. I always kept a spare key in the car. I know that was a bit naughty of me but I was scared of losing the main set you gave me and being locked out.

So, Jess, my darling. I hope you have calmed down. Even if Sam can't forgive me, I think that maybe you can. We had so much, let's not throw it away over a silly moment brought on by extreme stress.

We were so good as a partnership, Jess. We were meant to be together. I even gave up my mother to be with you, she didn't think you were good enough for me, but I didn't care.

Please leave your reply where you found this. I'll pick it up the next time I'm passing. I always ring the bell before I let myself in, just in case you're here.

My love for you remains as strong as it ever was and I think, deep down, you feel the same. Please don't throw it all away now. Take your time and remember what we had.

I love you.

Calvin.

Xxxx

When she had finished reading, Jess dropped the letter on the coffee table and burst into floods of angry tears. Sam wrapped her arms around her.

Eventually, Jess stopped sobbing, eased herself out of Sam's arms, and still sniffing, pulled a tissue from the box on the coffee table and blew her nose.

Sam picked up the letter. 'Do you mind if I read it?'

Jess nodded and blew her nose again.

'He's right, we did have a lovely relationship once.'

Sam snorted as she reached the part about her.

'Arrogant bastard... Sorry, what was that?'

'I'm just saying. It wasn't all bad. We were really close for a long time.'

'What! Jess, please tell me you aren't considering taking him back? You have to be kidding me.'

She stared hard at Jessica, who dropped her head and began to sob again.

Chapter 4

Martha lay on her side, her turban-covered head nestled into the deep pile of down pillows. Her bedside clock read four minutes past seven.

'Late again,' she said under her breath.

She rolled onto her back and studied the thick crack in the ceiling that she was sure had spread further over the last few days. She would have liked to get it fixed but the young man she had booked to give her a quote had looked like a bit of a rogue builder, although he claimed to be a member of the Master Builder's Federation. Martha didn't believe a word of it, there were a lot of rogues about these days. At one time you could get a local builder who would take pride in his work, knowing that if he messed up, the word would quickly get about, but now, all the trades seem to come from a minimum of twenty miles away and they wouldn't give a damn about receiving a complaint. Just look at that Rogue Traders program on TV. The country was full of cowboy builders.

Only last week, old Mrs Hardy a few houses down the lane had been told by a 'passing builder' that the roof of her old bungalow looked in danger of collapse. After an inspection, he blew out his cheeks, shook his head and told her it couldn't be repaired for a penny under ten thousand pounds. The silly old woman had agreed to have the work done, but luckily her son came over to visit at the weekend and he had brought in his best friend, a builder himself, to have a look. Finding no fault, he suggested they ring the police. Mrs Hardy's son, who was no saint, was reluctant to get them involved, so he just rang the number on the card she had been given, and cancelled the job, warning the builder that he was onto him and he shouldn't show his face around the area any time soon.

Martha scratched an itch just below her right eye and looked towards the door.

'Marjorie, where in God's name have you got to?'
she muttered.

She shook her head and thought about the meeting
with the solicitor later that day. With just the tiniest,
and long awaited, bit of luck she so thoroughly
deserved, she wouldn't have to worry about the cost of
repairing a crack in the ceiling ever again. She could
afford to get the modern equivalent of Sir Christopher
Wren to do the job if she felt like it. An unexpected
mention in her late mother's will could mean she would
never want for money again. The old girl had been
loaded when she died. The big, old farmhouse she had
lived in and the couple of acres of land around it, must
be worth at least three quarters of a million pounds
these days. Then there were the proceeds of her land
sales. The farm had once boasted a hundred acres but
Alice's astute selling of parcels of land had netted her a
fortune over the years. She had invested a lot of the
money in London property and stocks and shares. God
knows how much those assets were worth now.

'About time,' she said loudly as her sister, Marjorie,
entered the room carrying a rattling breakfast tray.

'I'm sorry, I... well, I dropped the pan with the eggs
in and had to cook some more, by the time I had
cleaned up, the tea was getting cold so I had to make
another pot.'

'I hope the eggs are properly cooked today.' Martha
scowled at her sister. 'Yesterday, they were so
undercooked they resembled mucus. How many times
do I have to say, boil them for three minutes and twenty
seconds, precisely.'

'Yes, Martha, I'm sorry, but the handle of the pan
was hot and—'

'Just give me the tray and stop wittering,' Martha
scolded.

Marjorie pulled open the thickly-lined curtains to
allow the early morning sun to light up the room.

'It's a nice day for an inheritance,' she quipped.

'Don't count your chickens just yet, Marjorie,' replied Martha. 'You know what the tight old so and so was like. Remember the time I went cap in hand to her when Roger claimed a quarter of this house in the divorce court? She wouldn't give me a penny to help me out of the mess.'

'It was good job I had some savings, wasn't it, Martha?' Marjorie walked stiffly across to the bed and sat on the corner.

Martha coughed on the piece of toast she had just put into her mouth.

'Don't go digging up all that again. You'll never let me forget that for once in your life, you helped me with something, will you? Put another record on, Marjorie, I'm fed up of hearing that one.'

'I'm sorry, Martha,' said Marjorie, quietly. 'I won't mention it again. I might not need to after we've been to the solicitor today though. I didn't think we'd get a penny from Mother, but we're both mentioned in the will. I fully expected her to leave everything to our Jessica.'

Martha put the crust of the toast back onto her plate and sliced the top off one of the eggs with a knife. Inspecting the consistency of the yolk, she nodded, and dug a teaspoon into it.

'Well, if we are the main beneficiaries, don't you go throwing your share about. I'll find some nice, safe investments for you. And, watch out for fortune seeking men. You would be taken advantage of far too easily.'

'I'm seventy-six now, Martha, I don't think any men will be interested in me.'

'You'd be surprised, Marjorie,' said Martha bitterly. 'If I can get caught out, there's little hope for you.'

Martha finished her egg and decided the quality wasn't quite good enough to warrant eating the second one. Instead, she poured tea into a delicate china cup, poured in a small amount of milk, stirred it gently, and took a large sip.

'At least the tea is made properly,' she said.

Marjorie got to her feet. 'I'd better get on with running your bath.'

'Leave it for twenty minutes, I don't want to bathe on a full stomach.'

'Yes, Martha,' replied Marjorie.

'You can get in after me.' Martha ordered. 'We'll share the water. Our gas bill was enormous over the last quarter.'

Marjorie walked to the door. 'I'll come back for the tray when you're in the bath, shall I?'

Martha nodded, picked up another piece of toast and bit into it.

'Off you go then. Make sure the kitchen is properly cleaned, I don't want to be stepping on bits of egg shell when I come down.'

When Marjorie had taken away the breakfast tray, Martha got out of bed, removed her nightgown and slipped into a striped bath robe. Removing her turban, she studied herself in the dressing table mirror, running her fingers through her sparse, white hair before holding a hand mirror behind her head. Cursing the latest, seriously expensive, but useless, scalp cream, she walked quickly to the bathroom where she dampened her hair in the sink before rubbing a generous handful of the supposed miracle, steroid cream, onto her head.

Martha had always been envious of her mother's shoulder length, chestnut curls. When Alice was young, people used to compare her to the Hollywood actress, Rita Hayworth, and indeed, there had been a remarkable likeness. Martha wasn't as fortunate, she hadn't been exactly unattractive when she was young, but she could hardly be classed as a beauty. Her hair had always been straight and thin, almost lank. Even in old age, Alice, her mother, had managed to keep a full head of hair, she had even retained some of her natural colour until she was well into her sixties.

Martha assumed she got her looks, and her hair, from Frank, her father, who had died somewhere in the

Atlantic the year after her birth. Maybe she got the hair problems from Frank's mother, Edna, was it? How was the hair gene passed down? She doubted it was a matriarchal thing, after all, her daughter and granddaughter both had dark, healthy, heads of hair. She decided to blame it on Alice anyway. They had always hated each other. There was talk of her mother practicing witchcraft in the attic of the farmhouse. Perhaps she had placed a curse on her first born, or simply used toxic chemicals when she washed her hair in the bath when she was a baby. Alice was capable of anything.

After bathing, she filled the sink and rinsed out the sticky cream with fresh warm water, then she returned to the bathroom, calling to Marjorie on the way.

'The bath's all yours, be quick, the water isn't too hot.'

In the bedroom, Martha pulled on a black and grey checked skirt and a white, silk blouse before opening a hat box that sat on the dressing table. She took out a steel-grey wig and pulled it over her patchy clumps of hair. She sat for a few minutes, tugging it first to the right, then the left, then the back. Finally satisfied, she applied a dab of rouge to her cheeks and went downstairs to the lounge where she turned on the radio and listened to the latest international news program. Radio 4 and the BBC TV news were her only source of information. She had cancelled the newspapers to save money some years before.

A few minutes later she heard Marjorie come down the stairs and five minutes after that, her younger sister walked into the lounge carrying a tray laden with Martha's favourite china tea service. She was wearing a maroon skirt, a cream blouse and a navy cardigan.

'I thought I'd use the best china as it's a special day,' she said.

Martha pursed her lips, looked Marjorie up and down, then shook her head.

'You aren't going to a solicitor's office dressed like that, surely?'

'What's wrong with it?' Marjorie looked down at her chest.

'It's not really fitting for the occasion is it? We're attending the formal reading of a will; we're not going to a coffee morning at the Women's Institute.'

'I... I thought.'

'Don't think, Marjorie. It seldom works out well for either of us.'

Marjorie looked confused. 'What should I wear then?'

Martha sighed. 'I'm not your dresser,' she said, testily. 'Wear the black knitted suit you wore to Mother's funeral. That will look much more business-like.'

'The hat had a veil on it,' Marjorie protested.

Martha slammed her hand down onto the dining table making Marjorie jump.

'Then don't wear the bloody hat.'

Sniffling, Marjorie left the room.

'And don't take all day about it,' called Martha. 'Nicola is picking us up at eleven.'

Marjorie's tear-stained face appeared around the dining room door.

'Why are we leaving so early, Martha?' She sniffed, pulled a handkerchief from the sleeve of her cardigan and wiped her nose. 'The appointment isn't until one-thirty.'

'We're going to have a look at our old home, Marjorie. I want to see what state the outbuildings are in. I've got big plans for that place.'

'You know you can stay with me as long as you need to, don't you, darling?' Sam took her arm from around Jess's shoulder. 'Sorry, love, it's gone to sleep.'

Jess smiled a weak smile and snuffled before taking a new tissue and blowing her nose again.

'Thank you, Sam. You won't have to put up with me for too much longer. I'll start looking for a place next week.'

'You've got a place. A lovely place. Don't let that bastard, Calvin, stop you living your life. Change the locks, get a bloody restraining order. Hire a hit man...' Sam aimed a finger gun at her.

Jess looked around the room, then hung her head.

'I've been so happy here. Everything was going so well, then... well, all this happened.' She put both hands to her face and began to sniffle again. 'I can't stay here, Sam. He ruined it, everything was so perfect and he went and ruined it.'

'To be honest, if I were you, I wouldn't let him have the satisfaction of knowing he can still get to me, Jess. But then, I haven't just lost my beloved Nana. Maybe I wouldn't be so dogmatic if I had.'

Jess got to her feet. 'I'll get all my stuff together.' She took another look around the flat where she had been so happy for so long. *I'll leave all the stuff in the kitchen for now*, she thought, then went to the cupboard in the hall and returned with a roll of black plastic bags. She tore a couple off, dropped the roll on the coffee table, and walked quickly through to the bedroom.

'Could you get all my stuff from the bathroom, Sam?' she called as she opened up her wardrobe and grabbed an armful of clothes from the rail.

Half an hour later, she stood in the lounge staring at half a dozen, full to bursting, bin bags that they had piled up at the top of the staircase.

'Six bags,' moaned Jess. 'Is that all my life is worth?'

Sam patted her on the back. 'Come on, Jess. You'll build a new life with someone worth sharing it with.' She picked up one of the bags and struggling with the bulk, hoisted it to her chest. 'Blimey! What have you put in here, your Neolithic fossil collection?'

'You picked the one with the jeans and winter coat in.' Jess forced a smile and grabbed two of the lighter bags. 'Come on, let's get them loaded up.'

Ten minutes later, the bags had been transferred to the car, the cupboards had been checked and the utility bills and solicitor's letter had been stuffed into Jess's shoulder bag. Sam waited at the bottom of the stairs as Jess took one last, lingering look around.

'Give me a moment, Sam,' she said quietly.

Sam nodded and returned to the car leaving the front door open.

Jess was lost in her own thoughts for a while, then made a decision. She looked back down the stairway to make sure Sam hadn't returned, then she sat on the sofa, opened the drawer under the coffee table, took out a notepad, a small white envelope and a pen.

Dear Calvin,

I cannot express how sad and utterly dejected I feel as I write this. I thought we would go on for ever. I really believed you loved me. I am devastated. My life has been turned on its head. I lost the two people I cared about most in the world in the space of an hour. I can't see any way back for us, Calvin, not after what happened. I could have forgiven the infidelity, I could have put up with the fact that you were short of money and couldn't pay your share of the bills again, I was used to that, but I can never forgive, or forget the way you acted towards Sam and me that awful afternoon. People who really love someone, as much you

*professed to, don't do things like that, Calvin,
no matter how tough a time they are going
through. You think you have had it hard? just
imagine, if you can, what my life is like now,
bereft of my darling Nana, pretty much
estranged from my entire family, an empty
heart and feeling very much alone. It's a good
job I had Sam to care for me or I don't know
what I might have done.*

*I can't move back into the flat, Calvin. It holds
one bad memory too many. I could never be
happy here again. I'm staying at Sam's for
now, but I'll get myself a new place soon. Don't
go thinking I've suddenly become rich, either.
I'm not. Surprisingly, Nana mentioned her
daughters in her will. I think they'll get the
farm and most of the money that she left. I'm
hoping for a few personal items to remember
her by, but that's about it. No fortune, no rent-
free flat, nothing. I'm going to have to rebuild
my life from scratch.*

*The rent is paid on the flat until the New Year,
that's when the lease runs out. I'm cancelling
all the direct debits for Council Tax, water,
electricity, gas, etc so if you want to stay here
until then you'll have to pay them yourself.*

*I won't come back here again, Calvin. You can
keep all the kitchen equipment; I'll get new
when I'm settled in my new place. I hope you
manage to find happiness. What we had was
so special that I can't find it in my heart to
hate you. Part of me still loves you, but I have
to steel myself to the fact that there is no future
for us. Please don't try to get in touch by phone
or in person. I'm going to try to remember you
as you were when we first met, not the
controlling, selfish man you became. Did you
change, or was that Calvin inside you all the*

*time? I'm going to give you the benefit of the
doubt on that one.
Take care, Calvin. I wish you a happy life and
I hope you find someone you can love and
respect. I'm sorry that I couldn't live up to
your expectations of me.
Love Jess. xxx*

Jess read the letter through, cursed herself for adding the kisses and thought about rewriting the whole thing in a more un-personal manner, but when she heard Sam call up the stairs, she whispered, *'sod it'* to herself, folded the letter in half and slipped it into the envelope.

She scrawled Calvin, across the front and just stopped herself adding more kisses. She had been so used to putting them on the bottom of every text message she sent him that it was an almost automatic thing to do.

'Coming.' Jess went to drop the envelope on the coffee table but remembering how Calvin had left her letter on the toilet seat of all places, she decided to do likewise.

Back in the car, she looked at her watch.

'Goodness, look at the time. I'm due at the solicitors in forty minutes and I need to get something ironed first. Everything will be creased after being in those bags.'

As Sam's Volkswagen pulled out onto the main street, a black BMW slipped out of the parking lot belonging to the next block of flats and parked up in the space that Sam's Golf had just vacated. Calvin slid out of the driver's seat, looked over his shoulder to make sure that Jess wasn't about to return, and pulling a single key from his pocket, let himself into the flat.

Chapter 6

By the time Nicola's battered old Ford pulled up outside, Martha's earlier good mood had gradually worsened and she had been pacing the strip of patterned matting in front of the window for a good fifteen minutes. Her vexation wasn't lessened when she spotted Nicola take a swig from a bottle before opening the door of the car to wave in her direction.

'Not only unforgivably late, but under the influence of alcohol as usual.' Martha sucked in through her teeth and scowled.

'Should I ring for a taxi then?' Marjorie asked, already knowing the answer.

'Do you think I'm made of money?' Martha turned her anger on the only target within earshot. 'We'll have to risk it with Nicola. I want to look around what's left of the farm and I'm not going to pay a taxi driver to sit twiddling his thumbs while I explore. Nicola can do that. It's the one thing she's good at, apart from drinking herself into oblivion. I don't know where she gets the money to afford the habit. That part time job at the supermarket must only just cover the rent.'

Martha stormed out of the house leaving Marjorie to close the door and scurry along behind as she marched across the tarmacked drive. By the time she reached the car, Nicola had climbed out and opened the rear door for her.

'Hello, Mum,' she said, nervously.

Martha pointed at her wrist watch. 'What time do you call this? We said eleven, not a quarter past.'

'I'm sorry, Mum, I got stuck behind a tractor on the lane.'

Martha gave her a withering look and slid into the back seat as Marjorie scurried around the back of the car to the other side.

'You're late, dear,' she said.

Nicola ignored her, climbed back into the car and started it up as Marjorie slammed the back door shut.

'Seat belt,' Martha snapped.

Nicola sighed, pulled the belt over her shoulder and clicked the tongue into place, 'Are we still going to Nana's, or—'

'We're going to *The Farm!*' spat Martha. 'It is no longer my mother's property. She gave it up the day she died.'

'It will be ours later on today, won't it, Martha?' Marjorie looked smugly at the back of Nicola's head.

'Oh, have you read the will already? That *is* good news,' Nicola replied. 'I hope you won't forget me when you come into your inheritance.' She looked over her shoulder towards Martha.

'You'll need to do something about that alcohol habit of yours before I hand over a penny,' said Martha, caustically.

Nicola concentrated on the road and refused to be drawn into another argument about her drinking. She drove steadily, a few miles an hour under the speed limit, but not slow enough to attract the attention of a passing police car. Instead of driving through the town, which would have been the quickest route, she turned onto a narrow, hedge-lined, lane that meandered through the countryside and led back onto the main road just past what used to be the town's railway station.

'I thought I'd take you via the scenic route. I love the colours at this time of year, don't you, Mum?'

Martha wasn't impressed. 'I didn't ask for a guided tour, Nicola. I know what you're up to. Now, just drive us to the farm for pity's sake.'

Nicola took a deep breath and pulled up a little too sharply at the T-Junction causing both passengers to lurch forward in their seats. Before Martha had a chance to criticise her driving skills, she swung the car to the right and went through the gears as the car sped along the long lane that led to what was left of the farm.

She pulled onto the asphalt drive with a squeal of brakes and came to an abrupt halt five feet short of the wide field gate that gave access to the rear of the farmhouse.

Nicola slipped out of the car and opened the rear door for Martha who strode purposely to the aluminium tube gate, pulled on the spring lever and pushed it open. She stepped onto the gravel drive and marched along the side of the old house towards another, smaller metal gate at the back. When she reached it, she stopped, placed her elbows on the top rail and looked into what had once been a busy farmyard.

'I bet this brings back happy memories, Mum,' said Nicola as she stood at the side of Martha.

'Not all happy ones,' Martha replied, quietly.

Marjorie pointed to an expanse of bare concrete on the far side of the yard. 'There used to be pig pens there, lots of them. And just to the side of the barn there was a milking parlour.' She was quiet for a few seconds. 'I liked it better then, it looks so empty now.'

Martha slipped the latch on the gate and the three women walked into the farmyard. She took in the rear of the sturdy old house then stepped across to a long, wide strip of concrete that had been breached here and there by thick clumps of grass.

'This was where the milking parlour stood. I was only a baby when it was built.' She stamped on the cold concrete. 'These foundations could still support a couple of new bungalows.' She turned a full three hundred and sixty degrees. 'The barn looks solid enough still. Maybe I could build one of those conversions there, people pay a fortune for those... and... I'm not sure how thick the concrete is where the sties were built but, if that area is going to be built on, it would probably have to be dug up. Old smells might linger.'

Martha turned back towards the old, red brick house. She looked down at the concrete beneath her feet, swallowed deeply and cleared her throat before she spoke.

'I can imagine my father standing here looking at the farmhouse, imagining that he'd be running the place one day. I bet it was his idea to build the milking parlour too.' She looked down at her feet again. 'I can almost feel his presence here. He probably stood on this very spot before my bloody mother forced him away... to die a hero's death in the cold sea.'

Marjorie, not to be outdone, walked across the farmyard and came to a halt in front of the barn.

'My father must have stood here at some time too,' she said.

'Maybe so,' uttered Martha, 'but he wouldn't have done anything to help build this place up, like my father did.'

'He was a pilot, he died a hero's death too,' Marjorie replied, sulkily.

'We don't know that. We just know he died. He could have been bombed at the RAF base for all we know. He could have crashed his plane into the sea, trying to run away from the German planes. We just don't know; we only have Mother's word for it, and we know what a liar she was.'

'It's just the same with Frank. There's no record of his death either. We just have Mother's word for that too,' replied Marjorie, sticking up for herself for once.

Martha was about to hit back, but decided that punishment for such insubordination could wait until later. Instead, she gave her a look that made Marjorie quake in her boots.

'Right, I want to have a good look around the place before we go to the solicitors.' She stepped off the concrete base onto the tarmacked yard and turned towards the single remaining field. 'There was a stable for Bessie, our shire horse, just along here. That could be another dwelling.' She turned back and surveyed the house again. 'Do you know what I see here? Apartments. Three apartments, and a studio in the attic, it's plenty big enough.'

'I wouldn't want to live in the studio,' said Marjorie, nervously. 'Not with all the witchcraft that mother practiced up there.'

'Don't worry, you won't be living in the studio,' replied Martha. 'You couldn't afford to.'

At one twenty-five precisely, Nicola parked up in the car park at the side of Wilson and Beanney, solicitor's office. She got out of the car and opened the back door for her mother, who slid off the seat, straightened and turned in one movement. She was an agile woman for her age.

'Do you want me to come inside with you?' Nicola asked as Marjorie alighted from the passenger side.

'Why on earth would I want you to accompany me?' Martha asked, coldly. 'I'm not completely gaga and I'll almost certainly understand the legalise much better than your drink-addled brain could ever hope to.'

She walked briskly towards the tinted glass doors of the office building. 'Just wait here... and leave that bottle you stashed away in the dashboard alone,' she ordered, without turning her head.

A bored-looking receptionist, sitting in front of a modern-styled desk, with a large computer screen in the centre, greeted them with a half-smile and buzzed a message through on the intercom. A couple of minutes later, a dark-haired, handsome young man wearing a mid-grey suit and brown brogues, came out of a connecting office and smiled at them.

'Good afternoon, ladies, would you follow me please, this shouldn't take too long,' he said, turning away as he spoke.

'Are you our solicitor?' asked Martha. She looked at him suspiciously. 'I expected someone... older, more mature.'

'Someone older,' repeated Marjorie.

The solicitor ignored the remarks. 'This way please, ladies.'

His office was a complete contrast to the one they had just left. The décor was very tastefully done, with grey walls and cream woodwork. From the walls, the serious, trustworthy faces of former partners stared down at them. The furniture was vintage and looked like it hadn't been changed since the business opened. Edwardian chairs with comfortable seats, were placed strategically around the room. The huge desk was made of solid, polished oak and in the corner was an ebony hat stand. The only modern feature in the entire room was the laptop computer that the solicitor opened as he reached the desk. Even the landline telephones looked to have come from the 1930s.

'Please, sit.' He held out a hand towards the two comfortable-looking chairs on the other side of the desk. He waited until they were seated before sitting down himself. 'It's a lovely day for the time of year.'

Martha pursed her lips. The person sitting opposite, whilst having good, old fashioned manners, seemed to be far too young to be holding a position of such responsibility.

'Young man—'

'Bradley.' The young man interrupted. 'Or, Mr Wilson, if we are to be formal. I'm happy with either.'

'Well, Mr Wilson,' replied Martha, curtly. 'I am Mrs Crew, and this,' she pointed to her left without looking at Marjorie, 'is my sister, Miss Mollison. Marjorie never married,' she added unnecessarily.

Bradley pressed a key on the laptop, studied the screen for a moment, then opened a drawer in the desk and took out a green folder.

'I am instructed to hand over a cheque to each of you, courtesy of your mother, Mrs Alice Mollison,' he began.

Marjorie began to fidget, wriggling about in her chair as though she couldn't get comfortable. Martha leaned forward an inch.

The solicitor took out two legal forms and two cheques from the folder. He slid the forms across the desk. 'Sign at the bottom, please... where I've marked with an X.'

Martha picked up a classic, black fountain pen from the desk, pulled a pair of narrow, framed spectacles from her handbag and began to peruse the document.

'One hundred pounds, paid to the beneficiaries of Alice Mollison, by the National and Provincial Insurance Company,' she read aloud. She signed the bottom of the form with a flourish, then handed Marjorie the pen and nodded to the second form. 'Sign it,' she ordered.

When the documents had been pushed back across the desk, Mr Wilson countersigned both sheets of paper, put them back into the folder, then handed one of the cheques to Martha and one to Marjorie, who giggled excitedly as she received it.

'Don't lose it... in fact, give it to me, I'll look after it.' Martha snatched the cheque from Marjorie's hand, studied both carefully to make sure they were identical, then folded them and slipped them into her bag. She shifted in her seat and looked expectantly across the desk. Mr Wilson typed something into the laptop, closed the lid and leaned back in his chair.

'Right,' said Martha in a business-like manner. 'Onto the substance of the will.'

Mr Wilson shrugged. 'I'm sorry, but that is the substance of the will, as far as you two ladies are concerned at least.'

Martha shook her head. 'Read it again,' she ordered.

The solicitor opened the folder, took out Alice's last will and testament, and read through it. It wasn't a long document.

'That's it,' he said. Reading aloud, he continued, 'My life insurance policy, provided by the National and Provincial Insurance Company, taken out in September nineteen thirty-eight to the value of, but not exceeding, one hundred pounds, shall be split evenly, between my surviving children as the policy stipulates.'

'And that's it?' Martha leaned forward and tried to snatch the document from the solicitor's hands.

Bradley pulled the document out of reach and slid it back into the green folder.

'That, is it,' he held both palms upwards. 'I know this must be something of a disappointment to you both, but that is all that was bequeathed.'

Martha got to her feet, her face crimson. She narrowed her eyes and stared hard across the oak desk.

'There's something fishy going on here. I believe I am being robbed of my inheritance. Be warned, this will be contested.'

'Contested,' echoed Marjorie, her eyes wide. She looked from the solicitor to Martha. 'Contested,' she repeated.

'There's nothing to contest, I'm afraid,' replied Bradley. It's written in very plain language and has a very clear meaning. You see, the entire estate, including the farmhouse, the London properties, the shares and the bank accounts, were placed into a Family Protection Trust, a few years ago. There are three named, trustees, but sadly, your name isn't one of them. The trustees are myself, Mr Beanney, my practice partner, and one other. The trust will run for one hundred and twenty-five years, unless it is dissolved by the aforementioned trustees.'

Mr Wilson got to his feet. 'Legally, the trust is bullet proof, Mrs Crew. You can waste money on your own solicitor if you want to, but you'd be throwing your money away.'

Marjorie's mouth opened and closed as if she was impersonating a goldfish. Martha hit her on the back of the head. 'Wake up, Marjorie,' she spat, then turned back to Bradley.

'Even if all this is true, and there is some fancy trust in place, which, you can be assured, I will be looking into. Surely there would have been interest on the insurance policy. It was taken out in nineteen thirty-eight for God's sake. Where is the interest? Have you taken it in fees?' She narrowed her eyes again and stared across the desk.

'Our fees are paid by the trust, Mrs Crew,' said Bradley. 'There is no accrued interest. The policy payout was set at one hundred pounds. It would have been one hundred pounds had she died the day after she took out the policy, and it remained at one hundred pounds right up to the time of her death. I'm sorry to be the harbinger of bad news, but that's the way these things work.'

He looked at his watch.

'I'm sorry but we will have to conclude out meeting now. I have another appointment.'

He walked smartly to the door, opened it, and smiled.

'Thank you for your time.'

Martha said nothing, but stormed past the solicitor, almost knocking him into the window blinds. Marjorie followed, giving him a snarl as she swept by.

Bradley watched as the two old ladies left the practice.

'Let me know when Ms Griffiths arrives, please.' He closed the door to his office and returned to his desk.

As Martha left the building, she turned her face skywards.

'Thank you, God. You never fail to disappoint.'

Nicola closed the lid of the glove compartment, wiped her mouth on the back of her hand and popped an extra strong mint into her mouth. She looked towards the office doors and her heart sank. Martha's body language didn't appear to be saying that the meeting had gone well. As she got out of the car to open the back door for her mother, Jessica's Toyota drove slowly into the car park. She pulled up next to Nicola and climbed out. Martha hurried across the tarmac towards her. She stopped abruptly a foot away and looked at her sternly.

'Jessica. We need to talk,' she said firmly.

Chapter 7

Jess walked quickly into the Wilson-Beanney reception, the words of Martha still ringing in her ears.

'Call me, the moment you know anything, Jessica. This is a concern for all the family, not just individual members of it.'

The bored-looking receptionist, a woman of about the same age as Jess, motioned her to sit and went back to filing her nails. Jess declined the offer of a seat and slowly paced the room, studying the mainly Victorian portrait prints that lined the walls. Two minutes later the intercom on the receptionist's desk buzzed.

'Melanie, has Ms Griffith's arrived.'

'Yes, Brad... Mr Wilson, she's here.' Melanie looked disinterestedly at Jess. 'Shall I send her in?'

Instead of replying, the door to the right-hand office opened and Bradley Wilson stepped into the room. He held out his hand and beamed a smile as he approached her.

'Bradley Wilson, I'm delighted to meet you.'

Jess smiled back, pleased that the image she had built up in her mind pretty much matched the figure that stood in front of her. He was tall, dark haired, with deep brown eyes and a dazzling smile. His mid-grey suit was cut in the modern style, the short, tight-fit jacket was undone showing off a slim waist and a muscular-looking chest that while well formed, didn't shout out daily gym routines.

She took his hand and shook it.

'I'm delighted to meet you too, Mr Wilson, but I have to admit to being slightly apprehensive about this appointment.'

Bradley motioned her towards his office door and allowed her to enter first. He closed the door behind him and walked smartly to his desk.

'I hope that feeling of apprehension dissipates quickly.' He smiled at her again and held out his hand towards a comfortable-looking chair on the opposite side of his desk. 'Firstly, and unfortunately, the formalities have to be gone through.' Bradley lifted the lid of his laptop and pressed a couple of keys.

'Could you give me your full name, please?'

Bradley took her through a series of security questions before tapping another key on his laptop and looking up at her.

'That's great. Ms Griffith's, I'm sorry about the personal questions but it has to be done. Is it all right if I call you Jessica?'

'Jess will be fine. Nana and her two daughters are the only ones that use my full Christian name. I don't really like it if I'm honest.'

'Jess it is then, and I'm Bradley, if you don't mind the informality. Your grandmother would be appalled at the familiarity.' He smiled his easy smile again showing off perfectly aligned teeth.

Jess shook her head.

'I can imagine. I hope they weren't too awful. They have very old-fashioned attitudes.'

'I've met far worse in my time,' Bradley replied. 'Now, down to business.' He pressed a series of keys on his computer then leaned back in his chair and clasped his hands in front of his stomach. 'Firstly, I'd like to congratulate you on having what was obviously such a delightful, loving, great grandmother. I can assure you she was full of glowing praise when we sat together to discuss her final requests.'

'Delightful! Really? Most people found Nana brusque, to say the least.'

'She was anything but. We got on like a house on fire. She said I reminded her of my great grandfather. They became good friends I believe.'

'They did,' replied Jessica. 'Nana liked him a lot. He was as much a friend as an advisor.'

'She gave us a lot of business over the years.' Bradley pointed to a pile of green boxes in the corner of the room. 'I went through it all when Mrs? Mollison set up the trust a few years ago.'

Jess leaned forward in her seat.

'About this trust, I don't really understand what it is, what it does, who runs it?'

'I'll explain all that in detail, Ms... erm, Jess. Firstly though, I'll give you a brief breakdown of the will and I'll leave the technicalities until later. I do have to go through the clauses in some detail but I'm not expecting you to understand all the legal terminology.'

Bradley opened a drawer and pulled out a thick green file. Noticing Jess's look of horror, he gave a short laugh and patted it. 'Don't worry, I'll give you the bare minimum, the condensed version.'

Jess blew out a sigh of relief.

'Basically, Jess, your great grandmother left you everything... everything except a small insurance policy that is to be shared between your grandmother and your great aunt and a ten thousand pounds donation to a farm worker's charity. All of the assets, including the farmhouse, five properties in London, her shares portfolio and the contents of her bank accounts have been placed into a Family Protection Trust. This is a legal device that protects the assets from being accessed by anyone not named in the trustee listing.' Bradley looked down at his file. 'I erm... believe she had concerns regarding your partner, Calvin?'

'Concerns... that's putting it mildly, Mr Wil... Bradley. She could see through most people and she certainly saw through Calvin.' Jess pulled a face and looked down at her hands.

'I see. Well, in that case I have to repeat that he will not be allowed to have any say in the running of the trust, nor the distribution of its assets.'

'He won't be around to do anything of the sort,' replied Jess. 'Calvin and I are no longer an item. We split up on the day that Nana died.'

'Excellent,' Bradley beamed. 'I mean... I don't mean excellent, that you... that you are no longer...'

He held up both hands palms facing out.

'I know what you mean, I'm not offended,' said Jess with a warm smile.

Bradley relaxed.

'Unfortunately, the same goes for any partner you might live with. The three trustees are myself, Mr Beanney and you, Jess. Should you require anything financially from the trust we will have to have a meeting before the transaction will be allowed. Please don't think we will be too restrictive. You are the main trustee and we will support any reasonable request.' He smiled earnestly at her. 'We are there to ensure that a third party doesn't attempt to gain personally at your expense.'

Jess laughed. 'Nana and I share a taste in men. She liked very few and trusted even fewer of them. She thought I might be taken advantage of. I disagree, but I'm not going to argue about it.'

'Everything we have in here,' Bradley patted the file, 'is for your benefit and your welfare. The trust will run for a further one hundred and twenty-two years, but you will be allowed to renew or review the trust to include any children or add their assets to it should they wish to do so.'

Bradley paused. 'It helps with death duties and taxes too.'

'I hadn't thought about any of that stuff,' said Jess with a look of bewilderment.

'As I said, I do have to give you a detailed statement but I'll keep it as short as possible.' Bradley smiled reassuringly.

'Mrs Mollison requested that the trust pays you an annual allowance of some twenty-five thousand pounds. Now, although this is taxable... it is income after all... the sums are for your personal use and there are no restrictions on how you spend it. Council Tax, water charges etc are to be met by the trust but you will pay for your own utility bills. The farmhouse is valued at eight hundred thousand pounds and is yours to live in or rent out as you choose, the cost of any repairs or alterations will be met by the trust. The properties in London are either leased out or rented and bring in an annual income of some one hundred and fifty thousand pounds. Shares your grandmother purchased over the years bring in a similar amount.'

Jess put her hands to her forehead and tried to concentrate as Bradley continued the list of assets and liabilities but she soon got lost in the seemingly endless projections of future earnings, tax exemptions and annual property valuations. As Bradley read on, she found herself looking at the black and white photographs on the wall. One in particular caught her attention. A good-looking man, with a winning smile, wearing a gangster style hat tipped over one eye.

'Godfrey,' she whispered to herself. She smiled as she recalled Alice's description of him. She looked around the room at the beautifully highly polished Edwardian furniture. She wondered if the layout had been the same when Alice sat in front of this very desk all those years ago. Then she remembered what Alice had written about that meeting, how she had seduced Godfrey to prove to herself that it was her, not him that held the power in the relationship. How they had made love on the oak desk. She felt herself flush as an almost video-like image of their coupling came to her mind. Her breathing quickened and her eyes closed.

'So, if you have any questions?' Bradley's voice brought her quickly back to reality. She blew out a deep breath, wiped at her brow and willed herself to speak calmly.

'No, I think you've covered everything,' she said at last. 'I'll have a quick look through the documents when I get home.'

'Excellent,' said Bradley as Jess straightened in her chair. She pointed up to the photograph she had picked out.

'Is that Godfrey?'

'Yes, that is he. Sadly, I never met him, but I've heard so much about him over the years from my mother and grandmother. He was quite a character, it seems.'

'That's the impression I got too,' replied Jess. 'Alice was quite taken by—' She stopped abruptly as she realised the connotations of her statement. 'She mentions him in her diaries.'

'I wondered why there were photographs of her hidden away in one of the files,' he said.

'Really! Pictures of Alice? Could I see them, please?'

Bradley got up quickly from his chair and rummaged about in one of the large green boxes. 'Here we are,' he said, holding a green file in the air.

Back at his desk he opened the file and pulled out three, large black and white photographs. He studied one before handing it to Jess.

'She was very beautiful. She reminds me of that film actress from the wartime movies you see on TV, what was her name?'

'Rita Hayworth,' replied Jess. 'Everyone commented on the resemblance.'

Bradley slid another picture across the desk. 'You look so much like her in this one,' he paused, looked from the picture to Jess, then back again. 'Stunning,' he said.

Jess felt herself blush.

The photograph was of Alice, leaning against an old Alvis car. She quickly understood why Alice had called it, Godfrey's 'Gangster Car'. She had seen similar ones herself in the old James Cagney movies.

'Then there's this one. Godfrey and Alice together. I think I understand why he hid them away.' Bradley smiled as he slid the photo across the desk.

The picture was of Alice and Godfrey standing by the gate at the farm. Alice was wearing a bright, floral summer frock with white shoes whilst Godfrey was in rolled-up shirt sleeves, he had his arm around her shoulders and they were looking at each other with such loving expressions that Jess immediately felt a lump in her throat.

'There's a note on the back,' Bradley said.

Jess turned the picture over.

1940. Gangster Godfrey and Alice Hussy, very much in love.

Taken by Amy Rowlings, the gooseberry.

Jess ran her finger over the photograph.

'This is beautiful. Could I make a copy? She had such a hard time back then but she looks so happy here.'

'Keep them,' said Bradley. 'I don't think my family would want to see them and I'd hate them to be destroyed. He kept them hidden away in the old files for a reason. Maybe you are that reason.'

Jess looked at the photographs again and slipped all three into her bag.

'Thank you so much,' she said, croakily.

She pushed a hand across the desk, Bradley took it gently in his.

'God bless them both,' he said.

Ten minutes later, with a folder full of documents in her lap and two full sets of keys to the farmhouse in her bag. Jessica cleared her throat and began to get to her feet.

'This is so emotional, forgive me if I burst into floods of tears.'

Bradley got to his feet and came around to the other side of the desk. 'I fully understand. She was your favourite person on earth and now what was hers, is yours.' He placed a hand on her arm as she stood. 'I hope you'll be very happy in the farmhouse. There will be improvements you will want to make, a new kitchen, bathroom, technology... Just call and Mr Beanney and I will sign off anything you ask for. We are here to serve you. We're not here solely to protect the assets.

Jess looked into Bradley's deep brown eyes. On impulse she leaned forward and pecked him on the cheek.

'I hope that isn't too familiar... I take after my great grandmother you see.'

Bradley grinned and looked at his watch. 'Look, it's four-thirty and I haven't so much as offered you a cup of coffee. Could I possibly make up for it by buying you a late lunch... early tea?'

Jess tipped her head to one side and studied him. 'Oh, I'm not sure I'd feel safe, out and about with the descendent of a gangster.'

'Bradley grinned again. 'I'll leave my machine gun in the office,' he said.

'Then, a late lunch/early tea sounds like a great idea, I'm starving. Where shall we go? I don't think they serve meals in the pub this late in the afternoon.'

'There's a hotel come restaurant along the road a bit. It's been there forever. They'll whip us something up, I'm sure.'

Bradley led Jess out of the office and across the reception. Melanie dropped her phone on the desk. Her eyes narrowed as they followed Jess across the room.

'Lock up, when you finish please, Melanie,' Bradley called over his shoulder as he opened the big glass door for Jess. 'I won't be back this afternoon.'

Chapter 8

In the car park, Bradley walked to a sleek, silver Mercedes, parked in his own personal space. 'Shall we go together or do you want to follow me? It isn't far.'

Jess thought for a moment. 'I'll follow you if that's all right? I have to go back to my friend's flat to pick a few things up before I go to the farm.' She pressed a button on her key fob to unlock her car.

Bradley got into the Mercedes and pulled out onto the main road.

Jess hurriedly fired up her little Toyota and waited as a white van passed the entrance before pulling out herself. The van turned into an industrial unit about two hundred yards along the road leaving her with an unobstructed view of Bradley's car.

About a mile further along, the Mercedes turned right at a faded, wooden sign that read, Café Blanc. Jessica had driven past it many times but had never been inside. She followed Bradley along a narrow, tree lined, asphalt track. Autumn was biding its time and many of the trees still held onto their leaves. At the end of the drive was a large, white painted building, the front of which was partly covered by crimson, climbing roses. White painted metal tables surrounded by wrought iron chairs were set out on a forecourt at the front. They parked up in an almost empty car park at the back of the restaurant and walked among the still-flowering rose shrubs that had been planted either side of a weather-worn, stone path and made their way to the oak-framed, panelled-glass, entrance.

'It's a beautiful afternoon for October. Shall we have our late lunch al fresco, or would you rather sit inside?' Bradley offered his hand towards the table lined forecourt.

'It's warm enough to sit outside, don't you think? It is lovely out here.'

51

Bradley smiled. 'I hoped you'd say that. Choose a table, I'll nip in and let them know we're out here.'

Jessica selected a table close to a low wall that bordered a neat, well cared for shrubbery, placed her bag on the table and sat down facing the old white building. Bradley joined her a few minutes later and pulled out a chair so he could sit facing her.

'Do you know, I have the strange feeling that I've been here before, but I'm sure that I haven't.' Jess swivelled in her chair and looked around.

'Maybe you came here with your parents when you were young,' Bradley suggested.

Jess shook her head. 'It's not the sort of place my parents would patronise. They found other things to spend their money on. Maybe I came here with Nana.'

A pretty waitress arrived with two menus and a notepad. Jess ordered a spicy veggie wrap while Bradley asked for a chicken satay salad.

'Would you like a drink with your meal?' The waitress waited; pen poised.

Bradley tilted his head and looked across at Jess. 'A cocktail, maybe? They do a lovely Martini here.'

'Just a glass of mineral water please. I'll be using the car until late evening.'

'Very sensible,' said Bradley and ordered up a diet cola.

Jess watched the waitress walk back to the restaurant, then threw her head back, her eyes wide.

'I suddenly realised why I thought I'd been here before,' she said.

Bradley looked at her quizzically.

'Nana's memoirs! She came here with Godfrey, I'm sure of it. She had a Martini, but she thought it was called a Martina. She'd never had a cocktail before.'

Bradley's jaw dropped. 'The Martina cocktail is our family's drink of choice when we all get together at Christmas. I have no idea who first mixed it, but it had to be someone in the family because you can't order one in a cocktail bar without explaining how it should be constructed.'

Jess laughed. 'In her memoir, Nana said that Godfrey was so delighted by her faux pas, that he was going to design a cocktail called a Martina. He actually mixed one for her at a New Year's party at the farm.'

Bradley grinned and raised his glass to Jess. 'That's one family mystery solved.' He looked up at the sky. 'It really has turned into a beautiful day. Wonderful weather and wonderful company. Who could ask for more?'

They chatted about the Mollison farm as they ate their meals. Bradley seemed genuinely interested in her future plans.

'So, you're going to move into the farmhouse immediately?'

'Yes, I think so. I'm staying with my best friend at the moment but I feel awkward, especially when her boyfriend stays over. I hate being a gooseberry.' She looked across at him as she placed her knife and fork onto her empty plate. 'Do you own your own place?'

'Sadly not. I did have a mortgage at one time. I was married for a short period and we bought a house on the outskirts of Gillingham, but the marriage was doomed to failure. We weren't mature enough to make it work, so we parted before the relationship got sour. We're still on speaking terms,' he added brightly.

'That's a shame, how old were you?' Jess wiped her mouth on the colourful paper napkin, screwed it up and dropped it onto her plate.

'I was twenty, she was nineteen. It was a whirlwind romance. As I said, doomed to failure.'

'So, you sold the house?'

'We did, and we lost a bit of money on it, not much, but we wanted a quick sale. I moved back home and stayed there for two or three years, then the apartment at Atwood Park became available. I'm happy enough.' He pointed Northwards. 'It's only half a mile away from the office, so it's very handy and I've got good neighbours. They're not the nosy sort.'

'My new neighbours aren't close enough to be nosy even if they wanted to be,' said Jess with a little laugh. 'One of the benefits of living on a farm.'

Bradley nodded. 'It's a lovely old building. I met Alice there when we drew up the plans for the trust.'

'You'll have to come over for the housewarming,' said Jess.

'Ooh, I love a party,' said Bradley. 'I'll look forward to that.'

'I'll give you a call at the office,' replied Jess. 'Don't expect a Hollywood party though, there'll probably only be a handful of people there.'

Bradley screwed up his nose and shook his head. 'Forget the office, can I give you my personal mobile number? We don't want my receptionist getting the wrong idea.'

Jess added him as a contact on her phone, then slipped it into her bag. 'It will be a couple of weeks yet.' She checked her watch then got to her feet. 'Thank you for the lovely meal but I'd better get off. Sam will be home from work now. I'm hoping she'll give me a hand moving my stuff.'

'If she can't help, I'm happy to offer my services,' Bradley volunteered.

Jess smiled. 'Thank you, that's very kind, but I'm sure Sam will help. What does my share of the meal come to?'

Bradley looked shocked. 'It's my treat. I really enjoyed your company.'

Jess waited at the entrance while Bradley went inside to settle the bill. When he returned, the pair walked back to the car park and stood awkwardly between the two cars. Eventually, Bradley offered his hand.

'It's been a pleasure to be of service. If there's anything else you need from us, any advice on how the trust works... well, you know where we are.'

Jess ignored his proffered hand, leaned forward and gave him a peck on the cheek. 'I'll be in touch as soon as I set a date for the housewarming. I'll know pretty much what I'm going to do to the old place by then. A bathroom upgrade is a must and the sooner I get some new appliances in that kitchen, the better.'

Bradley stood by the open door of the Mercedes as Jess climbed into her little Toyota. She closed the driver's door, snapped on her seatbelt, dropped the passenger side window and leaned across to give him a wave. 'Thanks for everything,' she called.

As Bradley climbed into his car, she put the Toyota into gear, eased her foot off the clutch and pulled away.

Two hours later, with a car full of clothes, a few food supplies and a chilled bottle of Pinot Grigio lifted from Sam's fridge, Jess pulled onto the asphalt in front of the wide, tubular gates at the side of Mollison's farm.

Climbing out, she pulled a set of keys from her bag and walked slowly to the front door.

Sam pulled two black plastic bags from the back seat of her own car, and carried them to the front step. 'Take a deep breath, love. It's all yours now.'

Jess looked back over her shoulder. 'I'm okay, Sam, I was just thinking about some of the happier times I spent here,' she pushed a silver key into the Yale lock. 'It will always be Nana's house to me.'

Jess opened the door and taking one of the black bags from Sam she stepped into the hall. She walked by the stairwell, opened the door on the left, flicked the light switch, and walked into the lounge, where her beloved Nana had spent the last year of her life.

'You know, Sam, the last time I came in here, all I could think about was Nana slumped in her chair, but now, although I can feel her presence, the gloom seems to have lifted.' She turned slowly, taking in all four corners of the room, the big old clock on the wall that had annoyed Alice so much as it ticked her life away, the hospital bed in the corner with all its gadgets, the sideboard with the new DAB radio that Jess had bought her, perched on top, the lion's foot coffee table that had held up so many tea trays over the years, the shiny, Marylyn Monroe wall art, and last but not least. Nana's armchair with the two large, green cushions that she had propped herself up with.

Sam dropped the bag she had carried in onto the floor and turned to get another one from the car.

'You'll be wanting to get rid of most of this stuff, I expect. Those armchairs have seen better days.'

'That particular armchair is going nowhere,' replied Jess. She looked around again. 'I have an idea who might find a home for the bed, and the sofa has to go, even Nana said so. I'll definitely be getting a new one. The first thing I need to buy is a new bed. The springs in Nana's old one play a tune whenever anyone lies down on it.'

'How many bedrooms do you have?' Sam asked.

'Four now, plus the attic, that's huge. There were five originally but Nana had one converted to a shower room a few years ago.'

'No bath? I love a shower, but I couldn't live without a bath to soak in.'

Jess walked to the open kitchen door. 'There is a bathroom. It was built onto the parlour on the other side of the kitchen,' said Jess. 'But it hasn't been used for thirty years or more. The bath is cracked and the sink is hanging off the wall. I could get that fixed up, though I might just leave that as it is and have a bath put in next to the shower upstairs. The downstairs bathroom was added during the nineteen-thirties and it hasn't been touched since.'

Sam pointed towards the stairs. 'Put one up there, love, maybe just get the lavatory working down here.'

Twenty minutes later, Jess and Sam sat on the old sofa sipping at glasses of Pinot Grigio, the nine black bags having been unloaded from the cars and stacked like a plastic Stonehenge in the middle of the lounge.

'Here's to your new home?' Sam chinked Jess's glass and took a deep sip. 'Ooh, that's hit the spot. It's a shame I can only have this titchy amount.'

'You can stay over if you don't mind a lumpy old bed,' said Jess. 'I'll have the sofa. It isn't a problem.' Jess looked hopefully at her best friend.

Sam thought for a moment, then drained her glass. 'Sounds good to me, pass that bottle.'

Jess poured herself a top up and passed the bottle to Sam, who filled her own glass to the brim.

'This sofa isn't the most comfortable thing I've ever sat on, and I can fully understand why you don't want to use the hospital bed, so why don't we share the upstairs bed? It wouldn't be the first time we bunked up together.'

'It's bad enough with one person sleeping on it,' Jess said with a laugh. 'It would be like a rusty spring orchestra playing Beethoven's fifth with two of us tossing and turning all night.'

Jess patted the pocket of her jeans. 'Bugger, I left my phone in the car.' She got to her feet. 'Tell you what. I'll nip up to the Tesco Extra while I'm out there and pick up a couple of bottles of PG, that one isn't going to be enough.'

'Grab some bacon too,' said Sam, as she kicked off her shoes and sprawled back on the sofa. 'Even PG can be improved with a bacon butty.'

Jess walked out to the car, started the engine and turned on the headlamps. She looked in the rear-view mirror before reversing onto the lane and was blinded by a wide beam of light as a long, sleek car roared past. Jess blinked a few times until her normal vision was restored, then cursed. She'd know that car anywhere. She remembered Calvin showing off after he'd made some modifications to make it sound like a supercar. It had to be Calvin, there was only a farm below hers on the lane and the occupants of that were in their eighties and hardly likely to own a BMW with modified mufflers.

No, it was definitely Calvin, but what the hell was he doing parked up next to the farmhouse?

As she headed up the lane towards the town, Jess decided not to tell Sam about the incident. She'd want to get the police involved, but Jess was reluctant. She blew out her cheeks as she turned off the lane and onto the main road that led to the supermarket.

'Bloody Calvin,' she spat.

Chapter 9

As Jess came out of Tesco Extra carrying her bag of shopping, she heard a familiar voice call her name, she turned to see Ewan Drake, an old school friend who had spent a few years working for a charity in Africa.

'Hello, Ewan, I haven't seen you since the day of your Uni presentation when Calvin created all that fuss in that café. How are you? I hope the lecture went well.'

Ewan flashed a quick smile. 'I'm good thanks. The lecture went very well, so well in fact, that I've been asked to do a series of them on different aspects of charity work.'

'That's great news, well done.' Jess smiled and patted his arm. Ewan looked down at her hand, then back to her face.

'Look, Jess... I heard through the grapevine that you're young, free and single again. I was hoping to catch up with you to ask... well, to ask if I could take you out to dinner one night.'

Jess bit her lip.

'I'm sorry, Ewan, but I'm not ready to move on yet. I was with Calvin for years and it's only been a few weeks since the split. I'm not really over him yet.'

Ewan's eyes narrowed.

'You're not thinking of having him back after what happened at the café are you? He was bang out of order, having a go at you like that, especially as the woman he'd been having an affair with was standing right next to him.'

'No, I'm not going to have him back, Ewan. Believe me, the situation got much worse when I got home.' She felt a chill down her spine as she remembered the day. 'As you say, I'm young, free and single and I'm going to stay that way for a good while. I don't need any more complications in my life at present, I've got enough on my plate.'

'I wasn't offering to marry you, Jess, it was only dinner. No strings.'

Jess's face softened. 'It's very sweet of you, Ewan, but honestly, I'm off men at the moment.' She put her hand on his arm again. 'It's not you, I'm not ready, that's all. I'm just going to get on with writing my book. I haven't had a chance to get started on it, what with Nana dying and then the break up.'

Ewan was appeased. 'Well, if you change your mind, I'll book us a table, somewhere nice. Do you still have my number?'

'It's on my phone, Ewan, but honestly, please don't hold your breath. I need to get my head sorted out, and that's going to take time.'

She pressed the button on her key fob and the lights on her car flashed as the central locking opened up. She gave him a quick smile and turned towards the car as he leaned forwards, lips pursed.

'Bye, Ewan. See you around.' Jess climbed into the car and dropped her shopping onto the front passenger seat. She closed the door quickly, pulled on her seat belt and started the engine as Ewan bent down to look into the car. Without a sideways glance, she indicated, then pulled out onto the evening traffic.

'I got two extra bottles; we may as well make a night of it.'

Jess waved the bag of shopping at Sam as she walked into the lounge.

'That sounds like a plan,' replied Sam, waving an almost empty bottle of wine in return.

Jess walked through the kitchen into what was once the parlour, but was now used as a store room. She opened the lid of the old chest freezer and placed the two wine bottles carefully on top of the bags of frozen vegetables.

'Remind me in twenty minutes, the wine is getting a quick chill,' she called.

'No need to shout,' said Sam, appearing behind her. 'Did you remember the bacon? I'm starving.'

'I got bacon and some fresh rolls,' replied Jess. 'Do you want to do the honours, or shall I cook?'

'I'll cook, seeing as you were kind enough to buy the stuff,' said Sam, taking a gulp of her wine. She walked back into the kitchen, took a frying pan from the hanging rack above the big oak dining table and set it on the hob.

'This cooker has seen better days too, my darling,' she said as she turned the knob and pressed the ignition button.

'I know. I've got to plan a refurb. I'll get a wall mounted oven and a halogen hob, but I'm not sure I have the patience to design my own kitchen. I think I'll get onto Robin's, let them handle it all.'

Sam dropped six rashers of bacon into the huge cast iron skillet.

'Blimey, this thing weighs a ton.'

Jess laughed. 'It's been in the family for generations, it's an heirloom.'

'It's a bloody wrist breaker,' her best friend replied. 'I'll tell you what. Back in the day, if the old man came in late from the pub and got clobbered with this, he'd think twice before he stayed out again.'

Fifteen minutes later, Jess transferred one of the bottles of wine from the freezer to the fridge and carried the other one through to the lounge.

'I'll call Sky to get my TV and broadband account switched over tomorrow.' She picked up a remote control and turned on the 32-inch flat screen TV. 'Until then, I'm afraid we only have a choice of five channels. Nana wouldn't even have Freeview installed.' She flicked through the channels before settling on an episode of the detective series, Vera. 'It's like the dark ages, isn't it?'

'I can't remember not having broadband,' said Sam. 'I must only have been a kid when we first had it installed at home.'

'Mum and Dad found other things to waste their money on,' replied Jess. 'I seem to remember a lot of squealing and squawking when Dad used the internet back in the nineties.'

Sam's phone pinged. She picked it up, read a text message, then sent a reply. 'Jamie, checking in to see how things are going. I sent him a wine glass emoji in reply.'

'He's a nice bloke, your Jamie, you've really landed on your feet there, Sam.'

'He's all right,' Sam replied. 'He's the marrying type though, and I'm not really sure that I am.'

'Don't let him slip away,' Jess advised. 'Nice men like that are a rarity these days. He's a keeper.'

Sam looked up from scouring WhatsApp. 'I know, I'm just not ready to be tied down yet, that's all. I'm not daft, Jess. I know I have a good one.' She looked back to the phone again. 'So, are you ready to get back onto the saddle, so to speak?' she gave Jess a wicked grin, made a semi fist with one hand and moved it up and down over the index finger of the other.

Jess rolled her eyes heavenwards.

'Not for a long while yet, Sam. I was just saying the same to Ewan Drake, outside of Tesco's this evening.'

'Ewan? That lanky, skinny, lad? The one who followed you around like a lost sheep at school?'

'That's him, only he's not so skinny these days, he's built like a rugby player. He went to Africa to do charity work.'

'Ooh, do tell. What was he after?' Sam sat bolt upright.

'He asked me out to dinner. But I refused,' Jess added quickly.

'Why? What's wrong with him? Fred West would be a breath of fresh air after Calvin.'

Jess pulled a face as she thought. 'He's a bit too clean cut, if you know what I mean? He's very serious all the time. For all his many faults, Calvin could at least make me laugh. I've never seen Ewan laugh in all the time I've known him.'

'I suppose you're right, you need a shared sense of humour, love. Jamie can tell some right dodgy jokes when he's had a few.'

'Ewan would take serious offence at a dodgy joke,' said Jess, sadly. 'He's on the woke side of things.'

'Oh, God, that's worse than finding religion,' said Sam. She looked up at the TV. 'Blimey! this is awful. Remind me never to slag off Netflix ever again.'

'I'd try to get Netflix on the laptop, but honestly, Sam, even tethered to the phone for internet, the speed would be so poor it would be buffering all the time.'

Sam pulled a face. 'I'm getting WhatsApp messages, but even the smaller videos aren't working.'

'It's like the back of beyond out here,' laughed Jess. 'Luckily the houses just up the road and the farm beyond this one, have broadband connections. It would have cost a fortune getting the fibre optic cable to me if they'd had to run it from the junction box outside the Old Bull pub.'

'Well, you can afford it now, Mrs Moneybags,' Sam said with a laugh. 'I'm sure your nice lawyer would have paid for it had you asked. What is he like, anyway? Is he cute, or is he an old duffer?'

'He seems very nice. He is rather good looking, a couple of years older than me, single... at least I think he is. He was married for a short time when he was in his early twenties but it didn't work out and they got a divorce. He has a flat down the Gillingham Road.'

'Blimey! You got all that from a will reading appointment? I shudder to think what you'd get out of him on a date. It would be like the Spanish Inquisition.'

Jess laughed. 'It wasn't like that at all. It came up in conversation when we were sitting outside Café Blanc, that's all.'

'Hang on a minute.' Sam put her glass on the floor and twisted around so that her face was only a foot away from Jess's. 'You didn't say anything about romantic meals at the Café bloody Blanc.'

'We'd both missed lunch… and it wasn't romantic at all… well, the setting was, but our meal wasn't. We just had a late lunch and a chat about things in general and that's it.'

Jess dragged her eyes away from Sam's intense stare.

'I see. So, when are you seeing him again?' Sam twisted her head so that she could see Jess's face.

'I'm not… at least… I've got to call him soon to get the repairs and improvements started on the farm. He gave me his personal mobile, so I can reach him…' Jess tailed off realising how it sounded.

Sam leapt on the pause and clapped her hands in delight.

'Well, it didn't take you long to get over Calvin did it? Listen here you, I want a full report on my desk within an hour of you either seeing, or speaking to him. Do you understand?'

Jess sighed and held up both hands.

'All right. But don't expect anything too exciting. He's only my lawyer, he's there to look after my assets.'

'Precisely.' Sam sniggered and winked.

Jess topped up their glasses and tried to steer the conversation in a different direction.

'I don't want to delve into the trust for everything,' I like to pay my own way if possible.'

'I'm only pulling your leg, love.' Sam patted Jess on the thigh. 'What are you going to do with yourself in this huge old place anyway? You'll rattle about like a pea in a whistle.'

Jess looked around. 'It is a bit big for one person. If I get too lonely, I might take in a lodger or a student… but, I'm going to be spending the next few months working on my novel, as well as writing any commissions the magazine editors might offer me.'

'It must be so nice being a creative,' replied Sam. 'I do envy you.' She took a sip of wine. 'Then again, I remember Uni, those impossible deadlines, you still have to work to those, don't you?'

Jess nodded. For the magazine and newspaper articles, yes, but I don't have a publisher for the novel. I haven't even worked out how the story is going to go; I have the source material in Nana's memoirs and there's definitely a novel in there. I just need to work through them all and pick out the bits I can manipulate into a story.'

'Watch out, kiddo, with your family you could end up in the courts if you type the wrong sentence.'

Jess pulled a face. 'Don't even think that. I'm going to be really careful about changing dates, place names and so on. I'll invent my own characters; it's not going to be Nana's biography. It's just background material really.'

Sam gave her a thumbs up. 'I'm sure it will be fabulous. Do I get an advanced copy?'

Jess grinned. 'Signed and dedicated to my batshit crazy best friend.'

Sam pouted. 'Aww, you say the nicest things.'

Just after midnight, with just half a bottle of wine remaining, Sam rolled off the sofa and got unsteadily to her feet.

'Right, Missis, I'm going up. Are you sure you don't want to share my bed?'

Jess waved a finger at her.

'All right, but keep your hands to yourself, you've had a few too many and I don't want you thinking you're in bed with Jamie in the middle of the night.'

'You should be so lucky,' said Sam. 'I'm a good girl I am.'

The two friends made their way to the staircase, flicking off the kitchen and lounge lights as they went. At the top of the stairs, Jess pointed to the left. 'That's the bedroom door, the loo is the one next to it.'

'Good, I'm bursting,' said Sam, as she pushed down the door handle.

While Sam was in the bathroom, Jess made a turn at the top of the stairs and walked along the landing to the window at the front of the house. Outside, a crescent moon shone brightly in an almost cloudless sky. Jess looked up the lane towards the Old Bull pub, then looked the other way towards the next farm along the lane. About fifty yards along, on the wide strip of bare land that had been cut out to allow tractors to turn, was the dark shape of a car. The headlights were off, but by the waxy moonlight, Jess could see a shadowy figure, reclining in the driver's seat.

Chapter 10

The next morning, Jess was just stepping out of the shower when her mobile rang. Wrapping a beach towel around herself, she walked quickly to the bedroom and with her dripping hair falling around her bare shoulders, she rummaged about in her bag until she found the phone. The caller was listed as unknown.

'Hello?'

'Jessica, I have to say I'm extremely disappointed in you.' The tone of Martha's voice did nothing to disguise the fact.

'Grandma?'

'You promised to call me immediately after coming out of the solicitor's office. I waited in all afternoon.'

'I promised no such thing, Grandma. You demanded that I call you.'

Jess heard a deep breath, then the sound of it being exhaled.

'I'm not going to argue over semantics, Jessica. I expected better from you. We're family... do I have to remind you of that?'

Jessica resisted the temptation to reply with a sarcastic comment. 'Of course you don't, Grandma.'

There was a long pause.

'Well?'

Jess took a deep breath. She knew the calls would keep coming until she broached the subject.

'Nana left me the bulk of her assets. There was a bit put aside for a farmworker's charity, but apart from that, everything else went to me.'

'Charity... how much?'

'Ten thousand pounds.'

'Ten thou... Dear God. My mother must really have hated me. Marjorie and I got a hundred, lousy pounds... BETWEEN US!'

'I'm sorry about that, Grandma but—'

'Well, you could do something to ease your guilty conscience,' spat Martha.

'I don't have a guilty conscience, Grandma. It was Nana's decision.'

'That doesn't stop you making things right, does it, young lady?' Martha's voice tightened.

Jessica sighed. 'I couldn't make it... right, as you call it, even if I wanted to. The assets are all tied up in a Family Trust. I get a yearly cash allowance from it and any maintenance or improvements to the farmhouse will be paid for, but any major decisions on the assets have to be made by the trustees, and I'm only one of three.'

'Pfft. How much is your... allowance worth?'

'I'm not going to divulge that, Grandma. I'm surprised you asked.'

Before Martha could reply, Jessica continued.

'I'll just say, that while it's a nice amount, and many families have to live on less, it's not enough for me to live the life of Riley. I'll still have to work.'

'So, sell the farm. Listen, Jessica, I have some wonderful ideas of how we could make a lot of money out of it. We could turn it into apartments, repurpose the barn and—'

'Nana would spin in her grave if the farm was sold, Grandma. That's the very reason it was placed into a trust. She loved this place and—'

'This place? So, you've already moved in?'

'Yes, I moved in last night.'

'Ha! You couldn't wait, could you? How long have you been planning this? Whispering in her ear, poisoning her thoughts. You didn't just get your feet under the table, you crawled underneath it.'

'Grandma! How could you say such things? You know I wasn't expecting to be left anything?'

'And yet, now you have EVERYTHING, you aren't prepared to share.'

'I can't share. I told you, every dec—'

'The trustees, yes, yes, I heard the excuse, but there has to be a way around it, there always is.'

Jess tried her best to keep her voice at an even tone. 'There are no ways around it, Grandma. As the solicitor told me, legally, it's watertight.'

There was a pause. When Martha spoke again, she used a softer tone. 'Forgive my anger, Jessica. I didn't mean to speak as I did. I'm just so frustrated by the whole affair. Do you know how much Marjorie and I have to live on? All right, we have a nice house, but I can't even afford a winter break. I had to cancel the newspapers and the milk delivery to save money. I haven't had a summer holiday for ten years. That's hardly fair is it?'

'I'm sorry about that, Grandma, but I really can't see how I can help you get onto a plane.'

'I can see plenty of ways, but... Listen, Jessica, it's high time the many wounds inflicted on this family, were healed. The feuding should stop. My mother is dead, please don't just step into her shoes and take up the cudgels. Let's heal the rift and become a proper family again. Don't take my mother's side.'

'I've never been on anyone's side particularly, Grandma. I was close to Nana, but the reasons for the hostility between you, were hers. Not mine. I'd like to see our family come together as well; I can't see any reason for bitterness or recriminations. Maybe we should all get together for a night out. I just found a lovely place to eat.'

'Night out? I see no reason for a celebration.'

'Just a nice cosy meal, me, you, Aunt Marjorie and Mum. I'm sure we could bury the hatchet once things have been talked over.'

'Hmm. All right, Jessica. Are you going to arrange it? Let me know where and when. I'll look forward to seeing whose head the hatchet is buried in.'

'Grandma!'

Martha let out an exasperated breath. 'It was a joke, you silly girl. Call me when you've organised it all... I can't afford to contribute, neither can Marjorie and your mother spends every spare penny on booze, so don't expect anything from her either.'

'I'll pay for the meal, Grandma. Don't worry about that.'

'Of course, you will. You can afford it now, can't you?'

'Goodbye, Grandma.' Jess hit the red button on her screen to end the call. Grabbing another towel, she began to dry her still dripping hair and marched down the stairs. Looking towards the black and white photograph of Alice that sat next to the DAB radio on the sideboard, she let out an angry snort, then sat down in the armchair opposite the one that Alice used to sit in.

'Oh, Nana, what have I just done?'

Chapter 11

After dressing, Jess made a bacon sandwich and a mug of strong, barista-style coffee and carried them through to the lounge on a small tray.

'Curse you, Sam. I'll have to get a fair bit of exercise to work this lot off.' Jess bit into the sandwich and searched on her phone for her Internet provider's number. After booking an appointment for the following Thursday to have TV and broadband installed at the farm and the service to the flat turned off, she took her empty tray back into the huge, old fashioned kitchen. She picked up a pen and notepad from one of the worktops, hoisted herself up onto the big oak table and began to make a list of the things she needed for the upgrade. When the list was complete, she blew out her cheeks and shook her head.

'It's a good job you're paying for all this, Nana,' she said aloud. 'I couldn't afford to do it on my own.'

Jess put the notepad on the table and slid off. Walking through to the parlour, she turned to the right and pushed open the door to the bathroom that Alice had got her local builders to install back in the 1930s.

'Well, Nana, what shall we do with this?'

She thought it might be easy enough to get it up and running again. A radiator was a must and a new bathroom suite, maybe with an overhead shower, it needn't be anything flash. She returned to the kitchen, made a few more notes on the pad, then carried it into the lounge where she added a new sofa and a queen-sized bed, both of which she would pay for from her own savings.

'That will do for now, Nana,' she said.

She sat on the sofa, pulled out her phone and searched for Robin's kitchens. After making an appointment with one of their designers for Thursday, she grabbed her bag, pulled on her coat and walked out to her car. Fifteen minutes later, she parked up outside the library where she knew she would get Internet access, and walked inside to check her emails and indulge in a bit of online shopping. There were two emails from the editor of a magazine she wrote occasional articles for and after making a quick decision, she sent off a short reply, accepting both commissions.

After sending out a couple of article queries that she had put on hold when Calvin had turned her world upside down, Jess logged onto Google and searched for a new bed. She considered hanging on for the Black Friday sale, but then she remembered how uncomfortable she had been, tossing and turning on Nana's lumpy, old mattress, and pulling her credit card from her purse, she entered her personal details onto the website.

Feeling pleased with herself and with excitement building about the upgrades to the old farmhouse, Jess returned to her car. With a shock, she saw that parked next to it was a black BMW. Before she could open the door to her Toyota, Calvin climbed out and with both hands in the air in a gesture of surrender, he walked around the front of Jess's car coming to a halt about six feet away from her.

'Jess, it's so nice to bump into you like this. You're looking well.'

'Go away, Calvin. I don't want to speak to you.' Jess pressed the button on her key fob to unlock the car.

'Don't be like that, Jess. I miss you. I only want to make sure you're all right on your own.'

'I'm fine, Calvin. Now, I'm busy. Goodbye.' Jess opened the car door, but before she could climb in, Calvin stepped forward and placed his hand on the roof.

'Jess. Look, I'll be honest with you. I'm struggling money wise. I don't have enough coming in to pay the rent or the utility bills.'

Jess stepped behind the open door so there was an obstacle between them. 'What's new, Calvin? You hardly ever contributed to the rent or the bills when I was there.'

'That's not true, Jess. I helped out when I could.'

'Helped out? You lived there with me. I can't ever remember saying that you could stay, rent free. Nana ended up paying your half of the rent every month and all you could do was wish her dead. Well, Calvin. You got your wish, she's gone, but so has the charity. You're on your own now. Deal with it.'

'Jess, please, don't make me beg.'

'It wouldn't make a difference if you did, Calvin.'

Calvin pulled his best sad face.

'What's happened to you, Jess? You've become so hard. You were never like that.'

'You happened Calvin. Now, as I said. I'm busy. The rent is paid until the end of the year, that's when the lease expires. I've already contacted the Estate Agents and they've agreed to leave it until then before they start looking for a new tenant. You can apply for it if you like and they'll consider your application, but you'll need to be in secure employment by then.'

Jess climbed into the car and tried to close the door but Calvin got hold of the handle.

'Jess, Jess, please. I still love you despite everything. Shall I book a table somewhere nice? We can talk things over in a civilised manner.'

'No, Calvin, I'm not falling for that.' She pulled on her seatbelt. 'I'd only end up paying for the bloody meal anyway.'

'Jess, help me out, please. Think about what we had. It was glorious at times.'

'You killed it, Calvin. Any love I felt for you, died when you attacked Sam in the flat. I saw the real Calvin then. Nana warned me about you months before, but I couldn't see past that bloody smile of yours. She said you'd show your true colours soon and she was right.'

'That interfering old witch, I'm glad she's gone, I—'

Jess's face turned into a mask of anger.

'Stay away from me, Calvin, and stay away from the farm. I've seen you twice, and the third time won't be lucky, because I'll call the police and have you arrested for stalking.'

Jess snarled as she pushed at the door, forcing him to step back. In a flash she leaned out, grabbed the inner handle and pulled it shut. Quickly pushing down the lock button, she took a deep breath, inserted the key and switched on the engine. A furious Calvin stood in front of the car in an effort to stop her pulling away. Jess hit the horn repeatedly until the noise attracted the attention of two middle-aged men who were walking back to their own vehicle. Calvin gave Jess the middle finger and stepped aside as the men changed direction and began to walk towards them. Jess dropped the driver's window, mouthed, 'thanks' to her two rescuers, then pulled out of the car park. She was still shaking when she arrived back at the farm.

Chapter 12

Nicola Griffiths groaned as her clock radio clicked over to six o'clock and heralded in the new day by blasting out the Rolling Stones classic, Street Fighting Man. She pulled the pillow over her head and pushed her arm from under the warmth of her quilt, making patting motions with her hand until somehow her fingers found the switch to shut off the alarm.

She closed her eyes and dropped off to sleep again only to be woken by a hammering on her door some ninety minutes later. Pushing the pillow from her head, she sat up and groaned as a bolt of pain flashed behind her eyes. The hammering continued.

'All right, all right, I'm coming.'

Nicola slid out of bed and holding her head in both hands as if to keep it in place, she shuffled across the bare floorboards of her bedroom towards the window. Tugging the dingy, full length curtain aside she looked down into the street to see Mrs Kaur, owner of the local mini-market, staring angrily up at her.

Nicola cursed, pulled up the sash window and stuck out her head, blinking in the morning sunlight. Her head began to spin and she just managed to shout, 'I'll be there in ten minutes,' before pulling herself back inside and throwing up on the floor.

She dressed quickly, pulling on the same clothes she had worn the day before, then she crossed the landing to the bathroom where she urinated, before standing in front of the aging bathroom cabinet mirror to study the all too familiar, hungover face reflecting back at her.

She shook her head slowly, a pained look on her face that was only partly due to the hangover.

'Christ, you look older than Mum,' she croaked. 'How much did you have last night?'

Nicola half-filled the sink then, taking a deep breath, hung her head over the bowl and splashed the bitterly cold water onto her face and neck before grabbing a towel and rubbing it vigorously against her skin. Leaving the bathroom door open behind her, she walked surprisingly steadily down the stairs to the kitchen. She filled the kettle, then remembering her promise to her employer, she slammed it down on the greasy hob and turned around to see if she could find her coat. She passed the rickety-looking dining table holding last night's empty, two litre cider bottles, and made her way to the lounge where she found her green Puffer jacket on the floor next to a badly stained sofa. Pulling it on, she patted her pockets to check for her keys, and stepping over the increasing pile of mail on the doormat, let herself out and crossed the street to the mini-mart.

Mrs Kaur checked her watch, then looked up as the tinkle of the bell announced Nicola's entry. If she had ever looked more disparaging, Nicola couldn't remember when it was, and there had been plenty of disparaging looks over the six months she had worked at the shop.

'Your shift starts at seven,' she remarked coldly.

'I know, Mrs Kaur. I'm sorry, I had a bad night.'

The shopkeeper shook her head and glanced towards the shelves of beer, wine and cider. 'From the looks of you it was a very GOOD night.' She pursed her lips. 'If you're late one more time, or, if you arrive at work so hungover that you can't see keys on the till properly, it will be the last time you do it. Do I make myself clear?'

Nicola nodded. She'd had half a dozen final warnings before, so she wasn't particularly worried about getting another. Her two predecessors had both been sacked for helping themselves to the cash in the till. Nicola hadn't stooped to those depths yet, though she had been sorely tempted when her purse was empty during the week before payday. Thankfully, her next-door neighbour, a soft touch called Maggie, worked at

Asda and would bring her a selection of food from stock that was about to expire. Nicola always offered to pay when her wages went into the bank at the end of the month, but Maggie would never accept. She was a church going Christian who saw the few pounds she spent on Nicola as an act of charity.

Nicola lowered her head as she walked past her employer, who wafted her hand in front of her face as she went by.

'For goodness sake, you stink of stale cider.' She grabbed a packet of extra strong mints and tossed it towards Nicola. 'Here, don't go too close to the customers until they've had time to work... oh, and ring them into the till. You're paying for them.'

Nicola took the mints without a word, then walked through to the back of the shop, hung up her coat and pulled on a fading, flower patterned overall with the Kaur's Mini-Mart logo on the breast. When she re-entered the shop, she found Mrs Kaur sitting on a high stool at the end of the counter. It was going to be a long day.

At one o'clock, Mrs Kaur begrudgingly took charge of the till while Nicola made the short trip home for her lunch break.

As she was crossing the street, Maggie came out of her front door wearing her green, Asda, fleece.

'Hi,' she called breezily. 'I'm just off to work, do you need anything bringing home?'

'You couldn't do me a massive favour and grab me a couple of two litre bottles of cider, just the cheap Lightning Bolt stuff. I've run out and I could do with some to last out the week.'

'All right, but you will have to pay me for them now. You shouldn't be spending money on alcohol when you've got no food in the cupboard.' She wagged a friendly warning finger at Nicola.

'I've got food, Maggie. The cider will last me until the weekend and I get paid then. I need to unwind when I get home from work or I don't sleep.'

Maggie knew that the cider wouldn't last until midnight, but she smiled anyway and waited until Nicola produced her purse and began to count out the seven pounds, twenty pence the cider would cost. She leaned forward and looked into the tatty, leather purse as Nicola's fingers searched the torn, satin lining for the stray fifty pence piece she thought was hiding there.

'Just give me what you've got, Nicola. It's all right, I'll make up the difference.'

Nicola nodded, gratefully, and turning away, walked the few yards to her front door and let herself in.

She had just taken off her coat and lit the gas under the kettle when her phone rang. She picked up the aging Nokia that Jessica had given her when she had acquired a new one, some years before, and pressed the answer button.

'Yes.'

'Hi, Mum, it's me.'

'Hello, Jess, this is a surprise, I've just this moment got in for my lunch break.'

'How's the old slave driver over the road?' asked Jess with a laugh.

'She's the same as always, the miserable so and so, she thinks she controls my whole life. I'm getting fed up with her lectures. If the blooming shop wasn't so convenient, I'd find a job elsewhere.'

'That's why it's called a convenience store, Mum.' Jess tried to keep the conversation light hearted.

'I'll tell her what I think of her one of these days and just walk away.'

'Don't do that, Mum. You're a bit better off in work than out of it.'

'It's a hard life, Jess. I'm struggling to keep up with the bills. I don't suppose you could—'

'What haven't you paid this time?'

Nicola sighed. 'The usual. I'm two months behind with the rent, I've got until next week to pay the council tax and they're chasing me for the water rates. They put the prices up every year but wages never go up to the same extent. It's scandalous.'

'How's your meters?'

'I put a few quid on the gas and electricity cards last week, so if I'm careful I'll last until payday.'

'Have you got credit on your phone? You need that in case of emergencies, Mum.'

'I'll buy a ten-pound top up on Friday,' Nicola promised.

'And what about food? What have you got in the cupboard?'

'Jess, stop interrogating me like I'm a special needs teenager,' Nicola stormed.

'I'm sorry, Mum, but I worry about you. It's only natural. I am your daughter.'

'If you were that worried, you'd put a few pounds in my bank account. You can afford it now, Jess. Don't be mean. You know we should all have shared the money that Alice left.'

'I don't know why you always call her Alice, and not grandma,' replied Jess.

'She was never a grandmother to me. Grandmothers dote on their grandkids. She left us high and dry when we had our money worries. That's the reason your father left and why I'm in such dire straits now.'

'I'm not going to argue about this again, Mum. Nana gave you money and Dad squandered it, gambling.'

Nicola sniffed. 'Well, she could have helped me when he left, but she did nothing, so don't expect me to mourn her passing.' She was quiet for a moment to let the message sink home, then she continued. 'So, what is it you want, Jess?'

'I rang to invite you out to a family dinner, Mum. I'm booking a table for four at the Café Blanc for this Friday evening. It will just be me, you, Grandma and Aunt Marjorie.'

'What's the occasion? Are we celebrating your inheritance or have you decided to do the right thing by us all?'

'I'm not allowed to do the right thing, Mum, I'll explain on the night. Nana tied all her money up in a trust fund. I couldn't give you a decent portion of it if I wanted to.'

'Typical!' spat Nicola. 'So, what's the point in this family dinner?'

'Mum, I just want us to be a family. I want all the back biting and nastiness to stop. Nana's gone and I don't want to be at the centre of hostilities like she was.'

'Is there a bar at this Café Blanc place?'

Jessica sighed. 'Yes, Mum, and don't worry about money. I'm picking up the tab for the evening.'

'I stopped worrying about money years ago, when I ran out of it,' said Nicola coldly.

'I'll see you on Friday then, I'll pick you up about six-thirty if that's all right?'

'I'll be here,' replied Nicola, 'but, Jess... can you help me out with the rent? I'm sure there's an eviction notice amongst the pile of mail on the mat.' Her voice became tearful. 'I daren't open it, Jess. I just let it pile up. Can you help me? I'm begging you; I'll have nowhere to go if they chuck me out.'

'Mum, you know I won't see you on the streets. Sort through that mail and give me the ones that are threatening court or eviction on Friday night.'

'Bless you, Jess. I'll pay them this time, I promise.'

'You won't need to, Mum. I'll pay them by bank transfer. You won't have to worry about going to the council offices and I've still got the estate agency's bank details from last time, so all I need is to know how much you owe.'

'Bank transfer....' Nicola's voice betrayed her disappointment.

'Mum, you know what you'll do with it if I give you cash. You really have to get yourself sorted out.'

'I can handle it, Jessica,' snapped Nicola. 'I don't have a problem; I can stop drinking whenever I want.'

'Okay, Mum, but take it easy will you, and don't have too much before I pick you up on Friday. The bar won't run out.' She paused. 'Bye, Mum, love you.'

The call ended. Nicola stared at the phone for a few moments then tossed it onto the sofa and walked through to the kitchen. She picked up the large, plastic cider bottles and shook them in turn. Disappointed, she dropped them onto an overflowing black bin bag near the back door, before opening the wall cupboard next to the sink and pulling out a half-full bottle from her emergency, vodka stash. She took a glass from the draining board, then uttering, 'sod it' to herself, put the glass down and took a deep swig from the neck of the bottle. Wiping her mouth on the back of her hand, she walked back through to the living room, took another swig of vodka, placed the bottle on the table, picked up the phone again and pressed the buttons to speed dial the only name on her list.

Chapter 13

Jessica spent Tuesday clearing out Alice's clothes and belongings. Because of the amount of time she had spent indoors over the last twenty years, the vast majority of her wardrobe items would be better suited to a company specialising in period drama costumes than the charity shop.

Jess bagged up the clothes, but placed the handbags, shoes and costume jewellery into a large box. Some of the items might be collectable and although Jess wasn't interested in any money that could be made, she wondered if a charity like Help the Aged could make use of them. She decided to take the garments to a clothing recycling bank, where any unusable items were shredded and mixed with fresh fibres to make new fabric.

In the afternoon, she sat at the kitchen table with her laptop and an old notebook that she had recovered from the attic on Nana's instruction. Written on the front, in Alice's beautiful handwriting were the words, Alice Mollison. Aged 19. Personal Memoir. 1939.

Jess made a large coffee, picked up the notepad and pen from the worktop and returned to the kitchen table. She opened the pad to a new sheet and wrote 1939 across the top of the page, then she opened the hardback notebook, only to find that the months from January to May had been roughly torn out. Jess was puzzled, she was sure that those entries had been there when she first brought the memoirs down from the attic. Then she remembered that Nana had asked for that particular volume to be left inside her bedside drawer a few days before she died.

'What was so bad you felt the need to hide it from me, Nana?' she asked aloud.

She decided to ask Gwen, Alice's carer, if she knew anything about it when she called her to see if she could make use of Alice's expensive hospital style bed.

Still puzzling over the missing pages, Jess took a sip of coffee and smoothed down the page titled, June 1939 and began to read.

June 1939
The summer has arrived at last. After a cool, damp April and May when we had to spend much of our spare time indoors, June brought sunshine and warm air with the promise of more to come. I set four of the farmhands to work shearing and dipping of our small flock of sheep and dehorning the young bovines while others were cutting the long grass in the fields left fallow, and piling it into tall haystacks that would be left to dry out before being made into bales and stored in the barn for winter feed.

Martha has been niggly for most of the spring. She loved being outdoors, it didn't matter where, as long as she could feel the breeze on her face. Her favourite place on earth was the farmyard. She loved to watch the chickens scurrying about, pecking and scratching in the dust, but she saved her most excited squeals for when she was up close to the pig pens. She adored our big boars, Hector and Horace and would scream with delight when I held her up to the bars of the pen while one of them rubbed its wet snout on her bare tummy.

She would get seriously annoyed when it was time to go back inside again and nothing would placate her. She had begun to crawl about in early spring and we had to build her a playpen to stop her getting into places we'd rather her not get into.

On her birthday, after an hour of tantrums, I stomped out to the piggery, grabbed two of the smallest piglets and carried them back to the kitchen. Miriam wiped off the worst of the muck with a damp cloth while Martha watched, mouth agape, from the confines of her new built prison.

When I put the piglets into the playpen with her, Martha screamed with delight and spent the next half hour rolling around the floor of the pen with them. She was so happy. I suddenly dreaded the thought of having to explain to her why the piglets were taken away when they had bulked up. I have to admit, more than one tear came to my eye when, after about forty minutes play, the three of them curled up into one large, pink ball and went to sleep.

On the Friday of that week, I had just finished cleaning out the piggery when I heard the tooting of a car horn. Puzzled as to who it might be, I walked across to the big barred gate, stood on the second rung and looked up the dirt track drive at the side of the farmhouse.

Parked at the top, near the lane, was a sleek, black Alvis. Standing in front was a man, wearing a pin striped suit. He took off his hat as he spotted me, and waved it in the air. My Gangster Lawyer and occasional lover, Godfrey Wilson, was paying me a rare visit.

'Hello, Alice,' he called.

'Hello, stranger,' I shouted. 'Go to the front door, I'll be there in a jiffy.'

I raced for the back door, stopping only to pull my dirty wellies off on the top step, then yelling, 'It's Godfrey,' to Miriam, I hared through the kitchen into the front room.

At the front door, I took a deep breath, patted the headscarf that protected my curls from the worst the pigpens had to offer, and yanked the door open with a flourish.

Godfrey stepped inside still holding his hat. Smiling, he looked me over. 'You look as beautiful as ever, Alice.'

I had completely forgotten that I was still wearing my dirty, work overalls that were covered with splodges of farm detritus. I looked down at myself and screwed up my face. If I could smell the pig muck on my clothes, he must be able to as well.

I pointed to the chairs that were tucked neatly under the round dining table and backed away towards the door.

'Take a seat, Godfrey, I'll be back in five... possibly ten... just let me get out of these... this...'

I stepped into the kitchen and ran through the parlour to the bathroom, pulling the buttons of my overalls open as I went.

'Miriam, make tea... keep him company... Help!' I hissed.

Miriam stepped away from the big Belfast sink where she was hand washing my smalls and picking up a tea towel to wipe her hands, she ushered me away and went to take my place in the lounge. Miriam was my live-in housekeeper, baby-minder, head cook and bottle washer, although she was paid for fulfilling her duties, she was more a part of the family than an employee. More than that, she was one of my closest friends.

In the bathroom I stripped naked as I ran hot water from the Ascot boiler into the sink. Picking up a flannel I soaped it up and had an all-over wipe down, paying particular attention to the bits and pieces that might have got a bit whiffy as I was going about my duties in the piggery.

Grabbing a towel, I gave myself a quick rub down and leaving my shed clothing on the bathroom floor, I hurried back through to the kitchen, holding the towel across my front. Miriam was standing at the big oak table, pouring boiling water into the teapot as I sped by, bare arsed.

She laughed as her eyes followed my bare backside across the kitchen. 'Would you like some talc dabbing on it?'

I gave her a look over my shoulder. 'Don't let him leave,' I said, and took the stairs two at a time, stepping onto the towel, tripping, and ending up on all fours, naked and frustrated.

Finally making it to the bedroom, I finished drying off, quickly brushed my hair into some sort of shape, sprayed a couple of puffs of perfume onto my chest, neck and wrists, and dragged my bluebell print dress over my head. Suddenly realising that I hadn't put on any underwear, I cursed, turned around towards the dresser, decided I didn't have time, and pulled a pair of shoes from the bottom of the wardrobe while staring up at the clock. I pulled them on as I hopped across the bedroom, checking myself in the mirror as I went.

Back in the kitchen Miriam was pouring the tea. I looked at her and held out the palms of my hands, a pleading look on my face.

'You'll do,' she said softly, and went back to making the tea.

As I walked breezily into the living room, Godfrey got up from his seat and gave me an approving look.

'Stunning, simply stunning,' he said.

I blushed, as I tended to under Godfrey's gaze. 'Miriam's bringing the tea,' I said, still trying to regain my breath after the hectic ten minutes I'd just spent.

Godfrey gave me his best smile, and my heart skipped a beat. 'I particularly like the odd shoes.'

I looked down and my heart sank. I had picked up one white Oxford heel and one black.

I felt myself reddening. 'I was... I... I've got another pair like it upstairs.' I turned and hurried out of the room giving Miriam a stare and pointing to my feet as I stomped past her.

Less than a minute later I was back, with matching feet. I walked back into the front room and bent forwards slightly, pointing at them.

'I decided to wear matching shoes after all,' I said.

Godfrey grinned. 'I just thought I'd let you know.'

I rolled my eyes heavenwards, walked towards him and kissed him on the lips.

'To what do I owe the honour?' I asked.

'I was hoping that we might have a ride out, to take advantage of the glorious weather. It's the first decent day we've had since last autumn. I couldn't bear to waste it sitting in a stuffy office.'

'Forget the tea, Miriam,' I shouted. 'We're going out.'

Back outside, Godfrey opened the passenger side door and waited for me to climb in before shutting it firmly and stepping around the back of the car to get to the driver's side. I lifted my bottom off the seat and smoothed my dress. Suddenly remembering that I wasn't wearing anything underneath, I screwed up my face and bit my lip.

Godfrey took his seat and turned towards me. 'Something wrong?' he asked, noticing my expression.

I shook my head. 'No, it's okay, I thought I'd forgotten something, but it doesn't matter now.' I smiled at him, then looked straight ahead, hoping against hope that the slight zephyr of a breeze that had been wafting around all morning, didn't pick up during the afternoon.

'Where do you fancy?' he asked. 'We could do a late lunch at the Café Blanc, or we could find a hostelry and have a drink or two.'

'By hostelry, I assume you mean, pub?' I replied.

'Indeed,' he said.

'Well, I'm not going to the Old Bull,' I said firmly. Going sans knickers in a strange pub garden is one thing, doing it in my local is another thing entirely.

'What about the Green Man near Aylesford. Would that be far enough away?'

I'd never been anywhere near Aylesford in my life, but it seemed to be quite a distant place and no one would know me there, so I nodded.

'That sounds perfect.'

As it happened, Aylesford was less then fifteen miles away and we arrived at the village pub about two miles outside of the town, half an hour later. The Green Man had a nice garden at the back and we sat amongst the early roses and hydrangea shrubs as we ate sandwiches and sipped at gin and tonic water.

After ordering my third gin (Godfrey only had two), and feeling utterly relaxed, I began to tell him about my life since we had last met back in October.

'It seems such a long time,' I said.

'If only you knew what a struggle I've had, keeping away,' he replied. 'I've reached the top of your lane three or four times only to turn back. I didn't know what your circumstances were, whether Frank had come back or not, so I thought it better to wait until you contacted me.'

'Frank never came back,' I lied, trying my best to keep the events of that dreadful Christmas Eve when he had attacked me and Amy, out of my thoughts.

'I wish you'd have let me know. I've missed you, Alice.' Godfrey leaned forward and took my hand across the table. 'Missed you so much,' he added.

I sighed audibly as my heart melted again under the influence of that smile.

'I missed you too, Godfrey, but I thought it best to let things lie, your circumstances being what they are. We couldn't allow ourselves to be seen together on a regular basis. We'd have been the talk of the town.'

Godfrey patted my hand. 'I have thought about leaving her you know.'

'Don't, Godfrey.' I pulled my hand away. 'I'd never be able to live with myself if I thought I'd caused your wife and kids to suffer. Families need a father figure. I know, I still miss my dad.'

Dad had died an alcoholic almost a year before, leaving me to run the farm on my own.

'I knew it could never work, Alice, not on a permanent basis, but it was nice to dream for a while.'

I reached out and took his hand again. 'We have today,' I whispered.

Twenty minutes later we had parked up at the edge of a small wood, just off a narrow country lane on the outskirts of the village. We climbed into the back seat, and without even a hint of small talk, threw ourselves at each other. Godfrey smothered my neck and face in kisses and after fumbling away at his trousers, slipped his hands under my dress.

'My goodness,' he gasped, eyes wide.

'I came prepared,' I said with a husky laugh.

He kissed me again, I hastily unbuttoned the front of my dress and spread myself across the back seat. Godfrey lay on top of me and with his hot breath on my neck and one hand on my breast he guided himself into me.

Our lovemaking was urgent, hurried and over all too soon, but I loved every brief moment of it. I had missed the closeness of his body, the musky smell it gave off as he began to sweat. When he was finished, he withdrew and, still panting, leant on one elbow and looked into my eyes.

'Alice, I love you. Did I ever tell you that?'

Chapter 14

On the Thursday morning, Jess got up early as Sky had promised their installer would arrive at any time between 7 AM and 1 PM. To her surprise, two engineers arrived in two different vans at ten-thirty. One to install the broadband and one to install the satellite dish.

Wade was in his mid-twenties with a broad chest, a thick neck and mop of red hair. He flexed the muscles in his arms as he smiled. He was obviously proud of his gym physique. Gordon was older, in his late thirties; he sported a paunch, his hair had grey flecks around the temples.

Jess set them both up with coffee and biscuits before they started work. While the installers were having a chat about recent difficult jobs, a large van pulled up and two more men arrived on her doorstep with the new bed, mattress and free, bonus bedding. With the aid of a twenty-pound note, Jess persuaded them to carry Alice's old, rusty-spring, bed and mattress down the stairs and dump them at the side of the house where she covered them in the plastic that the new items had arrived in. Making a mental note to ring the council and have them disposed of, she went back into the house just as her mobile rang.

'Jess? It's Bradley Wilson.'

'Hello, Bradley, is there a problem?'

'No, no, nothing like that,' he replied. 'I was, erm, well, I was wondering if you would like to have a run out for lunch on Saturday. My treat... only if you have time that is, I know you must be frightfully busy, I just thought...'

'Thank you, I'd love to come for lunch,' said Jess. 'It's a good job the offer wasn't for today, I'm up to my neck in installers, deliveries and kitchen quotes.' She looked out of the front window as she heard a vehicle pull up. 'Speak of the devil, the Robin's man is here. I'll have to go.'

'Would twelve o'clock be too early? I have a surprise for you. I'll come to get you at the farm.'

'Twelve is fine... bye, Bradley, sorry, got to rush.'

The Robin's Kitchen rep's name was Harry, a forty something man wearing jeans and a thick striped shirt. He stepped into the kitchen armed with an armful of brochures and designs. Dropping them onto the huge oak table, he looked around in wonderment.

'Blimey, this is a blast from the past.' He turned a full 360 degrees taking in the old 1930s cabinets and work surfaces. 'If you still had the old range in here you could open it as a museum.'

'I know,' replied Jess. 'I feel a bit guilty about ripping it all out if I'm honest.'

Harry opened a cupboard door, sniffed inside, then closed it again.

'You have got a bit of worm in the units, so it's probably a good thing to let them go.' He bit his lip. 'I think I have just the thing to replace it with.' He selected a brochure and opened it to a retro style kitchen with white units and solid oak worktops. There was even a double width range with a grill, two large ovens and a six-burner hob.

Jess looked at the brochure, then around the kitchen. 'It is beautiful. But it looks very expensive too.'

'It's not the cheapest on offer, but...' he did the full 360 turn again, 'this kitchen deserves it.'

Before he could go into full sales mode, Jess laid a hand on his arm.

'Could you measure up for it. I'll have a word with my financial advisor and see what I can afford.'

Harry pulled out his tape measure and Jess walked back through to the lounge where Wade was testing the new router with a program on his work computer.

'Almost done,' he said brightly. 'Would you like me to log you onto the router before I go? I always like to test the customer's computer is working before I sign off.'

'That's very kind of you,' said Jess, picking up her laptop and handing it to him. 'My ex teaches I.T. at Uni but I'm hopeless. I can use the programs I need, but that's about it.'

Wade looked around.

'You mean you live in a big old place like this, all alone? That must be a bit scary at times. The creaking of timber in the middle of the night and all that.'

'Oh, I've only just moved in,' replied Jess with a laugh. 'I'm hoping for less by way of nocturnal noises now my new bed has been delivered, the old one used to pop springs all night.'

'Really?' Wade gave her a leer.

Jess decided to leave the comment hanging in the air and looked over his shoulder at her laptop screen. 'It's logged on. My email just updated.'

Wade got to his feet and began to wander around the room holding the laptop in front of him. 'I'll check you can get a good signal everywhere before I go, save you having to order a Wi-Fi booster later. I've got one on the van if we need it.' He walked to the bottom of the stairs. 'Okay if I go up?'

Jess nodded.

Ten minutes later, Jess walked upstairs to find Wade sitting on her new bed, typing furiously on the laptop. She stood by the bedroom door and coughed. Wade jumped as though he had been given an electric shock. He recovered his composure immediately.

'Made me jump... Nearly done. The signal wasn't great in here, so I'm just optimising the Wi-Fi.'

'Sorry,' replied Jess with a little laugh. 'Optimise away.'

Wade finished typing, then carrying the laptop in front of him again, walked around the bedroom, watching the screen closely. At the doorway he stopped. 'Excuse me, I just need to do the landing.'

Jess moved out of the way and the engineer walked slowly out. 'I've already done the other bedrooms, what's in here?'

He stopped at a heavy, white painted door.

'The attic,' Jess replied.

'Am I all right to go up? If you get a signal there, you'll get one anywhere.'

Jess nodded. 'The door at the top is locked though.'

Wade opened the door and stomped up the bare wooden steps.

'There's a very good signal here,' he called.

'Fabulous,' said Jess as his heavy, boot clad feet stomped back down again. He pointed back up the stairs.

'Try it inside the attic. These Q boxes are very powerful.'

'I erm, don't intend to spend a lot of time in there... not just yet anyway.... It's a bit creepy,' she confided.

'You never know, you might want to turn it into a home office one of these days,' he replied.

Jess shuddered at the memory of the short time she had spent in the loft, shook her head and standing aside to allow the installer to get by, she closed the door behind him.

Back in the lounge, Wade placed the laptop carefully on the lion's foot coffee table, filled in a log sheet and passed it to Jess to sign.

'All done. I'll leave you a card in case you need anything, I'm a freelance installer, not tied to Sky, so I can drop in whenever I'm needed.' Wade handed her a copy of the log sheet with the business card, and let himself out. Jess stood on the doorstep while he loaded his tools into his van.

'Look, erm, Jessica, was it? If ever you feel lonely, or if you fancy a drink one night, just give me a ring.' He grinned and with a cheery, 'have a lovely day,' he climbed into his van, reversed into the lane and with his radio blaring, sped away.

Half an hour later, Gordon, the satellite installer called her in for a quick demonstration of her new Q box service.

'I usually do the lot,' he said, 'I was surprised to see Wade here too.'

'They might have sent him out because of the remote location,' said Jess. 'I don't know when the phone line was last tested.'

'Oh, I'm not complaining,' Gordon replied. 'Less work for me. I can get onto the next one now. I think it's an admin cock up though.'

'Well, I'm not going to complain either,' said Jess. 'I'm just happy to have everything up and running so quickly.'

After Gordon's departure, Jess walked through to the kitchen to find Harry picking up his brochures. 'I'll leave you this one,' he said, pointing to the one he had shown her. 'The quote is on top. Just ring if you decide to accept and we'll set things in motion. It will take a few weeks to get the stuff made, installation should only take a few days.'

Jess picked up the quotation and whistled.

'Phew, you were right about it not being cheap.'

'You get what you pay for. The new one will last you for many a year.'

Jess showed him out, then made lunch and settled down on the sofa to test out the newly installed satellite TV channels. She logged into her Netflix account, saved the details, then watched an episode of The Crown, while she ate her lunch. Sam texted as she was eating.

How's the installation? Are we Netflixed up yet?

Watching The Crown as I type, replied Jess.

I'll nip over on Saturday afternoon with wine.

Oops, sorry, I'm out on Saturday with Bradley, my lawyer. He's got a surprise for me.

I bet he has. Sam sent a wicked devil emoji.

Jess snorted. *I think you're confusing me with someone who has little control over their underwear.*

Go for it, Missis, he sounds delicious.

Jess smiled as she ended the messaging session with a wink emoji.

Speak later, need to organise house warming before the new kitchen is installed.

Jess, as a writer, refused to use the shorthand text method and Sam knew that it annoyed her so kept it to a minimum herself.

After lunch, Jess checked her emails, downloading the contract for the new magazine articles and replying to the responses to the queries she'd sent out. Walking through to the kitchen she picked up Alice's memoir from the table and skim read a couple of entries, before picking up her notepad and scribbling, Sept 1939 across a new page. She sat down at the table and began to make notes as she read.

September 1939

At eleven o'clock on Sunday September 3rd 1939, I opened up the kitchen for the farmworkers to enable them to hear an historic speech from our Prime Minister, Neville Chamberlain, or The Undertaker, as Amy had renamed him. Not all the lads worked on Sundays, some were rostered to tend the animals, milk the cows etc and I called them in when I heard the BBC inform us that there was going to be a speech of national importance.

We had been edging towards war for the entire year and Germany's invasion of Poland a couple of days before had made the prospect an inevitability. As we waited for the broadcast, my thoughts went back to the autumn of the previous year when the same man joyfully waved a piece of paper at the cameras whilst declaring, 'Peace for our time.' I wondered if he had brought a scrap of worthless paper with him this time around and what was written on it? 'Bugger!' must have been a distinct possibility.

Amy's nickname was perfectly suited. The scrawny man with the scrawny neck and the old-fashioned, turned-over collar, wouldn't have looked out of place marching solemnly in front of a hearse.

The few whispered conversations ceased as we heard his voice over the airwaves.

I am speaking to you from the cabinet room at 10 Downing Street. This morning the British ambassador in Berlin handed the German government a final note stating that unless we heard from them by eleven o'clock that they were prepared at once to withdraw their troops from Poland, a state of war would exist between us. I have to tell you now that no such undertaking has been received, and that consequently this country is at war with Germany.

There was a bit more, mainly relating to Hitler's warlike mentality, but we didn't really take that in, the first part of his statement said everything we needed to hear. We were at war with Germany again, even though we were promised that the 14-18 conflict had been the war to end all wars.

Amy pushed her empty tea cup across the table.

'Well, the undertaker has just assigned another few million people to an early grave. There has to be better ways to advertise your business.'

No one laughed.

Barney, our foreman gave his thoughts.

'Levity aside, Amy, this has been coming. Hitler is a nasty piece of work, and it really is high time someone stood up to him. We could have done it last year, but I understand that we weren't ready to take him on back then. I'm not sure we are now; I think we might have to try to persuade the Americans to come in again or we could be in trouble.'

'Thank goodness for the channel,' said Benny Tomkiss, one of the younger workers. He pointed vaguely towards the Kent coast from which any attack would surely come.

Miriam, a non-practicing Jew, whose father had spent the majority of his life working on our farm, waited for a few seconds of silence before adding her tearful thoughts.

'I'm so pleased we're finally telling him he can't just do what he wants. Last year, cousins of mine were thrown out of their businesses, their homes and their jobs, just for being Jewish. Do you all remember what they did on that bloody Kristallnacht? I'm so worried about them, I haven't had a letter since February. The Nazis are sending Jews to work camps where they are used as slave labour. How any so-called civilized society can allow this to happen is beyond me. He has to be stopped before millions of people are slaughtered just for belonging to the wrong religion.'

No one seemed to be able to look at Miriam as she delivered her tear-filled statement. We had all heard the rumours of Jewish people being hounded out of their homes and exiled to concentration camps throughout Germany. The newsreels at the cinema had shown graphic images of Kristallnacht. The vast majority of the British population were horrified by the news reports, but there were some, even in our small town, who seemed to blame all that was wrong with the world on the Jewish race.

I turned off the radio, thinking that as head of the farm, I ought to say something. My father would no doubt have delivered a rousing speech, saying we were all in this together and it was up to each and every one of us to do our bit to ensure that Hitler was defeated. Sadly, as a nineteen-year-old mother, I wasn't up to delivering rousing speeches.

'Firstly, I have to say that we all knew this was coming, sad and shocking as the actual announcement was. Secondly, I'm sure the government will announce soon that the farming industry workers are in a reserved occupation. The country will still need to be fed and our troops will need their ration packs so none of you will be forced to join up if you don't want to. I will however, understand completely if any of you feel you have to do your bit for King and country and you can go with my blessing, but please, if you can, wait until the recruiting offices are set up. We've still got the corn harvest to bring in before you go.'

I let out a deep sigh.

'Damn Hitler, damn Mussolini, and damn Stalin.'

As the lads drifted out into the yard, I sat down at the kitchen table thinking about the past year.

The farm had done well. The wheat crop had been as good as it ever had been and we'd had a bumper crop of piglets and lambs too. The new milking parlour/barn had enabled us to house thirty cows through the bad weather and the extra animals meant that our milk production had quadrupled. The electric pumps meant that milking was now a one-man job and Miriam's little butter and cheese enterprise had expanded. There had been a wedding in March when young Benny married his childhood sweetheart, Emily.

Martha was now a toddler with a mission to explore every inch of the farm. Her inquisitive nature was only matched by her temper if she was stopped from going into places she wasn't allowed to go.

Our relationship still bordered on indifference. She put up with me if she was in the mood, but no amount of encouragement or proffered bribes could get her to spend time with me if didn't feel like it. Her vocabulary wasn't great yet, but Mama, one of the easiest words to say, was the word she used least.

Since January, I had been accompanying my best friend Amy to the local picture palace to watch the latest Hollywood exports. To my delight and embarrassment, my movie star lookalike, Rita Hayworth, appeared in more and more of the movies on offer. I looked like Rita; my rolling shoulder length curls made the similarities almost photographic. We were so much alike that the owner of the picture house, a Mr Wallington, even offered to pay me to stand outside the cinema greeting prospective movie goers whenever one of her films was on show.

Future wise, I knew that financially, the farm would be better off. The government tended to look after us during times of conflict. They would almost certainly subsidise the crops and give us more money per ton for producing it. That wouldn't necessarily transmit to farm worker's wages and if we lost any of our men to the fighting, we might have to recruit from the elderly residents of the town, then again, the local factories would almost certainly switch to war production and that would mean the skills of the town's women and elderly men, would be much sought after.

I could never understand the government's attitude to farm workers. On the one hand they wanted them working at home producing for the country, but on the other hand, they were reluctant to pay them a little extra in order to keep them in our fields instead of fighting in foreign ones.

Amy, as a mill worker, wouldn't be allowed to leave to do any other work. Her skills would be needed in the manufacture of uniforms, parachutes or anything else the forces might require.

'I do hope this thing doesn't go on as long as the last one,' she said, sipping at a fresh mug of tea. 'I promised myself I'd be married before I was twenty-five and there will be a severe shortage of eligible bachelors once this bloody war gets going.' Amy was just coming up to twenty-two.

'You'll be all right if the Americans do come in,' I replied. 'Imagine Cary Grant or Jimmy Stewart turning up at an army camp nearby?'

Amy rested her chin in her upturned hands and sighed.

'Imagine,' she said.

Chapter 15

On Friday afternoon, Jess sat on her new bed with her laptop and queried a couple of magazine editors with ideas for articles before typing up the notes she had made whilst reading Alice's 1939 memoir. Yesterday evening she had begun to formulate the outline of her novel and had made some brief character notes.

Checking her watch, she left the laptop open on the bed, stripped, and walked through to the upstairs bathroom to get a shower. Twenty minutes later, she returned wearing a bath sheet and a smaller towel around her head. The bath sheet slipped as she stretched to remove the towel turban. She let it fall and sat in front of Alice's old dressing table mirror to brush her shoulder length chestnut hair.

As she got up from the pink, padded stool, she noticed a blue light on her laptop. The screensaver had loaded, so she pressed a key to allow her to see her desktop. The blue light normally only came on for a Zoom or FaceTime meeting, or when she was recording a short video for one of the occasional podcasts that she was asked to appear in.

Puzzled, she checked the running programs, but nothing that required the camera was in use. Jessica closed the lid of the computer and opened it again. The light remained on so she restarted the laptop to find that the blue light had disappeared. Thinking she had rectified the error she got to her feet, and standing naked in the bedroom, began a stretching routine she had learned at the gym.

After ten minutes of exercise, Jess stopped the stretching, and flexing her shoulders in a circular motion, turned back towards the bed, only to find the blue light had come on again.

'Dammit,' she said to herself.

She could do without the laptop playing up. It wasn't a new model by any stretch of the imagination but she had hoped it would see her though for another year or so. If it was beginning to develop faults it might be time to replace it. She couldn't risk her precious new novel being irretrievably lost. Wrapping the big towel around her again, she picked up the laptop, walked down the stairs to the front room and dug out her portable, back-up hard disk from the drawer under the coffee table. She made copies of all the files she had added since her last backup, then sent the new notes she had made the previous evening to her wireless printer.

Satisfied that her data was now secure, Jess left the laptop on Alice's old writing desk and went back upstairs to get ready for her evening out.

She chose a scooped neck, Shamrock green dress that hung just below the knee. Anything shorter than that could get her a ticking off from Martha. She still vividly remembered her twenty-first birthday party at the Old Bull, when she had turned up wearing a mini skirt and a sheer blouse and had been subjected to the most embarrassing lecture about modern day standards.

'I can see what you had for breakfast, Jessica. Now, go back home and change before the rest of the guests arrive. We don't want them thinking we've booked a stripper, do we?'

With the memory of her grandmother's stinging rebuke still echoing around her head, she grabbed her shoulder bag, coat and car keys and stepped out of the house.

It was only a short drive to her mother's terraced house on Burnett Road. Although the street lamps glowed dimly in the misty, autumn air, there were no lights showing through Nicola's front window. After attempting, but failing to lift the rusted, lion's-head door knocker, she rapped on one of the dirty, fan shaped, glass panes at the top of the door. After a full two minutes, her mother opened it with a gap just wide enough to peer through.

'Ah, it's you. That's good, I thought it might be the old witch from the shop wanting me to do extra hours. Mandy hasn't turned up for the evening shift, she texted me to say that she's ill. She isn't, she's out with that new bloke of hers.' Nicola opened the door and ushered her daughter inside. 'Hurry, don't let her know I'm home.'

Jess stepped quickly inside and Nicola shut the door behind her.

'Is that why you're sitting in the dark?' she asked.

'No, I'm out of electric,' her mother replied. 'I was going to get some this evening, but with Mandy not turning up, I decided not to go over there in case she insists that I work.'

'Just tell her you're going out with me,' said Jess.

'That wouldn't stop her putting pressure on me to do Mandy's shift,' said Nicola. She grimaced. 'I owe her a few hours for being late and for knocking off early when I felt ill the other day.'

'Give me your electricity key and gas card, Mum,' Jessica demanded. 'I'll go over and buy some credit for you.'

Five minutes later, Jessica was back with the fifty pounds on the electricity key and the same on the gas card. She looked on sadly as Nicola inserted them into the meters and the living room lights came on.

'Mum, please let me know when you're running low again. You can't be without light and heating in winter.'

'Jeanie Desmond has a fake card, or so she claims. She never seems to run out. I might ask her to get me one.'

'MUM! Don't even think about it. With your luck the bloody thing would set off an alarm at the EDF engineer's office.' She looked around the untidy room. 'Did you sort through your mail?'

Nicola picked up a thick pile of letters and handed them to Jessica. 'I don't know what they say, I daren't look.'

Jess stuffed them into her shoulder bag. 'I'll sort them all out in the morning, but listen, Mum. You have to look after yourself better than this.'

'No lectures, please, Jessica. I'll get enough of those from my mother tonight.'

'I wasn't going to lecture you, Mum. I worry about you that's all.'

'If you're that worried you could send a bit of money my way.'

Jessica sighed. 'I may as well give it straight to the off licence and save you the bother of handing it over.'

Nicola sniffed. 'If my circumstances were better, I might not feel the need for alcohol. It's the only way I have of forgetting about how bad things are.'

Jess shook her head. 'You start wallowing in self-pity when you drink. It makes it worse.'

Surprisingly, Nicola didn't take offence. She pulled her best coat from a hook on the back of the front door and slipped it over the freshly ironed, floral print dress.

'I've always liked you in that dress,' said Jessica with a smile, pleased that her mother had at least made an effort. Her speech wasn't slurred and her eyes looked relatively bright.

'It's the only decent thing I've got left,' Nicola replied.

Jess patted her on the back. 'Shall we have a girlie day out soon, do the sales? They seem to be on all year round.'

As Nicola smiled, it seemed to wipe away ten years of aging.

'I'd like that,' she said.

She was still an attractive woman, Jess thought. She could easily find another man if she wanted to. The problem was, she only had room in her heart for one man, and he had walked out a few years ago.

They arrived at the Café Blanc at six-fifty to find Martha and Marjorie waiting for them in the foyer. Martha glowered at them as they entered.

'About time too. We've been here for twenty minutes; I was beginning to think you had called it off.'

'Hello, Grandma. Hello, Aunt Marjorie.' Jess smiled and stepped forward to offer a hug. Martha pushed her hands in front of her to stop any such attempt. Marjorie, who had already held her arms open to accept one, suddenly stepped back behind her sister as if for protection.

'Twenty minutes,' she tutted and shook her head.

Nicola undid her coat and stepped out from behind Jessica.

'Hello, Mum,' she said quietly.

Martha looked her up and down with a look of distaste.

'I see you're wearing that dress again. Still, it appears that you are relatively sober, so we shouldn't be too critical.'

Jess bit her tongue as Nicola looked down at her feet.

'Come on,' she said, trying to sound as jovial as she could. 'Let's go in. Our table should be ready.'

She pushed open the spring-loaded, panelled door and held it while the others came though. A suited, bow-tied host stepped towards them; Jess smiled at him.

'I booked a table for four. Griffiths.'

'Ah yes,' the host smiled and led them to a table in a nook on the far side of the restaurant.

'Are you trying to hide us away,' snapped Martha looking around the room.

The host smiled. 'No, Madam. Ms Griffith's requested a more secluded table for a quiet family meal.'

Martha tightened her lips and waited for him to pull out her chair. To her annoyance, he didn't.

'The waitress will be with you shortly.' He placed a menu and a wine list on the table in front of all four seats, then smiling again at Jessica, he walked back the way he had come.

Nicola picked up the wine list as soon as she was seated.

'Don't go ordering a bottle for yourself,' said Martha curtly. 'We don't want any drunken dramas tonight.' She looked around from the confines of the nook. 'Isolated as we are.'

Jessica looked up as the waitress appeared.

'White, red or pink?'

'White,' said Martha, 'and don't go spending a fortune on it.'

'White,' agreed Marjorie, who didn't like white wine that much.

'I prefer red, but I'll go with white if that's what everyone else wants,' said Nicola.

Jessica, sitting next to her, patted her hand.

'We'll have a bottle of the house red and a bottle of the house white,' she said.

Before the waitress could turn away, Marjorie piped up.

'What's pink?'

'Rosé,' said Jessica, 'would you like to try some?'

'She'll have the same as me,' said Martha, giving her younger sister a glare.

'Do you have those miniature bottles of rosé?' asked Jessica.

The waitress nodded. 'Yes but,' she leaned forwards to whisper. 'They cost the same as a half-bottle, you're better off getting one of those.'

'Just the small one for now,' replied Jessica. She smiled across the table to her great aunt. 'We can always get a half bottle if you like it.'

Martha shook her head. 'Money to burn.'

Marjorie got to her feet and smoothed down her plaid, smock dress, then sat down again. She looked around excitedly. 'It's been ages since we've been out in the evening, hasn't it, Martha?'

'It has,' replied Martha, looking directly at Jess. 'But there is a good reason for that.'

Jessica blew out her cheeks and let the air out slowly.

'All right, Grandma. I was hoping to get through the meal before the conversation turned to money, but as it has, let's get started. What, exactly, do you expect me to do?'

Martha, snorted.

'Expect? I expect nothing, Jessica, but I *hoped* that you'd be sympathetic to my...' she looked sideways at Marjorie, 'to *our*, plight.'

'I could use a bit of help, too, as you know,' added Nicola.

Martha glared at her daughter.

'You've been at it already have you, trying to undermine us? I thought we had an agree—' She cut herself off mid-sentence.

Jessica tried to make light of it and gave a little laugh. 'So, you were all set to gang up on me, were you?'

'It seemed to be the sensible approach,' said Martha, staring hard at Nicola.

'Well, whatever approach you decided on, the answer is still the same, Grandma. I can't access the money in the trust fund without the agreement of two, third party trustees, and they will make their decisions on Nana's instructions, and those instructions state, that no money of substance is to be handed over to any of her daughters or granddaughters. I couldn't do it if I wanted to.' Jess held out her hands palms up.

'There is always a way.' Martha leaned across the table towards Jessica. 'We just have to find it.'

Jess bit her lip, and waited to speak until the waitress had finished pouring the wine. Nicola drained half her glass in one go, while Marjorie took a tentative sip of the rosé.

'Ooh, I say. That is gorgeous,' she said, and took another, larger, sip.

'I think we'll take the half bottle too,' Jess said.

'And I'll have a gin and tonic, double measures,' added Nicola quickly.

When the waitress had gone, Jess sipped her own drink and looked across at Martha with a serious look on her face.

'Right, Grandma. It's like this. I get a certain amount from the estate every year. I have to pay tax on it, but I can supplement it with any earnings I make from my writing, so, as I don't have to pay rent anymore, I'm a lot better off than I used to be.'

'That goes without saying,' replied Martha. 'Listen, Jessica, we don't want your money, we want our share of the estate, or at least some of it.'

'I can't do that, Grandma,' said Jess firmly. 'But!' she held up her hand to request silence, 'if it's a holiday you need, then I might be able to give you the money for that from my annual allowance.'

'I wasn't thinking of a weekend in Rhyl,' said Martha, testily.

'Nor was I,' replied Jessica. 'I think I can get you two on a reasonably priced cruise in January if you'd like that.'

Marjorie lurched forwards almost knocking her wine glass over.

'A cruise? Where to? How long? Will I need a new hat?'

Martha looked suspiciously at her granddaughter.

'It's a start, I suppose. But you're not buying us off that cheaply.'

'A cruise,' Marjorie whispered as the waitress returned with the extra drinks and asked if they were ready to order.

They decided to skip the starter. Martha ordered Dover Sole for herself and Marjorie, while Jess went for a vegetarian pasta dish. Nicola took a deep pull on her gin and ordered the same as Jessica.

'Better put something inside to soak it up,' she said.

They ate the meal in silence. Nicola just picking at hers. After a few minutes, she looked over her shoulder towards the bar, then announced she needed to visit the toilet.

Jessica watched as she made her way to the bar. After a quick word at the counter, she visited the lady's room, then returned to the bar where she tipped back a glassful of clear liquid before walking back to her seat. The waitress appeared a few minutes later with another glass of gin. Martha, who hadn't seen her at the bar, noticed the refill.

'Steady on. We aren't on a hen night you know.'

Nicola curled up her lip. 'Stop telling me what I can and can't do, Mother. I'm a big girl now.'

'Then bloody well act like one,' snapped Martha.

Nicola picked up her glass and raised a toast. 'To our Jessica. Who holds all of our futures in her beautifully manicured hands.'

'Don't, Mum.' Jessica reached out towards Nicola.

'Don't what?' Nicola drained the gin and reached for the wine bottle.

'Don't be like that, Mum. You know I'll look after you if I can.'

Nicola poured the wine unsteadily, spilling some of it onto the tablecloth. She picked up the glass and took a mouthful.

'Like filling my meter with gas?'

'If that's what you need, then yes.'

'Have you been stupid enough to give her money? You know what she'll do with it,' said Martha.

Marjorie poured herself another glass of rosé and took a big gulp. 'She'll pour it down the drain,' she giggled to herself. 'We know what Nicola does with money, don't we, Martha?'

Martha gave her a look. 'Easy with that stuff or you'll end up like her.' She nodded across the table towards Nicola.

'Grandma, Mum, stop it,' Jessica pleaded.

Martha put her knife and fork side by side on the plate and dabbed at her mouth with a linen napkin.

'I'm warning you, Jessica. Don't give her money.'

'I'm going to try to work out a financial plan for her,' said Jessica. 'The first thing is to get her out of that awful house; it's damp, it's dirty and she deserves to be somewhere a lot nicer than that.'

Martha shrugged. 'Where? She wouldn't pay the rent wherever you put her.'

Jessica thought for a moment.

'Well, the farm used to own a few cottages that were let to the labourers. They belong to the trust now. I can have a look to see if any of those are empty or if the tenant lease is coming up for renewal.'

'Oh, isn't that just dandy!' spat Martha. 'The old soak gets to live rent free for the rest of her life and all I get is a bloody boat trip.'

Marjorie waved her glass in the air. 'A bloody boat trip,' she echoed.

'It's a bit more than a boat trip, it's a three-week cruise,' said Jessica quietly.

'Semantics,' replied Martha.

'I had an idea of how we could get you some money the other night,' said Jessica.

Martha's ears pricked up.

'Well?'

'I thought... Well, why don't you release some equity from your house?'

'MORTGAGE IT!' Martha was furious. 'Do you know how long it took me to pay off the last one?'

'I gave you some money to help, didn't I?' slurred Marjorie.

'Shut up!' Martha shouted, red faced.

Jessica tried to calm the situation.

'It was only an idea, Grandma. The money is no good to you after you're gone. I just thought you might want some of it now.'

'What I want,' Martha banged the table with her hand. 'Is what I'm owed. My birth right. My share of the farm.'

'I can't give you that,' said Jess quietly.

Martha's face became a deeper shade of red. 'Young Lady, I—'

Before she could vent, they were interrupted by a loud, male voice coming from the restaurant floor.

'Jessica. My darling daughter. How wonderful it is to see you.'

Jessica closed her eyes as the voice got nearer.

'I heard you were having a celebration. Fancy not inviting your old dad.'

When Jessica looked up, he was standing at her shoulder. He threw his arms around her and leaned in so that his mouth was next to her ear.

'Jess, I need some money and I need it quickly,' he hissed.

Chapter 16

'Hello, Dad.'

As her father pulled back from his embrace, Jessica looked him over. Physically, he had changed a little since she'd seen him last, some four years ago. His face was thinner, his hair a little greyer and he had definitely lost weight. His clothes seemed to hang on him and the stubble on his cheeks along with the deep bags under his eyes gave him a haunted look.

Nicola got unsteadily to her feet and reached out to hug him.

'Owen, I've missed you so mu—'

He looked quickly over his shoulder like a hunted spy.

'It's Bill, now,' he hissed. 'Bill Stevens. I changed my name by deed poll, remember?'

'Oh, we remember all right,' said Martha, looking at him with distaste. She picked up her glass, sipped the wine and then pulled a face. 'So... BILL... What brings you back after all this time? As if we didn't know.'

'I came to see my daughter. I've missed her.'

'You heard about her inheritance you mean.' Martha wasn't to be taken in.

'My reasons for coming back are no business of yours.' Bill tried to hold Martha's steely glare, but looked away after only a few seconds. He almost pushed Nicola back into her seat, looked around again and seeing only the restaurant host taking any notice of him, he pulled a seat from the next table and dragged it across to sit next to his daughter.

Nicola put a hand on his arm. 'I've missed you, Ow... Bill.'

'So you said.' Bill shuffled his chair closer to Jessica. 'Jess, I need a private word.'

'Not here, Dad... Please. This isn't the time or place.'

'Where then, and when? Come on, Jess, I'm desperate. I can't hang around here too long. You know that.'

'Are they still looking for you after all this time?' Martha was listening in. She might be almost eighty but her hearing was as sharp as it had ever been.

'Keep out of it, Martha. I told you, my business is no concern of yours.'

'No concern of mine. Hmmm. So, the fact that I lent you money to help pay off your gambling debts and you gambled it away and created fresh debt, is nothing to do with me. The fact that because of the despicable way you treated her, my daughter is now an alcoholic, has nothing to do with me. The fact that you fully intend to drag my granddaughter into your poisonous world, is nothing to do with me. Well, think again... BILL... Those issues have a lot to do with me.'

Jess tried to calm the situation before the restaurant management became involved.

'Grandma, it's all right. I know what he's after.' She looked into her father's dark eyes. 'Dad, I can't give you any of Nana's money because it's locked away in a trust and I can't access any of it without the backing of the other two trustees.'

Bill rubbed his stubbly chin and narrowed his eyes. 'Who are these trustees?'

'My solicitor, Bradley Wilson and his practice partner,' replied Jess, calmly.

'You're telling me that Alice left you everything but you can't get your hands on any money? I don't believe a word of it.'

'It's true nonetheless,' said Jess. 'I do get an annual allowance and I get to live at the farm, rent free, but that's it. Nana made it clear what can and can't be done without all three trustees agreeing.'

'That evil bitch. She's still laughing at us.'

'Dad, there's no need for that.'

'Jess, I'm desperate. I can't tell you how desperate. You don't mess around with the people who are chasing me for money. They make this lot up here look like a credit union.'

'I'm sorry, Dad, but as I said—'

'There must be a way, there's always a way.' Bill looked pleadingly at Jess. 'Come on, love. You wouldn't want to see me hurt, would you?'

He picked up the bottle of wine from the table and took a deep swig. Wiping his mouth on his sleeve he took another drink, then rested the bottle on his lap.

Nicola reached across the table to pick up the bottle of white wine that was still half full. She poured a good measure into her glass, then put the bottle next to her plate and gave Martha a defiant look. A shell-shocked Marjorie looked from Jess to Bill to Martha.

'Who's Bill? I'm confused.'

'Then you're in your usual state of mind.' Martha shook her head and turned her attention to Jess. 'If you do find a way to release money from the trust, don't forget, I was at the front of the queue. Don't allow yourself to be coerced into giving in to that snivelling idiot. You may as well hand it straight to the nearest money lender.'

Bill shot a glance over his shoulder as he heard the scrape of a chair behind him, but it was only a customer leaving her seat to visit the cloakroom. He put his hand on top of Jess's.

'Please, Jess. I'm begging you. Just a few thousand. I promise, I'll make a clean start afterwards. I've seen the error of my ways. I've had enough of running and hiding. Honestly.'

'PAH! You pathetic individual.' Martha shook her head again.

'Dad, I don't have a few thousand to give you even if I wanted to.' Jess got stood up and nodded towards the waitress. 'I think it's time we all went home.'

Bill got to his feet with a furious look on his face.

'So, that's it. You're just going to throw me under the bus? Can't we at least talk about it?'

'Of course we can talk about it, Dad. Come to the farm tomorrow morning, but I'm telling you now, my answer will be the same, because there is nothing I can do.'

Bill looked around as if trying to plot his escape.

'I'll be round in the morning then. I'll stay with Nicola tonight.'

Nicola beamed, reached out and took his hand. 'You can stay as long as you like, Owen.'

He snatched his hand away.

'It's Bill for Christ's sake.'

A few seconds later, the waitress arrived with the manager.

'Is everything all right, Ms Griffiths?'

Jess nodded. 'Everything's fine. This is just the way our family reunions go.'

'Then you have my sympathy.' The manager took the bill from the waitress and handed it to Jess. She scanned it, then followed him across to the far end of the bar to pay. As she was tucking her card back into her purse, she heard Nicola call from further along the bar. She waved a bottle of red wine in the air.

'Add this on, Jess,' she said.

In the car park, as Jess opened the back doors of her Toyota to allow Martha and Marjorie to climb in, Bill popped up from behind a Ford KA and slipped in to take the middle seat meaning it would be a bit of a crush on the drive home. The car wasn't really made for five adults. Nicola, clutching her precious bottle of house red, almost fell into the passenger seat. Jess closed both the back doors, climbed into the driver's seat, then reached across to help her struggling mother find the slot for the seat belt. She switched on the lights and with a deep sigh, started up the engine.

At her grandmother's house, Marjorie, and a still furious Martha, got out of the car and walked towards the front door without a word.

'Goodnight, Grandma, goodnight, Aunt Marjorie,' Jessica called as the pair entered the porch.

Martha inserted the key in the lock, pushed open the door, then turned around.

'I'll call you in the morning, young lady. Don't do anything stupid.' With that, she stepped into the house and slammed the door behind her.

As soon as Jessica pulled away from her grandmother's house, Bill started work on her again.

'Jess, honestly. Just this one favour. I'll never ask for anything again.'

'You'll never ask for anything until the next time you're in trouble,' said Jess quietly as she pulled out of the side street onto the main Gillingham road.

'You can trust him, Jess,' slurred Nicola. 'He's your father after all.'

'I remember trusting him when he said he was taking my piggy bank away, to get it paid into my post office account. But not only did he smash the pig and take out a year's savings, he emptied my account too.' Jess wiped away the tear that appeared as she remembered the incident.

'Jess,' said Bill, soothingly.

'I'd saved that money to buy a doll. The doll you promised me for Christmas but never arrived.' A stream of tears rolled down her cheeks. 'I'd saved eight pounds, Dad. Eight pounds and you stole the sodding lot.'

'Jess. I'm sorry, but—'

Jess pulled off the main road, turned onto Burnett Street and pulled up outside her mother's house.

'What did you get for eight measly pounds, Dad?' Jessica wasn't going to let it go now.

Bill opened the car door and slid across the seat.

'You got your bloody doll, didn't you?'

'No thanks to you. Nana, bought it for me.'

'Leave it, Jess.' Nicola pressed the release catch on her seat belt three times before she managed to free herself. She opened the passenger door and crawled into the street with her bottle tucked safely under her arm.

Bill closed the rear door then walked around to the passenger side and leaned into the car.

'I'll see you in the morning, Jess. You, err, couldn't come here instead, could you, save me the bus fare?'

'No, I bloody couldn't,' said Jess with feeling. 'Don't leave it too late either. I'm out for the afternoon and I have to get ready.'

'Oh, you have a new boyfriend already? Nic told me about Calvin. I never did like him. He was a wrong 'un.'

'It takes one to know one, Dad. Shut the door please. I'm going home.'

Chapter 17

Jess made the short trip home with tears streaming down her face as she remembered the hardships and betrayals she had been forced to endure as a child. In bed that night, she found sleep to be impossible as her overworked brain trawled up the memories of her childhood.

One occasion in particular refused to be sent back to the dark cupboard in the back of her mind where such distressing memories were securely locked away. She could picture the event as if it had happened a few seconds earlier.

Jess was in her room, reading a second-hand book she had been given for her birthday. The majority of her toys and books that held any value were stored safely at Nana's farmhouse where she would sleep over most Friday and Saturday nights, as well as a week at a time during school holidays.

Her attention was caught by an argument her parents were having in the next room. Her father's voice was raised, there was nothing new in that, but it was the pleading response from her mother that made her want to listen in. She crawled out of bed, opened her door a crack, cocked her head to one side.

'It's only for a few weeks. I can't see why you're so opposed to the idea.'

'It's disgusting, Owen. I'm not going to do it.'

Jess heard a thud as if something heavy had been thrown onto the floor.

'Come on, Nic. Just a few weeks. I'll be hanging around to make sure you're safe.'

Nicola began to sob.

'Owen. I'm not going on the game and that's that. It doesn't matter if it's one night or every night for a year. I'm not going to do it. My reputation around here is bad enough as it is.'

'But it's the only way out,' Owen roared.

'You do it then,' Nicola screamed back at him. 'I'm sure there are plenty of men willing to pay for your services.'

'Now you're being ridiculous. Come on. Just try it. It probably won't be as bad as you think.'

'No, Owen.'

'You'd rather see me in hospital than do this little thing for me. That's nice. You know what the Duncan brothers are like. I'll be lucky if I can ever walk again.'

Jessica had no idea which game her father was demanding her mother take part in, but it didn't seem to be a game that she wanted to play. The voices quietened for a while, then Owen spoke again, this time with a more persuasive tone to his voice.

'Nicola, come on. Put something sexy on. We'll just go out and have a look to see what it's like. You don't have to bring anyone home tonight. Just stand near the railway station with the other girls. They're not a patch on you, Nic. You can do it, just have a drink first. It will be fine. I'll be watching out for you.'

'What about Jess? We can't just leave her.'

'I'll look after Jess if you bring anyone home. Come on, you can do it.'

Jess decided that she didn't like the idea of being left alone while her parents went out to play games. They had left her alone when they went out to a New Year's Eve party and had promised to be back by a minute after midnight, but Jess had stayed awake, frightened and alone, jumping at every creak the old house made, until they finally got home at three in the morning.

She pushed her door open and made her eyes into slits as she stepped along the landing to her parents' room.

'Mummy, I have a pain.'

'Jessica! Go back to bed,' her father ordered.

'But I have a pain, I think I'm going to be sick.'

The door flew open a few seconds later and her mother appeared pulling a dressing gown over black lingerie.

'Oh, Jess, come on let's get you back to bed. Mummy will sit with you until the pain has gone. Do you think a glass of warm milk will help, maybe an aspirin?'

She led Jess back to her bed and lay down alongside, stroking her hair to soothe her.

'I don't want you and Daddy to play the game, Mummy.' Jess began to cry.

Nicola looked across at Owen, standing in the open doorway, then turned her attention back to her daughter.

'I don't want to either, my sweetheart. So, we won't play it. I promise.

Chapter 18

The next morning, Jess was woken by the rattle of the door's heavy knocker echoing up the stairs from the hall. Rubbing her eyes, she picked up her phone to check the time.

'Seven-thirty. Who the hell?'

She sat up, remembering not only that her father was calling in, but the dreadful memories that had haunted her sleep. She swung her legs off the bed, and yawning, stood up and stretched. The banging became more intense, then the sound of a muffled voice came through the letterbox.

'Jess.'

'Sod it, you can wait,' she muttered, reaching for her dressing gown.

She walked through to the shower room, had her first pee of the day, cleaned her teeth, then took a leisurely look at herself in the wall mirror. She dragged a brush through her hair, then walked back to the bedroom just as her phone rang. She picked it up to see 'unknown caller' on the screen. Refusing to answer, she stepped onto the landing and walked to the front window. Outside, on the asphalt parking bay, her father was looking angrily at his phone. He pressed a button and Jess's phone rang again. This time she answered.

'Yes.'

'Jess, It's Dad, love, are you going to let me in?'

'What time do you call this, Dad? It's Saturday you know?'

'I do know, but you said you had to get ready to go out?'

'Good heavens, Dad. It won't take me four hours to get ready.'

There was a pause, then he spoke again. 'Well, can I come in?'

Jess sighed and hung up. She slipped her phone into the pocket of her dressing gown and walked slowly down the stairs, stretching as she went. She paused at the front door, in two minds whether to let him in or not. The old memories hadn't yet returned to the locked room in the recesses of her mind.

'Hello, Dad,' she sighed as she opened the door.

He saw the indifferent look on her face and turned on the charm, leaning forward to kiss her cheek. Jess pulled her head back while his was still a foot away.

'Tea?' she asked.

'If you're making it?'

He looked around as he walked into the lounge.

'She's had the place knocked about a bit since the last time I came inside. The stairs used to come off the kitchen. There was no hall here, just a door out to the front yard.'

'That was about twenty-five years ago,' replied Jess. 'The old stairway had a problem and had to be taken out, so she had the place redesigned. You can still work out where the old stairway used to be in the kitchen. Haven't you been in here since then? I'm sure Nana said you and Mum came around to borrow some money when I was little.'

'I didn't come in. Your mother had to persuade the old witch to give us a few quid.'

Jessica's lips became a thin line.

'She helped you out, Dad, and what did you do? You gambled away the money she gave you to pay the mortgage, so we ended up getting evicted.'

Bill looked like he was going to argue the point, but decided against it.

'Water under the bridge,' he said.

'There's been a lot of water flowing under that particular bridge over the years, Dad.'

Jess walked into the kitchen, filled the kettle and switched it on as Bill walked around, opening a drawer here, a cupboard there.

'It could do with a revamp,' he said.

'It's having one,' replied Jess. 'I got Robin's Kitchens to do an estimate.'

Her father whistled. 'That won't be cheap.'

'It won't,' Jessica agreed as she poured boiling water into two mugs.

Bill pulled out a chair and sat down at the huge oak table. He rubbed his hands over it as Jess put his tea in front of him. 'I bet this has lived through some interesting times.'

'Nana gave birth to Grandma on that table,' Jess replied, running her own hands over the surface.

Bill pulled his hands away as if he'd received an electric shock.

'She always was a strange one. Can you remember? Martha and Marjorie used to claim she was a witch and practiced magic in the loft.'

'Of course I remember. I remember everything.' She curled up her lip as she looked across the table at her father. 'I remember the Christmases with no presents. I remember the birthdays without parties and just a second-hand book or two as a present. I remember going to school hungry because there was nothing in the cupboard for breakfast, I remember—'

'All right, all right. Times were hard. Lots of families suffered back then.'

'Yes, but in our case, there was no need for anyone to suffer. You had a good job but you spent all of your wages at the bookies or the racetrack. You sold, or pawned everything we ever owned to fund your habit. You lost our house. You made our lives a living hell, never knowing what depths you would stoop to in order to put your next bet on.'

Bill reached out a hand. 'Come on, Jess, it wasn't all bad. You had some good times too. Didn't you?'

'All my good times were spent here with Nana.' Jess felt a lump in her throat, so sipped at her tea to hide it.

'I wasn't the best father, or husband, Jess, I admit that, but I did want the best for you. That's why I was always chasing the impossible dream. To enable us to have nice things.'

'You were an addict, Dad. There's no getting away from it. I was lying in bed last night thinking about it all.'

'Forgive and forget, eh, Jess? A lot of water—'

'The bridge flooded, Dad. then it collapsed under the torrent.'

'Jess.'

'Last night, I remembered something I had buried so deep I hoped I'd never get a hint of it ever again.'

'Don't...'

'You tried to get my mother to go on the game just to raise a few quid for a bet on the three-thirty.' Jess almost spat out the words.

'Now, that's not true, Jess.'

'I remembered it like it happened yesterday. I had to come to your bedroom door, pretending to be sick or you were going to take her out onto the streets.'

Bill's head fell.

'I wasn't in a good place then, Jess.'

'You're not in a much better place now by the sounds of it. How much do you actually owe?'

Bill shrugged.

'How much are you asking me to raise, Dad?'

'Forty thousand.'

'FORTY THOU—'

'I was going to buy into a card school, Jess. A big one, with big gamblers. It would have been a regular event. My share would have been twenty percent of the deposits every night. Punters had to pay us to take part. I couldn't lose.'

'But you managed to drag victory into the gaping jaws of defeat, yet again. You really are the world's biggest loser, aren't you?'

'It really wasn't my fault this time, Jess, honestly. I borrowed the money for my stake, but, the night before I was due to hand it over, there was a dummy run, with some of the prospective clients. I sat in... The whole thing was rigged, Jess. I was set up.'

Jess looked away and shook her head.

'You stupid fool.'

'I know, I wasn't thinking straight, Jess. They screwed me good and proper, but the thing is. I owe them now, they want their money, and these aren't people you can say no to.'

'I can say no, and I'm going to. Sorry, Dad, but you made your bed, now you can lie in it.'

'Jess. Please. I'm begging you.' Bill's eyes became liquid pools.

'No. Even if I could get the money from the trust, I wouldn't. What the hell would I say to the other trustees?'

'Make something up. Say you want to invest in a business venture I'm setting up. You'll think of something.'

Jess walked into the lounge with her father in pursuit.

'Goodbye, Dad.'

'Don't you dare treat me like this, after all I've...'

'After all you've done for me? My God, that's rich.' Jess walked down the hall and yanked open the front door. 'OUT!' she commanded.

Bill walked slowly out of the house. On the bottom step he stopped and turned.

'Jess, I know you think I'm trying to save my own skin, but I'm worried about your welfare too.'

'Why? These people have no idea who am I and where I live.'

Bill pulled a face. 'That's not quite true, Jess. To buy some time I had to tell them about your good fortune. They know all about you.'

Jess scowled. 'I thought you couldn't get any lower than trying to force your wife into prostitution, but you've managed it. You've handed your daughter over to gangsters.' Jess stepped back into the house and slammed the door, then leaning against it, she began to sob.

Chapter 19

Jess walked slowly through to the lounge and plonked herself down onto the old sofa.

'Oh, Nana, I didn't know it was going to be this difficult,' she said softly.

She curled up her feet and wriggled her bottom in an effort to get comfortable but the saggy cloth and bent springs in the sofa made it impossible.

'This has to go, Nana,' she said aloud and grabbing her laptop she began to search for a new sofa. She had only looked at a couple when her phone rang. She ignored it, thinking it was her father trying to put pressure on her again, but when the phone stopped ringing then started again, she picked it up, glanced at the screen and held it to her ear.

'Hello, Grandma.'

'Jessica. I'm just checking that you're all right.'

'I'm fine, Grandma.'

'He didn't turn up with a grasping bookie in tow then?'

'No, he came alone... Look, Grandma, I didn't promise to give him money. I haven't got any to give him.'

'Good. He's a nasty piece of work. I'll never know what Nicola saw in him.'

Jessica's voice softened. 'He might not have been like he is now when he was younger... though, I can never remember him being any different.'

'He was a charmer when he was young. Your mother fell for it. He knew which of her buttons to press. Take care, Jessica. Men are like that.'

Jess thought about how her relationship with Calvin had deteriorated and nodded without replying.

Martha's tone suddenly sweetened. 'When you agreed to sit down and talk to your father, it made me think that it's about time you and I had a private chat.

There always seems to be someone else around when we meet.'

'That would be nice, Grandma, but it won't change anything.'

'We don't have to talk about money all the time, Jessica. We seem to have drifted apart over the last few years and I regret that.'

'I'd like a nice cosy chat. I wish we could have done it when Nana was still here.'

'It was never going to happen when my mother was around,' replied Martha. 'We never saw eye to eye over anything, she was—'

'Don't, Grandma, please.'

'We do have to discuss her sometimes, Jessica. You only ever heard one side of the story.'

'I'd like to hear about your life, Grandma, I hardly know anything about it really.'

'There's a lot more to it than you could ever imagine. Mother had no idea what sort of life I had after I left home.'

Jessica was sympathetic. 'That's a shame, I think she would have been interested had you given her a chance.'

'We never got on. She didn't like me, even as a child, and the feeling was mutual.'

'I think you'd be surprised, Grandma. You ought to read some of her memoirs. She worried about your relationship and did what she could to try to improve it.'

Martha was having none of it. 'Miriam brought me up. My mother was hardly ever around.'

'She had the farm to run, Grandma. That took up most of her day. She gave you as much time as she could, I promise you.'

Martha snorted. 'I'd like to see what excuses she used to cover her guilty conscience.'

Jessica sighed. 'Look, I've got to get ready to go out. Can we meet up in the week?'

'Come to see me on Tuesday afternoon. I'll send Marjorie on an errand for an hour, though she'll almost certainly get lost.'

'I'll pick you up at eleven and drive you over here, Grandma. Marjorie can't get lost if she's left at home, maybe you could bring her with you? It would be nice to see you both.'

'It would be better if she's left out of it. She'd only get confused. She isn't the sharpest knife in the drawer.'

'Oh, Grandma. Don't be like that. Aunt Marjorie is lovely.'

Jessica heard her grandmother sigh.

'Goodness knows what sort of life she'd have led if I hadn't been there to look after her. You might think I'm harsh, but she needs a firm hand. She'd be lost without me.'

'I don't know much about Aunt Marjorie's life either. Maybe I should have a sit down with her one day.'

'Bring a pillow and a mug of Ovaltine with you when you do. She hasn't lived the most exciting of lives.'

'I'm sure there's more to it than you're letting on, Grandma... Look, I have to go, I have to get ready.'

'Ready? Are you out on a date or something?'

'I'm going out for lunch with Bradley Wilson.'

'That solicitor fellow?'

'Yep. We're having a drive out to a country pub for a meal.'

'Hmm, I can see the attraction, he is a professional man and not bad looking. You could do a lot worse.'

Jessica laughed. 'I'm not out to marry him, Grandma. It's only lunch.'

'Well, he seems a better prospect than that worm of a boyfriend you just got rid of.'

'I'm not looking for a new boyfriend either,' Jess replied. 'I'm still trying to work out how I let Calvin get away with what he did for so long.'

Martha was silent for a moment. When she spoke again her voice was almost conspiratorial.

'Listen, Jessica. See if you can get him to find a way out of this trust thing. I'm sure—'

'Goodbye, Grandma. I'll see you on Tuesday.'

Jess hit the red button on the screen to end the call and leaned back on the sofa. Shaking her head at Martha's attitude, she picked up her laptop again and began to surf for sofas.

Twenty minutes later, Jess had chosen, ordered and paid for a sofa. She checked her banking app and realised with a shock how much she had spent recently. She would have to bring up the subject of money with Bradley after all. Some of her annual allowance was urgently needed. Her credit card bill had arrived that morning too.

Standing at the door of the kitchen, Jess stared across the room trying to imagine the new sofa in situ.

'Sorry, Nana, but it had to be done,' she said aloud. Her eyes were drawn to the big, expensive, hospital bed that Alice had slept in for the last twelve months of her life. She had decided to offer it to Nana's carer, Gwen to see if she could find a use for it, but had forgotten to call her. She picked up her phone and hit her contact number. Gwen answered after three rings.

'Hello, Jessica, is anything wrong?'

'Hi, Gwen, no, nothing at all. I've been meaning to call you all week. I'm living at Nana's house now.'

'So I heard, Lovely, there are no secrets in this town you know.'

Jess laughed.

'The thing is, Gwen. I'd like to catch up, there are one or two things I'd like to talk to you about. The main one being this bed of Nana's. Do you think you could find a place for it? I'd much rather it goes to one of your clients than have it picked up by a charity.'

'OOOH! That's very kind of you, Jessica. I took a new client on when Alice passed. She's another Alice, Alice Scrimshaw and she really could do with something like that. She's a bit heavy for me and those buttons and

switches that raise and lower the bed would be a big
help.'

'Then, it's yours,' said Jess. 'When do you think you
could arrange to have it picked up. Do you need a man
with a van? I can organise that.'

'No, Lovely. Alice's grandson has a big van, he does
removals. I'm sure he'd be happy to pick it up. How
much do you want for it?'

'I don't want a penny, Gwen, it's yours to do with as
you see fit.'

Jess could visualise Gwen's astonished face. She
never could understand why anyone would want to
reward her.

'I'll tell Alec that it's not theirs to keep of course. It
was far too expensive to just give away. Alice has a few
month's yet, but after that, old Mr Parfitt will be
needing one. He's starting to struggle now, even with
the stairlift.'

'I'm sure you'll use it wisely, Gwen, and I'm happy
it's going to someone who will appreciate it.'

'You said there are a couple of things you want to
talk to me about,' said Gwen with a worried tone in her
voice.

'Oh, it's nothing important, Gwen. Just the odd
thing or two about Nana. She seems to have torn some
pages out of one of her memoirs and I can't find them.
They were there when I brought them down from the
loft.

'I don't know anything about those, Lovely. Alice
never mentioned them to me.'

'Not to worry,' said Jess. 'As I said, it's not
important. Give me a call when Alec has an hour free.
We can have a coffee and a chat while he loads it onto
the van. I think he'll need assistance though. It will be a
bit awkward for one.'

'Alec has two sons. They'll help I'm sure.'

'Great. All right, Gwen, take care now. I'll see you
when you come over.'

'Bye bye, Jessica, and thank you again.'

After the call, Jessica picked up her laptop and carried it upstairs. Putting it on the dressing table she had another look at the new sofa she had ordered. The blue light problem seemed to have fixed itself so, relieved at not having to raid her dwindling finances again, she closed the laptop lid, patted it for luck and walked through to the bathroom to shower.

She dressed in newish, light blue jeans, a white blouse with a pink, floral embroidery above the right breast and black, low heeled shoes. She kept her phone at the side of her as she brushed her hair and applied the minimum of makeup, as she couldn't remember if Bradley had said he'd call when he was on his way.

At twelve on the dot, Jess heard the toot of a car horn, and grabbing a navy jacket and her shoulder bag she let herself out of the front door to see Bradley standing proudly at the side of a vintage, Alvis car.

'Oh, Wow!' Jess exclaimed. She had read all about what Alice had called the Gangster Car but she had no idea it was still on the road after all these years. She stood for a few moments as she admired the beautiful, shiny, black automobile. There didn't seem to be a mark on it.

Jess looked up to the skies and smiled.

'I have a Gangster Lawyer too now, Nana.' She grinned at Bradley as he walked around the front of the car and opened the passenger door for her.

'All that's missing is the hat,' she said with a laugh.

Bradley looked puzzled. 'The hat?'

'Godfrey always wore one. That's why Alice called him her Gangster Lawyer. With his pin striped suits, hat and that car, he looked like he'd just stepped out of a James Cagney movie.'

'Ah, I see,' said Bradley with a grin. 'Sorry, no hat.'

Jess climbed into the car and sat down. She reached over her shoulder for the seat belt, but not finding one, looked at Bradley with a puzzled look on her face.

'Cars of this vintage aren't required to have them fitted,' said Bradley as he started the engine and put the Alvis in reverse.

'Are you sure?' Jess felt a bit uncomfortable without the reassuring strap over her shoulder.

'Trust me, I'm a lawyer,' grinned Bradley. 'It feels a bit odd doesn't it? But don't worry. I'll be careful.'

Jess looked over her shoulder towards the back seats and suddenly remembered what Alice and Godfrey had got up to in the car all those years ago. The day Alice had got dressed in such a hurry that she forgot to put on her underwear. She quickly turned her head to the front, but the vision in her mind wouldn't go away. She could feel herself beginning to flush.

'Are you all right?' said Bradley taking a sideways glance. 'You look a bit hot. I'm afraid there's no air con.'

'I'm fine,' said Jess, reaching to her right and winding down the window. 'I was in a bit of a rush, that's all.'

They drove through the winding back lanes of the town until they hit what used to be one of the main routes to Gravesend. They followed that for a few miles before turning off again and pulling up at a riverside pub in a pretty little village with picture postcard thatched cottages and a Norman church.

The Lobster Pot had a beer garden and boasted a mainly seafood menu, although, thankfully for Jess, who was struggling to become a vegetarian, the pub provided a sparse vegan menu as well.

Jess found Bradley refreshingly interesting after the narrow mindedness of Calvin. He genuinely seemed to be sympathetic to her views. He listened intently as she told him about her life at Uni and some of the scrapes she had got herself into on the anti this, and that, marches.

She looked across the table at him as he ate during a short lull in the conversation. He was handsome, there was no getting away from it. He had an easy manner about him, and refreshingly, unlike Calvin, he seemed willing to discuss subjects that he wasn't particularly knowledgeable about. Calvin was only interested in promoting himself or his own ideas and frequently talked over Jess when they were out with friends. Bradley had hardly mentioned his own life and seemed much more interested in finding out more about her.

As she was studying him, she suddenly heard Alice's voice in her head.

'Beware men who never talk about themselves, Jessica. You will invariably find that they have something to hide.'

She put the thought to one side. While she didn't know Bradley very well, he had been honest enough to offer up the information about his previous, short lived marriage, and Alice liked him enough to trust him with her financial and legal affairs, much like she had with his great grandfather, Godfrey, though 'affair' had other connotations as far as he was concerned.

Bradley looked up from his plate as if he had heard Alice's words. He noticed that Jess had been studying him with corners of her lips turned up in a soft smile.

'What?' he said, smiling himself.

'Oh, nothing,' Jess replied. 'I was just thinking of something that Nana had said.'

'I liked Alice. Want to share?'

Jess shook her head. 'No, it was a private thing. Just one of her little pearls of wisdom.'

Bradley grinned showing off his perfect, white teeth.

'I'm sure she had many of those to impart. I hope you listened.'

'Always,' replied Jess. 'Especially when she talked about men.' She smiled mischievously and looked away from him.

After lunch, they took a walk along the river, stopping to watch a pair of swans swimming side by side at the edge of the reed bed.

'Aren't they beautiful,' said Jess. 'I think it's lovely that they pair for life. They don't fall out or treat each other badly like human couples.'

As if listening to their conversation, one of the swans looked towards them and floated a few yards closer.

Bradley pointed to it. 'You don't know what she's thinking though do you. She might still be brooding about him having a late night in the reed beds.'

Jess punched him lightly on the arm and laughed. 'Or she might be thinking. What a handsome chap my partner is. I can't wait for mating season.'

Bradley faked shock. 'Jessica Griffiths!'

'I'm like my Nana,' she said. 'Her best friend used to call her Alice Hussy.'

Bradley laughed again and turned back to the path.

'You know, Ms Hussy. You really are very good company. I could get used to this.'

He smiled warmly at her then began to walk at a slow pace. Jessica took two quick strides to catch up with him and slipped her arm through his.

'You're not bad company yourself,' she said.

After the riverside walk, they returned to the Alvis and Bradley drove back towards home via the many narrow country lanes and B roads. After a while, Jess remembered about the kitchen quote. She dipped into her bag to pull it out.

'I've taken the liberty of getting a quote for a new kitchen. Make sure you're sitting down when you read it.'

'It will be fine, whatever the cost,' replied Bradley. 'Maintenance is covered within the trust terms.'

'Also... I erm... I could do with a bit of my annual allowance if that's okay. I had to buy a new bed, get the broadband fitted, then there was the sofa and...'

'I'll get on to it on Monday morning.' Bradley flashed her a quick glance then focussed on the road again.

Jess cleared her throat. 'I probably shouldn't tell you this, but I'm under pressure from my relatives. They all seem to think there's a way around the trust terms and conditions. They think I can magic up money from thin air.'

'There's no way around it. Regarding pay-outs at least.'

'What about property,' said Jess, eagerly. 'My mother is living in a proper dump; okay, she has her problems, but she deserves better than that. It's damp, it smells and it costs a fortune to heat.'

'What do you mean by property? Are you looking for somewhere for her to rent?'

'Not exactly, rent... She can't afford a lot. I was hoping to help her.'

'There are properties in Spinton and one in Gillingham. I can check the leases... hang on... I know for a fact that one of your tenants is leaving in January. She's an elderly lady and she's going into a nursing home after Christmas. She's staying with her family until then, but we can't really chuck her stuff out onto the street. The lease runs out on the thirty-first of December.'

'Is it close by? It's not too grand is it?'

'It's a two-bedroom cottage. It used to be leased out to one of the farmworkers. Alice mentioned that her own father had allowed a retired farmhand to live rent free in it for the rest of his life.'

'That would be Miriam's father. Miriam was one of my Nana's best friends. She lived at the farm after her father died.'

'I'll certainly look into it for your mum,' said Bradley. 'It does carry a market rent, but... well, I suppose it's your decision what level it is set at. You're the owner. You won't get any argument from me.'

Bradley reached out and patted Jess's hand. 'Had it been your grandmother, I might have put up more of a fight.'

Jess laughed. 'And she has such nice things to say about you.'

Back at the farmhouse, Jess invited Bradley in for a coffee. Bradley was reluctant at first. 'My mother will be worried about the car. It's a family heirloom and she thinks that it's her responsibility.'

'Ten minutes?' Jess produced her doe eyes. Bradley immediately crumbled.

He waited on the doorstep to allow her to go in first, then closing the front door behind him he followed her through the lounge to the kitchen. Jess handed him the brochure that the Robin's man had left.

'That's what's costing so much money,' she said, filling the kettle.

Bradley looked at the brochure, then around the kitchen. 'Good choice. It will look beautiful,' he said.

Jess held out her hand towards the huge oak table. 'Please, sit.'

Bradley pulled out a chair, sat down and ran his hands over the well-worn surface of the table. 'I've sat at boardroom tables smaller than this,' he said.

'I bet no one ever gave birth on a boardroom table.'

'I don't suppose... hang on. Are you saying...?'

'Nana gave birth to Martha on that very table,' said Jess proudly.

'Why? I mean... what...?'

'She refused to have the baby on the upstairs bed because her mother had died on it and she didn't want to pass any bad luck onto a newborn.'

Bradley touched the table again and shook his head.

'Then, a few hours after Martha was born, she found her father dead in the front room.'

Bradley looked towards the door that connected the two rooms.

'Oh, my goodness, what a day that was for her.'

'I know,' said Jess. 'She ended up being a single mother, running a hundred-acre farm with all the stresses and strains that go with it. She'd have been a feminist icon in this day and age, but back then, she had to take the baby's father's surname, even though she wouldn't marry him, just to make it look respectable.'

Jess stuck out her chin and her voice cracked with emotion. 'She built her own business empire on the back of such harrowing circumstances.'

'I'm not surprised you're so proud of her. I met her and liked her, as you know. She was a very impressive lady.'

Jess wiped away a tear and tried to swallow the lump that had appeared in her throat.

'She was, very impressive... and I loved her so much.'

Bradley was on his feet in an instant. He wrapped his arms around her and hugged her tight. Jess dropped her head on his shoulder and soaked it with tears.

'Everything has happened so quickly,' he said, 'you haven't had chance to properly mourn her.'

'I don't really need to mourn her.' Jess pulled her head from his shoulder and looked into his eyes. 'She's here, around me all the time. I just miss her voice, her advice... she had absolute faith in me. I just hope I can manage to live up to it.'

'You have made an excellent start,' said Bradley softly. His face inched closer, then, falteringly, his lips touched hers. He pulled away and looked into her glistening tear-filled eyes, then his lips found hers again.

Ten minutes later, Jess followed him out to the Alvis. Bradley turned as he reached the bonnet of the old motor and blew her a kiss.

'Here's looking at you, kid. Isn't that what they said in the gangster movies?'

'Something like that,' Jess replied. She gave a wiggle of her fingers.

'I'll call you on Monday, straight after I release the annual funds into your bank account,' he said.

As he turned towards the car he stopped dead, a look of horror spread across his face.

'Whatever is the matter?' Jess took a few steps forward to see what had shocked Bradley so much.

Cut into the shiny, black paintwork, running the full length of the beautiful, ninety-year-old car, was an ugly, jagged, key scratch.

Chapter 20

'My mother will go ballistic.' Bradley ran his hand along the scratch.

Jessica looked up and down the lane. 'Who would even think about doing such a terrible thing to something so old and beautiful?'

'I can't understand it either,' said Bradley. 'And, where did he... I'm assuming it's a he, come from? We only left it alone for twenty minutes. I can't remember seeing another car on the lane when we pulled up.'

'Will it be expensive to fix?' asked Jess.

'It won't be cheap. I really don't know if you can still get the matching paint. This stuff is enamel, I think.' He ran his hand along the side of the car again. 'Ninety years without so much as a stone chip and then someone does this.'

'I feel guilty now,' said Jess. 'If there's anything I can do to help. I'll contribute to the repair costs.'

Bradley looked up from the car. 'You really are very kind, but the fault is all mine. We only take her out to car shows or the odd run in the London to Brighton rally. I think I was trying to impress you, what with Alice's connection to the car and everything.'

Jessica bit her tongue. The connection was stronger than he knew. Especially her connection to the back seat.

'I'll slip it into the garage while my mother is out. She's got one of her charity things today. I can hopefully get it to a specialist before she notices,' Bradley said as he opened the driver's door.

'She can't blame you for this, surely? It's just the work of a mean-minded vandal after all.'

Bradley pulled a face. 'She did ask why I needed to use the Alvis. I told her I just fancied a spin in it.'

'She doesn't know you were meeting me then?'

'No, I, erm, didn't mention you. It would only have led to an inquisition. Mothers want to know every detail, don't they? Next thing she'd be checking my Facebook and Twitter feeds. She's a little over protective, especially since my first marriage went sour.'

'You'd better not tell her I was with you at the time, then. I don't want her poking about in my social media.' Jess laughed, trying to make light of the revelation.

'She'd check you out, that's for certain.' Bradley joined in the laughter half-heartedly. 'I'll just refer to you as a client for now. I think it's best.'

'For now?' Jessica walked to the side of the car and put her hand on Bradley's arm. 'You want to see me again then, even after this?'

'If you're willing.' Bradley gave a half smile. 'I'm sorry I was a bit off when I saw the damage. It's my mother... you don't know her.' Bradley looked as though he was dreading the encounter.

'I'm sure you can win her around. Use that lovely smile of yours. You could melt the hardest of hearts with that.' Jessica leaned forward and brushed her lips against his. 'I'll look forward to our phone conversation on Monday.'

'Phone con... Oh, right. Your annual allowance. I'll get straight onto that first thing. It should only take a couple of minutes. I only have to get Simon's signature to process the release of funds. Simon is one of the practice partners and the other trustee.'

'Thanks for sorting it so quickly,' replied Jess. She backed away and he pulled the door shut before starting the engine and reversing out into the lane.

As Jess watched him drive away a waving hand appeared out of the driver's window.

Jess returned to the kitchen and put the kettle on feeling a mixture of excitement and sadness. She didn't like the sound of Bradley's mother, but she was used to dealing with forthright women. Nana had been a very strong woman in thought and deed, but she had always allowed Jess to live her life without too much interference. Martha, on the other hand, was a control freak and would have liked to have had a far bigger say in her upbringing. She touched her lips and remembered the almost electric sensation she had felt when they came in contact with Bradley's.

'What do you think, Nana?' she said softly. 'I really like him. I hope he isn't overly influenced by his mother like Calvin was. I hope I haven't found another mummy's boy.'

As if in reply, a loud gurgling sound came from of the sink. Jess laughed. 'What was that, Nana? I didn't quite catch it.'

After coffee, Jess settled down at the big oak table with her notebook, pen and Alice's 1939 memoir. She opened her notebook and made a new heading.

Autumn 1939.

Jess sat with pen poised as she began to read.

September 1939

The weather had been kind to us throughout September allowing us to finish the harvest early. Also, during September, the government issued a directive, demanding that all men aged between 18 and 41 must register for National Service, meaning everyone in that age bracket would be liable for conscription. Later in September the National Register was compiled, preparing the way for ration books to be issued.

My workers were exempt from military duties, farming being classed as a reserved occupation, but it didn't stop the youngest, Benny, George, Tommy and Harry from signing up. I admit that I used every trick in the book to stop them from registering, even trying emotional blackmail on Benny who had only been married for a few months and his new wife was expecting. It wasn't solely for commercial reasons; I genuinely classed my workforce as members of my extended family. I cared about them and I would have been heartbroken had anything happened to them.

We said our goodbyes the day after the farm's harvest party. Barney, my stoic foreman, a man who could be guaranteed to keep his emotions in check, made a speech that my father would have been proud of and speaking in a brittle voice, wished them all the luck in the world and a speedy return home.

I gave each one a big hug, whispered 'stay safe, please come back to us' and handed them each a brown packet containing two, pound notes, to see them through their first few weeks training. Two pounds was a week's wage and I hoped it would allow them to buy beer in the NAAFI to help lift their spirits after a hard day spent learning how to kill the enemy. As it happens, I found out a week later that all of the young men gave the money to their wives or mothers.

I spent the rest of that afternoon in the kitchen with Martha on my lap, praying to any deity who happened to be listening, to spare my boys and send them home safely.

That evening, Miriam's man friend, Michael, telephoned. It was an emotional call telling Miriam he had to see her urgently. Miriam, thinking that her beau was about to ask her to marry him at last, rushed out of the house without changing out of her work clothes or even brushing her hair. She returned an hour later, in tears.

'Miriam?' I got up from the kitchen table and held out my arms to her as she came through the door.

'He... we... Look, he doesn't want to marry me; he's still being loyal to his dead wife. He was just upset because both his sons signed up to fight and they left for training today, just like our lads.'

'Oh, Miriam, I'm so sorry,' I said inadequately.

'We'll never be married,' she sniffed as she took off her coat. 'If anything happens to those boys...'

'Your son has signed up too, Miriam. You have something more to share now. Concern for your children, it might bring you even closer together.'

'Do you think it will, Alice? I'm not so sure. He feels guilty for seeing me as it is, he thinks his wife disapproves of us, somehow. If anything should happen to Michael junior, or David, he might begin to think it's a curse sent down from above.'

'Their mother would never do that. If she is capable of anything, surely it will be a protecting influence?'

'Oh, I do hope so, Alice. I hope my old dad is watching over my Dennis, too.'

I gave her another hug and a kiss on the cheek. 'He will be, Miriam. He will be.'

That night, I lay in bed thinking about all the mothers in the town that were about to say goodbye to their sons. For many of them it would be the last word they ever shared. I pictured Benny's pregnant young wife standing on the doorstep receiving the dreaded telegram informing her that her beloved new husband had been killed or was missing in action. I imagined Tommy's mother dropping to her knees. She wasn't the strongest of women. Like my own mother, she had had a terrible time in childbirth. The trauma she had endured had affected her mentally and she suffered regular periods of depression, some of which had seen her taken into the psychiatric hospital at Gillingham.

At three in the morning, I got up to make tea, sleep was never going to come. As I stepped into the kitchen, I found Miriam already there. Noticing my red eyes, she gave me a sad smile and picked up the teapot.

'Come on, love. I've made a nice cup of tea, that will make you feel better.'

Tea was Miriam's cure-all. She was convinced it was a quick fix for most emotional difficulties. That night it worked, although I think it was more her company and her warm arms around me that scared away my demons.

My birthday fell on a Saturday and as that was a regular night out with my best friend Amy, we decided to stick to our usual routine and spend the evening at the pictures, ending up in the Old Bull for the last hour.

The film was Goodbye Mr Chips with Greer Garson and Robert Donat. Many tears fell during the screening. Especially when Mr Chip's wife and baby died. I was still wiping my eyes when we left the cinema and crossed the road to buy fish and chips before the bus came.

We sat on a low wall opposite the bus stop as we ate our supper. Amy chatting away whilst blowing on a chip to cool it.

'So, Alice Hussy, have you seen anything of your Gangster Lawyer since I saw you last?'

I had just stuffed a couple of chips in my mouth, so she had to wait for an answer while I panted like a racing greyhound to try to stop the blisteringly hot food burning my tongue. Eventually, I managed to swallow them whole.

'No, I haven't seen him since you last asked on Thursday evening.' Amy had been down to visit after work.

'He's going off you, I can tell.'

'He does have a wife and kids, remember?'

'If he really loved you, he'd be there every day, professing his love, whispering poetry through the letterbox.'

I looked at her quizzically. 'Have you been reading Shelley again?'

Amy sniffed and popped the last of her chips into her mouth.

'Might have,' she said.

'I can always tell,' I said. 'You get all mushy.'

'I do,' agreed Amy. 'Though it might be...' she pointed downwards, 'I always get a bit emotional at this time of the month.'

We screwed up the sheets of newspaper our chips had been served in, dropped them into a metal litter bin and walked quickly across the road as our bus turned the corner further along Middle Street. We joined the queue of chatting cinema goers and a short time later we arrived at the Old Bull, where I was greeted with a chorus of Happy Birthday as we walked into the lounge.

I was surprised to see Big Nose Beryl standing with the factory girls at the bar. Beryl doesn't have a particularly big nose, but gets the nickname because she can't keep it out of other people's business. She usually frequented the Red Lion in town. Amy had been gunning for her for months.

'Happy Birthday, Alice,' she gushed as I took my G and T from Amy who always bought the drinks on my birthday.

'Thank you, Beryl,' I replied and waited for the follow up barb, there always was one with Beryl.

'How old are you now, nineteen is it?'

'Twenty, Beryl.'

'And, how old is little Martha? I bet she's getting big now.'

'She's fifteen months, and yes, she is growing quickly.'

Amy took my arm and began to lead me across to a group of girls we went to school with. Most of them worked at the factory with Amy, although a couple had jobs in the shops in town. Beryl hadn't finished though.

'Has Martha's dad been in touch recently? I heard he'd written to someone saying that he met a woman in Dover and was starting a new family there. You'd think he'd ask for a divorce first, wouldn't you?'

Before I could say anything, Amy turned around, took three large paces forward and stuck her face up close to Beryl's. Beryl suddenly looked like a cornered fox, her eyes darted left and right as if looking for a way out.

'Frank is with the Merchant Navy, working out of Liverpool, so take your malicious gossip and stick it where the sun doesn't shine.' Amy spat the lie through gritted teeth. Frank was dead, but Amy and I were the only people who knew it.

Beryl backed off.

'I'm only saying what I heard,' she whimpered.

'You're a scheming, despicable, two faced, liar.' Amy stuck out her chin and fixed Beryl with a glare that would have scared Joe Louis, the world's most famous boxer. 'Don't think I've forgotten the lies you told about me at work. There will be a payback one of these days if you don't start keeping that snake-like tongue of yours in check.'

Jan, one of the women that Beryl had been drinking with, reached to grab her coat from the peg on the wall.

'I'm nothing to do with this, Amy. You know me, love. I'm not a muck spreader.'

Amy continued to glare at Beryl who looked around desperately for support. When none arrived, she slammed her drink down on the counter and followed Jan to the door.

'I didn't mean anything by it, Alice, honestly. I was just telling you what I had heard.'

'Keep it to yourself next time, she isn't interested.' Amy delivered her parting shot and turned back to me.

'Blimey,' I said, mouth gaping. 'Where did that come from?'

'Oh, she's been asking for it for ages,' Amy replied. 'And, I did tell you that my hormones are all over the place at the moment.'

We turned towards Joyce and the girls who were still laughing at Beryl's embarrassment.

'What did you get for your birthday?' asked Joyce.

'All sorts of useful stuff, from winter socks to bath salts. Amy got me Glenn Miller's Moonlight Serenade record from America. I haven't stopped playing it all day.'

'Oh, I'd love to have a record player,' said Joyce wistfully. 'I have to make do with the versions they sing on the radio. They're pretty good, but the BBC Light Orchestra isn't exactly Glen Miller, is it?' She turned towards the bar to get a refill, singing the first line of the ballad.

We stayed in the Old Bull until chucking out time, which was unusual for us. The six of us spent a happy hour and a half singing our favourite songs. Stan, the landlord, came in to tell us to, 'keep it down', after receiving several complaints from the miserable shower of men in the bar, who thought they owned the pub and hated the thought of women having a good time without them.

Amy gave me a big hug at her front gate and I walked on down the lane to the farmhouse. When I stepped into the kitchen, Miriam was hopping from one foot to the other in excitement.

'Oh, thank goodness you're home. Mr Wilson, your lawyer, has been ringing you for the last half hour. I think he has something important to discuss with you.'

'Has he really?' I looked at the big clock on the wall, it was ten to midnight, I usually got home well before eleven thirty.

'It must be important for him to call at this time of night. I had to get out of bed to answer the telephone. If I hadn't been looking after Martha, I'd have come up to the pub to let you know.'

I patted Miriam on the arm reassuringly.

'Go to bed, Miriam, I'll sit up in case he calls again.'

I made myself a cup of Ovaltine and walked through to the front room. As I sat down at the old round table, the telephone rang.

'Hello?'

'Happy Birthday, Alice. I hope you've had a lovely day.'

'It's been fun, mostly,' I replied.

'I'm sorry I couldn't get over. I'd have loved to have spent a bit of time with you today. We attended a wedding. I didn't get home until after nine.'

'There's no need to feel sorry, Godfrey. I know how things are. I honestly didn't expect you to drop by.'

'Even so, I'd much rather have been in your company than the dreadful people who attended the wedding. Society people are so boring. They only ever talk about what they possess, or hope to possess in the near future.'

'Well, it's very nice of you to think of me,' I replied. 'But it's late, Godfrey, your wife will be wondering what you're up to.'

'I told her that awful wine had given me heartburn. It's true too, it did. I switched to cocktails half way through the evening.'

'Did you have a Martina?' I laughed to hide the embarrassment I still felt after asking him to buy me one at a posh restaurant we had visited. The young naïve me had mispronounced Martini. Godfrey had promised to invent a cocktail with that name in my honour.

'I haven't actually got round to mixing one myself yet, but when I do, you will be the second person to test it out.'

I yawned, then apologised.

'You'd better get to bed, Alice, I'm being very selfish, I know full well what unearthly time you have to get up in the morning. I just felt the need to hear your voice, that's all.'

'I'll be fine, Godfrey, I'm used to early mornings. It was very sweet of you to call. Good night.'

'There is one more thing,' he said with a note of excitement in his voice. 'I had to register for the military yesterday. I'm within the age range for the call up. Because of my education and family ties, they're going to send me for officer training. I have to report to a military camp in Chatham for the preliminaries and a medical on Thursday, so... well, I hoped I might see you before I go.'

'Not you as well!' I almost shouted down the telephone line. 'Damn Hitler, damn Chamberlain. They are determined to take away everyone I ever cared about.'

'It's my duty, Alice. I missed out on the first war by just a few months but they managed to snare me this time.'

'Bugger duty,' I said angrily. 'You can't go, Godfrey, I...' I tailed off knowing that nothing could stop the inevitable.

'Can I see you on Monday?' he asked, quietly.

'Of course, you silly man. Make it after lunch. I'll have done with the pigs and I'll have time to change. I can't have you going to war remembering me in my filthy pig-stained overalls. Make it about two o'clock if you can. I'll get Miriam to take Martha for a long walk.'

'Monday it is then,' Godfrey replied. There was a long silence and I began to think we'd been cut off. Then his smooth, velvety voice returned to my ear.

'I love you, Alice. Good night.'

Chapter 21

At seven o'clock on Saturday evening, Nicola took a deep swig from her glass of strong cider and unfolded the paper wrapping from the two portions of fish and chips she had just bought from Jackson's chip shop on Middle Street.

Tipping the contents onto two warmed up dinner plates, she carried them through to the front room, placed them carefully down on the coffee table, then went back to the kitchen to retrieve her cider. When she returned to the living room, Bill was typing something into his phone.

'Eat them while they're hot, Owen. I mean, Bill,' she said. 'Don't waste them, they cost a fortune these days. Fish and chips used to be a cheap family meal back in the—'

'For God's sake, stop wittering on, woman. Can't you see I'm conducting business here?'

'Sorry... Bill.' Nicola picked up a chip and nibbled on it.

'They've never tasted the same since they switched from cooking them in fat to oil.'

She dropped the half-eaten chip onto her plate and leaned back on the sofa with her glass in her hand. 'Shall we see what's on the tele?'

Bill stood up, grabbed his dinner plate and stormed into the kitchen. 'I said I was busy.'

Nicola sighed and switched on the TV as the contestants taking part in Strictly Come Dancing, were giving their all. Nicola let the sounds of the excited audience wash over her for a few minutes, then, leaving her cooling dinner on the coffee table, she walked back through to the kitchen. Bill had finished texting for the moment and was washing his dinner down with a glass of Nicola's strong cider as he scoured the day's newspaper for the evening dog racing cards.

'Haven't you got anything better than this muck?'
he asked, pulling a face. 'It's sour.'

'I had a bottle of wine from last night's meal, but
you drank it when we got home,' she reminded him.

'Nip over to the shop and get something a bit better,
will you?'

As Nicola held out her hand for the money. Bill
widened his eyes.

'What? Come on, Nic, you know I'm skint.' He
spread butter onto a thin slice of bread and heaped a
pile of chips onto it. Folding it in half he bit into the
sandwich and pointed towards the door. 'Beer will do...
and not that cheap crap either.'

Ten minutes later, Nicola returned with a six pack
of lager and another bottle of cheap, strong cider.

Bill looked up from the race cards as she entered
the kitchen.

'What kept you? I missed the 19.34 race.' He
checked his phone for the result and shrugged.
'Wouldn't have won anyway. I picked traps five and
two.' He looked up from the phone at Nicola who was
still holding the cans of bitter. 'I hope you got cold ones.
Pour one out, put the rest in the fridge.'

Nicola rinsed a glass under the cold tap, snapped
open a can and poured him a glass of beer. Placing it in
front of him on the kitchen table, she opened the
refrigerator door and put the remaining cans on the
almost empty shelves.

'When do you have to go home?' she asked. 'I
thought we could do something tomorrow.'

'I'll be busy tomorrow,' Bill replied. 'Look, Nic, can
you transfer a few quid to my bank account. There are
three or four dogs I really fancy tonight, but I'm short of
funds.'

'I'm short of funds too, Owen.'

'Bill.'

'I'm short of funds too, Bill. I had to buy groceries,
and fish and chips... and your beer.'

'You got paid yesterday didn't you?'

'Yes, but most of it goes on rent.'

'I thought our Jess had sorted that out for you. Come on, Nic. I only want a hundred quid, I'm not after your whole month's pay.'

'I don't have a hundred quid. I had to pay Mrs Saur for the credit I ran up over the month.'

'How much have you got then?'

'About forty. I don't get my Universal Credit until next week.'

Bill sighed. 'Forty will have to do then.' He held up his phone so that Nicola could copy down his account number.

'How do I do it?'

'Do what?' Bill looked puzzled.

'How do I transfer the money?' Nicola said nervously. 'I don't have my bank on my phone. It's too old.'

'For God's sake, Nicola, you really are useless. I'll have to go to the bookies shop. Give me your bank card, I'll draw the money from the cash point.'

An hour later, Bill let himself into the house. Ignoring Nicola, he walked straight through to the kitchen and took a beer from the fridge. Snapping the ring pull, he took a deep gulp, and sat down at the table. Nicola followed him in, forcing a smile.

'Did you win?'

Bill scowled at her.

'No, the races were fixed. That track is famous for it.'

'So, why did you—'

Bill threw the half full can of beer at her, hitting her on the cheek.

'Get out of my sight,' he said.

Holding her hand to her face, Nicola ran to the stairs, then, turning back, she grabbed a cider bottle by the neck and hurried up the steps.

At one o'clock, she was dragged into wakefulness as she felt a weight on top of her.

'Owen,' she whispered, as she opened her eyes. She held a hand up to touch his face. Ignoring her, he pulled up her nightdress, pushed his knee between hers and forced her legs apart.

'There's no need to be so rough I'm not going to fight you,' she said soothingly.

Bill, guided himself into her and began to thrust. Less than a minute later he rolled off, and pulling up his trousers, walked out of the room.

The following morning, Nicola got up late, she walked into the front room to find Bill sitting on the sofa using her best coat as a blanket.

'Get the kettle on, will you? I'm parched.'

Nicola walked through to the kitchen, filled the kettle and plugged it in. 'Tea or coffee?' she called.

'When have I ever drunk tea?' he shouted back.

By the time she had made coffee and carried it through to him, he was up and dressed. Her best coat was in a heap on the floor. She picked it up, smoothed it down and hung it on the back of the door.

'Do you remember Paul Austen and Neil Redmond? Are they still about?' he asked.

'Probably, if they're not in prison. What do you want them for?'

'Oh, nothing much. I just thought I'd catch up, that's all. Do you have any idea where they're be if they are around?'

'Paul will be at home with Irene, his long-suffering mother, I imagine. I'm not sure about Neil but I can't see any decent woman taking either of that pair on.'

'Does she still live on Ironmonger Row?'

'I don't know. I think so. I haven't seen her for a few years now.'

Bill sat quietly for a few moments. 'Her house was the one with the red tiled roof, wasn't it? They had to have a new one after Paul set fire to his attic bedroom.'

Nicola nodded. 'I remember that. He was smoking in bed, drunk.'

'Right, I'll nip over to see him, it's only a couple of streets away. I have to be careful still. I don't want to bump into the Duncan brothers after what went on back then.'

'One of them is in prison, for sure,' said Nicola. 'I think the other one was crippled in a gang related attack a couple of years ago. It was on the news at the time.'

Bill clapped his hands, grinned a huge grin, then picked up his coffee mug. He sniffed at it, then put it down again.

'Cheap crap,' he said.

At eleven o'clock, Bill set off to see if the Austens were still in the area. He returned less than half an hour later with a smile like a crescent moon on his face.

'Get the beers in, Nic, it's time to celebrate.'

'I don't have any money for beer... Bill. You took the last I had.'

'Never mind,' said Bill, pulling a twenty-pound note from his wallet. 'I was saving this for emergencies, but I won't be needing to now.' He thrust the money into Nicola's hand. Get more of that lager for me and grab yourself some cider... No! make it a bottle of wine, but don't go over the top.'

Nicola folded the banknote in half and stuck it into the pocket of her cardigan. 'You found Paul then. I take it that it's good news?'

'The best.' Bill punched his left palm with his right fist. 'I don't think I'll have to worry about money again after this week.'

As Nicola was crossing the road to the convenience store, she suddenly stopped dead. *Was it Dougie Duncan that had been crippled in the gang fight or was it one of his attackers?* She racked her brains but for the life of her she couldn't remember. She decided to ask Mandy, who was on the till that lunchtime.

Mandy could remember the incident clearly. 'No, Nic, Dougie walked away without so much as a scratch. One of the London gang had to have a leg amputated afterwards. Tony Duncan was jailed for his part in the melee, but Dougie got off scot free. He lives in a big place off the Gravesend Road.'

Nicola walked back to her house wondering how she was going to explain her mistake to Owen... no, Bill, she would have to stop calling him Owen. As she pushed the front door open, she decided not to mention the Duncan brothers for now. He was in such a good mood. She didn't want to spoil it.

Chapter 22

Jessica slept in late on Sunday morning. She was woken at ten by the sound of a car horn. Slipping out of bed, she stepped across the landing and opened the curtain to look out onto the front of the property. Blinking in the bright autumn sunshine, she looked down onto the asphalt to see a long white van. Standing in front of it, waving up at her, was Gwen.

Jess threw on a thin, cotton dressing gown and hurried down the stairs. Greeting her with a hug on the doorstep she said hello to Alec, the driver of the van, and led the way to the lounge where the hospital bed was stripped and ready for removal.

As Gwen carried a pile of bedsheets out to the van, Alec and his son took hold of the special mattress that helped reduce pressure sores and, twisting it onto its side, lugged it across the room.

'I can see you lads have done this before,' said Jess.

'Too many times,' replied Alec with a grunt. His son had turned a little too early as he stepped into the hall.

Gwen stood aside as the two men came out of the front door with the mattress.

'We're going to try to get the bed out in one go,' Alec said, grumpily. 'We'll be here all day if we have to strip it down to parts. I've got a darts match at twelve-thirty.'

Gwen hurried back inside and picked up a pile of pillows. Jess, looking guilty, felt the need to explain why she wasn't helping.

'I'm not really dressed for it. I've only got a short nightie on under this.' She opened her arms to show her unfastened dressing gown. 'I can't find the belt.' Too late, she realised that Alec and his son had re-entered the room.

'Well, that was worth coming for at least.' Alec winked at her as he passed.

The bed was easier to get out than they had thought it might be, and with a bit of manoeuvring and only a couple of scrapes on the doorframe of the lounge, they soon had it loaded onto the van.

'There's a massage mattress topper too,' said Gwen. 'It's rolled up in the cupboard under the stairs. Alice didn't like it. She said it made her feel funny.'

Alec snorted with laughter and opened the door to the cubby under the stairs. Dragging out what looked like a rolled up li-lo, he stuck it under his arm and stood looking at Jess as though expecting a tip.

'Thanks for coming,' said Jess with a smile. She squeezed past him and stood by the open front door with her fingers on the handle.

Alec grunted, and mumbled something about it being a wasted day off as he carried the massage mattress out to the van.

Jess felt the weight of Gwen's hand on her arm and turned towards her. 'Never mind him, Lovely. His mother will be grateful for the bed, as will I. She's a big woman. The electronic risers on the bed should stop me putting my back out.'

'Would you like a coffee before you go, Gwen? It's ages since we had a chat.'

'Oh, go on then.' Gwen smiled and shouted out of the door towards the two men. 'I'll be over in half an hour, just get it set up in your mum's lounge. I'll need you to give me a hand to move her from her old bed to this one though, so don't clear off too early.'

'I've got darts,' Alec moaned as he climbed into the van.

'Darts are more important than your mother's welfare?' Gwen pulled a fake smile and waved them off. Jess closed the door, then letting her dressing gown fall open, walked through to the kitchen to put the kettle on.

'The room looks empty without the bed it in,' she said, as she brought the coffee mugs through to the lounge.

'I know, it seems to have been there forever,' Gwen replied, taking one of the mugs and sitting down on the lumpy sofa. She fidgeted for a while, trying to get comfortable. 'This sofa has seen better days.'

'I've got a new one coming,' said Jess. 'It is being made as I speak.' She winked at Gwen. 'I've got a new kitchen coming too in a few weeks. She hurried back to the kitchen and returned with the brochure.

'Ooh, I say. We'll hardly recognise the place.'

'It needs doing,' replied Jess. 'There's woodworm in the cupboards.'

'I didn't mean that you shouldn't,' said Gwen. She looked around the lounge. 'Alice was always saying the place needed a makeover. She was just too old to be bothered with it.' The carer smiled at an old memory. "Jessica will know what to do with it. She has good taste." That's what she told me.'

Jess smiled sadly. 'I do miss her so, Gwen.'

'Me too, my lovely. But...' she looked up at the ceiling. 'She'll be around if you need her for anything.'

Jess swallowed the lump in her throat and nodded.

'How did the family take the news? About the will, I mean. I assume Alice didn't change her mind during those last few days.'

'She didn't, and they didn't take it well at all, Gwen. Grandma Martha and Marjorie took it particularly badly. They really thought they had landed on their feet when they heard they'd been mentioned in the will.' Jess finished her coffee and taking Gwen's empty mug from her, she placed them on the coffee table before sitting down again. 'Grandma's face could have curdled fresh milk. She's spoken of nothing else since. She's convinced I can just conjure up money out of thin air.'

'She wasn't concerned enough to come and see her mother when she was ill,' replied Gwen, who had heard all about the family feud from Alice.

'My dad was the worst though. He was a bit scary to be honest.'

'Owen? So, he's back is he? Word spreads fast.'

'He calls himself Bill these days. He was worried about bumping into the Duncan brothers. He's owed them money for years. That's why he ran away originally.'

'Does your mum know he's back?'

Jess nodded. 'She was the one that told him about the family dinner I organised. She was so pleased to see him but he treated her like dirt, just like he always has.' Jess's lips became a thin line. 'Still, things are going to get a bit better for her soon. The trust owns a cottage that will soon be empty. I'm going to let her have it.'

'That's lovely, Jessica,' replied Gwen. 'I'm sure it will help to get over her problems with... Well, you know?'

'I hope so, Gwen. I really do.'

Gwen suddenly looked unsure of herself. She wrung her hands on her lap, looked across at Jess, then quickly back down at her chest.

'I, erm... You know when you asked about those missing pages from Alice's memoir and I said I didn't know what had happened to them? Well, I do know. I'm sorry I lied, but Alice made me promise I wouldn't tell you what was in them.' She took a deep breath and let the air out slowly. 'I'm still not sure I should talk about it, but as it's you, and you have the rest of the memoirs...'

'Don't feel you have to tell me if it's going to be on your conscience, Gwen. It's just that... well, I really do want to know everything there is to know about her. She's my hero and when I write my book, she's going to be the star of it, albeit with a different identity.'

'I'm sure she'll forgive me when we finally meet up,' said Gwen, looking heavenwards again.

'Wait a minute, let me make us another cup of coffee. You won't have had lunch yet either. Can I make you a sandwich?'

Gwen looked at her watch. 'Oh my, I'm supposed to be back to supervise Old Alice's bed changeover. I completely forgot.'

Jess got to her feet and rushed to the hall. 'Give me five minutes to get changed, I'll nip you over there, then

I'll give you a lift back and you can tell me all about Nana while we have lunch. How does that sound?'

'It sounds perfect,' said Gwen. She picked up her phone and rang Alec's number.

An hour later, Jess and Gwen sat at the big oak table in the kitchen and tucked into a plate of cheese and onion sandwiches. Gwen smiled fondly as she picked one up.

'Alice would have thrown this back at me,' she said with a little laugh. 'Ham was her thing. She thought she'd been short changed if I ever made her a sandwich without meat. She loved her mustard too. The strong, yellow, English stuff. *"Don't ever try to feed me any of that insipid, French sludge,"* she used to say.'

Jess smiled at Gwen's anecdote. 'I can see her saying it.'

Gwen sipped at her coffee and put the half-eaten sandwich back onto her plate.

'Now, about those missing pages.'

'Do you still have them?' asked Jess.

'No, Lovely. She asked me to burn them, unread, and I did as I was asked. I threw them into my wood burner at home.'

'But what was so terrible about them, Gwen? Nana had a very troubled life back then, I'm not going to go into detail, but if she thought what was in those pages would upset me, then it must have been truly awful.'

'Not awful in a nasty sense,' replied Gwen. 'She didn't kill someone, or anything like that. The thing is... well, she suffered from a period of depression.'

'Depression... and she had to hide that from me? I'd have understood, especially knowing what she went though.'

'She said it was a period of severe Melancholy. That's what they used to call it back then. She wouldn't see a doctor about it, she was terrified that he might book her into the Funny Farm... her words, not mine, Jessica.'

'Oh, Nana, you silly thing. There was no need to hide it from me.'

'It was classed as a weakness when she had it. Even doctors would tell you to snap yourself out of it. Anyway. This is what happened.'

Gwen took another sip of coffee and stared into the distance.

'It was a day or two before she died. You remember she had to have the antibiotics for that awful chest infection? You had brought down the two books she'd asked for from the attic, and she handed one to you, then put the other one in her bedside drawer.'

'That's right,' said Jess. 'She said I didn't need to see that one yet.'

'Well, after you had gone home, she called me in and asked me to get the book from the drawer. When I pulled it out, she told me to sit down and flick through the pages until I got to June, then I was to turn back one page and tear out all the sheets before that one. I asked her why, but she just gave me that look of hers, there was no point in arguing, so I tore them out and handed them over. She stared down at them for a full five minutes with an anguished look on her face as though she was remembering the events she'd written about. Then she told me to get one of the large brown envelopes from the kitchen drawer. When I got back, she had folded the pages in half. She handed them to me and ordered me to put the sheets directly into the envelope without looking at them. I did as I was told, I sealed it, then she took my hand and made me promise to burn it as soon as I could. I had to swear on my husband's life that I wouldn't open it. Then she let go of my hand and said, "Jessica must never be allowed to read it." No one in my family can ever know I was on the verge of being locked away for ever in the lunatic asylum.'

Gwen looked out of the back window as she thought.

'They couldn't do that, could they?' I asked.

'Alice lay back on her pillows and looked at the ceiling. "Gwen," she said, "they could do anything back then. At one time, a woman suffering with the baby blues, could be sent there. In Victorian times, a man could have a woman committed for infidelity, claiming she must be mad to have done it. That had stopped by the time I got Melancholia, but anyone with severe depression was pretty much considered to be insane and were shipped off to the nuthouse without so much as a by your leave."

'She said, "I couldn't let that happen. What would have happened to the farm? To Martha? They would have put her in an orphanage."' Gwen looked at Jessica through teary eyes. 'The poor woman.'

'I'm so angry about this, even though it was a different time with different standards,' said Jess, putting her hand on Gwen's.

'The main reason she didn't want you to read it was because she had recorded all of her suicidal thoughts. She didn't want to put you through the anguish of reading them. She said that she was in a really bad way, mentally, and she had sat in the bathroom with a little pot of the barbiturates her doctor had given her when she had complained about not being able to sleep properly. Somehow, she got through without overdosing on them. She said it was probably the thought of her prize boars, Horace and Hector being shot that stopped her taking them... and Martha of course. Anyway, by the summer, she began to feel a little better. She put it down to the lighter nights and mornings but there must have been more to it than that.'

Jess thought about Alice, at eighteen, pregnant, frightened and alone. There was no support in those days. Women were stigmatised and thought of as being wanton. On top of all that, Alice had been left with the huge responsibility of running the farm after her father had drunk himself to death. Jess took a deep breath and let the air out in a huge sigh.

'Poor Nana, she was under so much pressure.'

Gwen nodded. 'She said I deserved an explanation after asking me to burn the papers. Then, as I said, she made me promise not to talk about it. She still felt such a strong sense of shame. She was so proud of being seen as a strong woman in a time when all women were considered to be inferior to men.'

She looked up at the wall clock and gasped. 'Is that the time? I'd better get home. Gareth will be wondering where I am. He'll be hungry.'

'Can't he get his own dinner for once?' asked Jess with more anger in her voice than she meant.

'No, he'll burn the place down, Lovely. It's not that he won't do it, more that he can't.'

'Nice excuse if you can get away with it.' Jess wasn't convinced.

'He does other stuff, Jessica, things I can't do around the place. And he runs all the errands, does the bins, decorating, that sort of thing. There are a lot worse, believe me.'

'I'm sorry, Gwen.' The two women got to their feet and hugged. 'I'm not mad at your Gareth. I'm still stung by Nana's confession about her mental state. I wish she felt she could have shared it with me.'

'Pride, my dear. Don't think bad of her. She kept her secrets right to the end, but it was to protect you, as well as her own reputation.'

Jess led Gwen back through the front room, reaching for her bag as she went.

'There's no need to put yourself out, Lovely. I can walk this time.'

'Don't be silly, Gwen. You've done me two big favours today.' She thought for a moment. 'I'll tell you what. Do you think your Gareth could do without you for one night? I'd love you to stay over. We could have some wine, watch a little TV and have a proper chat about Nana. I'll get a new bed for one of the spare rooms. Please say yes.'

'I'd love to, that sounds like a really good idea, just give me a call when you can fit me in. I'm usually off on a Saturday night.'

'I'm having a housewarming party soon. You and your Gareth have an official invite to that too.'

Gwen blushed. 'Ooh, I say. A party. We don't get invited to many of those.'

'Well, you're top of my list for this one,' said Jess. She gave Gwen another hug and followed her out to the car, pulling the door shut behind her.

When she returned, twenty minutes later, she parked up the car and was just about to walk to the front door when the old bed and mattress she had left out for the council caught her eye. The plastic covering had been stripped from both the mattress and bed. The plastic bags of old bedding had been torn open and the bed had been made as though it was still in use. Jess opened the metal tube gate, pushed it open and pulled back the duvet to find two, small, straw, scarecrow-like figures lying pressed together underneath. On the front of each head, was a childlike drawing of a face, held in place with a thick elastic band. Between the two heads lay a sheet of paper onto which had been drawn a large heart. Written in thick marker across it, was a single word. US.

Chapter 23

'Someone did *what?*'

'Hang on, I took a pic, I'll send it to you, Sam.'

Jess sent the picture of the made-up bed to their joint WhatsApp group.

'That's just creepy,' Sam said after a few moments. 'No need to guess who did it, is there? Have you phoned the police yet?'

'Not yet. But I am getting a little bit concerned. Calvin was hanging around the farm the night I moved in and someone... I can't say it was him... someone scratched a deep gauge down the side of Bradley's beautiful old car when it was parked outside.'

'Call the cops,' said Sam, firmly.

'I might just have a word with him first. I know he was a control freak but this doesn't seem like him somehow.'

'For pity's sake, Jess. This is seriously weird. Promise me you'll ring the police.'

'I'm not sure, Sam. I want to know it's definitely him before I accuse him of anything.' Jess heard her best friend sigh.

'Well at least get a security camera up on the wall so you can see who's ferreting about. Tell me you'll do that at least.'

Jess could visualise Sam's frustrated face. 'I'll do that... Actually, I know just the man. He's an electronics technician.'

'So was Calvin. Be careful, they might be a type. You know, Technocreep Incorporated.'

Jess laughed. 'This one is a broadband installer, though he's a contractor and does all sorts of other stuff. He left me his card.'

'Ring him as soon as you hang up this call,' Sam demanded. 'You need that camera up, ASAP.'

Jess rummaged in the drawer under the coffee table and pulled out Wade's business card.

164

'I'll ring him now. He's a bit of an oddball. He asked me out when he'd finished installing the broadband line.'

'He what? You don't half attract them, Jess. Listen, Missis, go to that electronics repair shop in town. At least he has a bricks and mortar business.'

'Bits and Bytes? The man who runs it is Calvin's mate,' replied Jess. 'I'll go there if I have to, but only as a last resort.'

'Do you want me to come over and stay for a few nights while you get your security sorted?'

'That's kind of you, Sam, but there's no need. I'll be fine, honestly.'

'Well, the offer stands. All you have to do is call.'

'Thanks, Sam. You're a star.' Jess blew kisses into the phone, then hung up.

'This is Wade. I'm not here right now, leave a message.'

'Hi, Wade. It's Jessica Griffith's you installed my—'

'Hi, Jessica.' Wade suddenly came online. 'No problems with the broadband I hope?'

'Oh, hello... Wade. No, the broadband is working fine. It's just that... well, one or two things have happened over the last couple of days and I'd like to have a security camera fitted on the wall overlooking the property.'

'Seriously? Well, you are a bit out of the way down there. It might be burglars, sizing the place up.'

'Don't say that,' replied Jess with a nervous laugh. 'I doubt if the person, or persons involved want to rob me. It's more of a personal thing.'

'Oh, right. How soon would you need it doing? I've got a pretty full schedule this week.'

'I'd like it fitting as soon as possible really. Look, thanks for answering so promptly. I'll give Bits and Bytes a ring in the morning. I think they do all sorts of electronics stuff.'

'Don't go to them, Jess. Is it all right if I call you, Jess?'

Without waiting for a reply, he continued.

'They'll charge you a fortune to fit it and they'll put a big mark-up on the actual camera.' He paused. 'Look, Jess. I fit a lot of security stuff, inside as well as out. I have a nice outdoor, weatherproof camera in stock, it's high definition, has fantastic night vision, and comes with a big memory card and a month's free cloud service with the manufacturer. You don't have to subscribe to that. Any images will be sent to your laptop too.'

'Sold,' replied Jess, 'but when could you fit it?'

'How does twenty minutes sound?'

'Really? Look, Wade, I don't want to spoil your Sunday. I can wait a few more days.'

'I'm happy to do it,' said Wade. 'You don't want to take the chance if you have a stalker.'

'I didn't say I had a stalker, but thank you. I'll get the kettle on.'

Wade was as good as his word and twenty minutes later his van pulled onto the asphalt drive of the farm. Jess opened the front door and smiled to welcome him.

'Thanks again for being so kind. The kettle's on.'

Wade, wearing just a t-shirt and jeans despite the cold weather, flexed his muscles and looked down at his own broad chest as he walked towards her.

'I'll get the thing mounted first. I've brought you a wireless camera because your Wi-Fi is really good. We even got a signal up in the attic. I'll have to drill a hole through the wall as it will need to be plugged into the mains.'

'That's fine by me,' said Jess. 'Where were you thinking of putting it. I have a plug socket on the landing.'

'Can I have a quick look?'

Jess stood aside to let Wade get by. He took the stairs two at a time, checked the position of the double power socket on the landing, then opened the window at the front of the house and stuck his head out to get his bearings.

'The socket is perfect,' he called. Wade came back down the stairs and walked back to the van, showing off his wide shoulders.

Jess held her hand in front of her mouth to muffle the giggle that she couldn't stop. Wade was a body builder, that was obvious, but did he have to walk like he was carrying two rolls of invisible carpet all the time?

He returned a couple of minutes later, lugging a big drill and a dust sheet.

'That's a big one,' said Jess with a smile. 'I'll leave you to get on with it. Just call if you need anything.'

Wade nodded his ginger head and carried his equipment up the stairs. By the time Jess had walked through to the kitchen and opened up her laptop, the drilling had begun.

'It's mounted on the side wall, but I've angled it so that it covers the parking space and the land on the other side of the gate, where your old bed is lying.' Wade stood, arms folded, showing off his biceps.

'Fabulous. How much do I owe you?'

'I'll leave an invoice. I trust you to pay.' Wade sniffed. 'Can I smell coffee?'

Jess filled the kettle and switched it on.

'I still have to set it up with the router and install the app on the laptop.' He pointed to Jess's computer. 'Okay if I...'

Jess nodded and continued making the coffee. 'No sugar, is that right?'

'I'm sweet enough,' replied Wade. 'Hey, I must have made an impression the last time I was here for you to remember that.'

'I've only made coffee for three people since I moved in,' replied Jess. 'It wasn't much of a memory feat.'

Wade took the coffee without acknowledgement and began the camera set up. One computer reboot and two router restarts later, the software was installed and Jess was able to see outside the house from her laptop screen.

'That's a fantastic view. It's so clear.' She patted Wade on the arm, then instantly regretted it.

'Wait until you see the night vision. It's so good you could pick out a snail crawling across the floor.'

Wade took his time finishing his drink. 'Did you consider my offer?' he asked as he wrote out and tore off an invoice from his pad.

'Offer?'

'I asked you out, remember?'

'I do remember, Wade, and it was very sweet of you. But as I said. I'm not looking for a new relationship at the moment. I'm still getting over the last one.'

'It's only a bloody night out.'

Jess took a step back as Wade turned his angry face towards her.

'I understand that, Wade, but honestly. I'm right off men at the moment.' She smiled reassuringly at him. 'It's not you. It's just men in general.'

'Men are all right when they come out on a Sunday afternoon though?'

'I didn't ask you to come out today. You offered.'

Wade got to his feet and snatched up his invoice pad.

'I forgot to include my unsocial hours rate on the invoice.'

'Send me another one with everything included then, Wade. I don't want you to be out of pocket, I'm very grateful, honestly.' She smiled at him, then continued. 'I might have a bit more work for you soon, anyway. My laptop's playing up. The blue camera light comes on at random. I'd like a bit of advice... you know, whether to scrap it and get a new one, or whether the fault is worth fixing. I don't want to spend a lot of money on it.'

Wade's demeanour changed. He was the man in charge of the conversation again.

'Camera light? Is it running any video app in the background when it comes on?'

'No, that's the strange thing. It seems to be a random event. Mainly in the evenings, but not exclusively. It works fine with WhatsApp, Zoom and Messenger and switches off when the session is ended, but then it will come on again without a reason. I don't mind buying a new one if I have to, but I'd rather not. I've spent too much recently.'

Wade sat down again and pressed a few keys on the laptop. The camera app appeared on screen showing his face. He shut it down again, then re-opened it.

'It's working fine at the moment. I'd need to take it away with me to run a few diagnostic tests. It's not a common thing, it's more likely to happen if you have some spyware or malware on your computer, but again. I'd need to test it properly.'

Jess pushed the lid of the laptop down.

'Ah, never mind. I can't be without it at the moment. I'm researching for a novel and I've got a few magazine articles to write. I'll give you a shout when I've caught up with everything. How long would you need it for?'

'A day or so, no longer.'

'Okay. I'll get everything that's already in the pipeline sorted, then I'll call you.' She smiled again and led him to the front door. 'Thanks again for coming out.'

Wade stepped through the doorway, then stopped and turned on the bottom step.

'Look, I'm sorry I got shitty a moment ago. I wasn't proposing to you, it really was just the offer of a night out. I don't know what I've done wrong recently, but I seem to get knocked back every time I ask a girl out.' He looked at each of his muscle-bound arms in turn, then back up to Jess's face. 'I'm not that repulsive, am I?'

Jess thought carefully before she spoke.

'You're not repulsive at all, Wade. I'm sure you'd be very good company. It's just that—'

'I know,' he interrupted. 'You're off men.'

Jess nodded. 'I really am,' she said.

Wade stared at her for a few moments, then turned away and, suddenly remembering the two invisible rolls of carpet, opened his shoulders and waddled across to his van.

'Sorry again,' he called as he opened the driver's door. 'I really didn't mean to seem so aggressive. I was just disappointed, that's all.' He started the van, turned it around, then his head appeared out of the wound down window.

'That invoice stands. Forget the new one.'

With that, his stereo blared out a drum and base beat and he sped off up the lane.

Jess closed the front door and strolled through to the kitchen. Sliding her mouse on the table, she clicked on her new camera app and studied the image that immediately appeared on her computer screen.

'Right,' she said. 'Let's see what my new toy can capture.'

On Monday morning, Jess got up early to check if there had been any alerts sent from her new security camera, but there was nothing recorded on the app, so she showered, had breakfast and switched on the TV to watch the morning news.

At nine-thirty, Bradley rang to ask her to check her bank account, as he and Simon, his fellow trustee, had approved Jess's request for her annual allowance to be paid.

'Wow! I've never seen so much money. I have to say I was getting a bit concerned, I've been far too profligate, lately. I'll have to rein in the spending, thanks for sorting it out for me.' Jess smiled as though he could see her. 'How did your mum take the bad news?'

'She wasn't happy, and that's putting it mildly. Let's just say I was sent to bed without supper. I was hoping to get it into the garage before she got back, but she came home early and saw the damage before I had the chance to park up.'

'I'm so sorry about all that, Bradley. It's probably down to me in the end. There was another situation over the weekend and I've had to have a security camera fitted.' She explained about the old bed and the pair of scarecrows.

'No doubt you've thought about it, but could this be your ex? I'd like to give him the bill for the repairs if it is.'

'He doesn't have the money to pay, even if he is responsible. I'm going to talk to him later today.'

'He'll just deny it, surely?'

Jess nodded at the phone. 'He will, but he acts in a certain way when he's been caught out. He gets angry, and starts to bluster whilst making out the world is against him.'

'Be careful, Jess. Exes can be tricky.'

'You get on well with yours, don't you?'

'Yes, we're still good friends.'

'Good, that's how it should be,' said Jess.

Bradley was quiet for a moment, then he spoke again.

'The cottage we were discussing will be available from January the first. The old lease runs out on the thirty-first of December. I've spoken to Simon about your plans for it and neither of us have an objection. There should be some rent paid, and it has to be a reasonable amount, according to the trust terms, but you can set the level. It's up to you what you think is reasonable.'

'Lovely, Mum will be thrilled to get out of the dump she's in. Thanks so much. Will you need to draw up a contract?'

'We used an agency to let it last time. We won't do that as there is obviously a cost involved. We can just copy and paste the agency's relevant terms and conditions into a new contract and issue it via the trust. The main points will be about not subletting, keeping the place in good repair, etc.'

'Brilliant. I'll give her the good news later today. She'll look after the place, I'm sure.'

'There was one other thing,' said Bradley. 'It regards your grandmother. I think I've thought of a way to get her off your back and at the same time, allow her to have some money.'

'Ooh, that sounds interesting.' Jess's ears pricked up.

'If, and it's a big if... she is prepared to sign her house over to you on the understanding that it will be placed directly into the farm trust, we should be able to release some of the equity to her. It would also mean you had control of the property after she passes.'

'That's a very interesting idea, Bradley. Thank you for that. I'll ask her about it when I see her on Wednesday. I know she's worried that if she goes first, the place will be left to Marjorie and she really doesn't trust her to make the right decisions on her own.'

'Here to help,' replied Bradley. 'I'd better get off; I've got a rather tricky divorce settlement to sort out this morning. A local couple who've been clients of ours for decades. He's ninety and she's ninety-two. Apparently, she has been unfaithful.'

'Good grief, at ninety-two?'

'Her husband says she's got a toy boy, although the man in question is eighty-three himself.'

Jess shook her head. 'Good luck with that one.'

'All part of the service. Enjoy your new-found wealth, Jess.'

'Would you, erm, I mean, could we meet up soon?' Jess asked.

'That sounds wonderful. I think I'll need a shoulder after the negotiations this morning.'

'How about tomorrow evening? I'll rustle something up.'

'Seven-thirty?' said Bradley. 'I'm over at Gillingham all afternoon. I won't be back until sixish, then I'll have to change.'

'Seven-thirty is it, and good luck with your gallivanting geriatrics.'

After the call, Jess sat on the lumpy old sofa as she plucked up the courage to ring Calvin. After ten minutes of trying to find excuses not to, she picked up her phone and tapped his name on her contact list. After today, she decided she would block him.

'Jess? Oh, my goodness, it's nice to hear from you. How's everything? Have you settled in?'

'Calvin, this isn't a make-up and mend call. I want to ask you something, but I want to ask you face to face.'

'That sounds ominous,' replied Calvin.

'Just a conundrum I need an answer to.'

'All right, Jess. You know I'm good at puzzles. Do you want me to come to the farm?'

'NO!' Jess replied, quickly.

'The flat then? I wanted to talk to you about that, the estate agents have—'

'Not the flat. Meet me at the lychgate at the church, that's the gate at the back, not the main entrance. I'll be there in half an hour if that's okay? It's only a two-minute walk for you.'

'The lychgate? That's where they bring all the dead bodies, isn't it?' He laughed nervously. 'Should I wear a bullet proof vest?'

'That depends whether you think you need to, Calvin.'

Jess cut off the call and breathed out. She was surprised at how much hearing Calvin's voice had affected her. As she put down the phone, she noticed her hands were shaking.

She went upstairs and pulled an old pair of jeans and a baggy woollen jumper out of the back of the wardrobe, then washed her face to remove the few dabs of make-up she'd put on that morning. She didn't want Calvin to think she had made any sort of effort for him.

Jess parked her car up on one of the free parking spaces at the side of the church, and walked the hundred yards or so around the metal, paling fence towards the lychgate. When she arrived, she found that Calvin was already there, he smiled warmly as she approached, and held out his arms.

'Jess, it's lovely to see you.'

She ignored his arms and stopped about six feet away from him. She smiled at an old lady as she puffed her way past them on her way up the hill, then turned to face her ex-partner.

'I've got two simple questions, Calvin, and I expect two simple answers.' She held up a finger. 'One, did you run a key down the side of a nineteen-thirties Alvis car on Saturday?' Jess held up a second finger, 'and two, did you set up a ridiculous tableau using the bed I'd left out for the council, sometime between Saturday night, and Sunday morning?'

Calvin looked genuinely perplexed.

'Tableau? What do you mean, tableau?'

'You know what a tableau is, Calvin. A set piece, a scene, like an artwork. A bloody tableau.' Jess felt herself beginning to shake with anger.

Calvin shook his head. 'A tableau? No, I haven't... I don't know what you're talking about.'

'And the car? Were you hanging around the farm on Saturday afternoon? If you were, you picked on the wrong man, Calvin. The car belongs to Bradley Wilson, he's a lawyer, and a very good one.'

'I wasn't anywhere near the farm on Saturday, Jess.' Calvin looked her straight in the eyes.

Jess was almost convinced. He usually added the epithet 'honestly' when denying something he was actually guilty of. She watched his face carefully.

'You have been hanging around the farm though, Calvin. I saw your car parked in the layby.'

'I've been nowhere near the farm. At night or any other time.'

'Bullshit, Calvin. You were watching me.'

'No, I wasn't, Jess, honestly, I wouldn't do that.'

'I've told you once, Calvin and this is your last warning. Stay away from me.'

'Warning? What do you mean, warning? I haven't been anywhere near your precious farm. I've got better things to do with my time.' Calvin's face became crimson, whereas earlier he had calmly answered her questions.

'Just keep away, Calvin. It's just your luck to be in the wrong place at the wrong time. If I get any more nasty surprises, I'm going straight to the police and if you happen to be around at the same time as they are, well, it won't look good for you.'

Calvin's eyes narrowed. 'Have you got a stalker, Jess? Look, maybe I can help. I could sit in the layby, I'd let you know when I was coming over, I could keep an eye on the place for you.'

'No, Calvin. Just stay away. Please.'

Calvin held up both hands, palms towards her. 'Okay, okay, if you want to do things your own way.'

'I always did want to, Calvin, but you thought you knew better. Look where that got you.'

Calvin dropped his hands. 'Speaking of where things got me. Jess, I really do need your help. I'm not asking for forgiveness, not that I think I need forgiving for too much, but I'm really going to struggle to get the down payment on the flat in time for January. Do you think you could give me a sub. Just to pay the deposit. I've got regular, private tutoring work coming in now, and I think I've landed a job looking after the Comp school's I.T. equipment next term. I just need a bit of help to see me through Christmas.'

'No, Calvin. You've had all the favours you're ever going to get from me. The last one, was not reporting you to the police after you attacked Sam.'

'Attack, fending off, the truth is somewhere in between. You know that.' He looked at her pleadingly. 'Come on, Jess. I know you. You're not a hard-hearted person. You wouldn't see me on the streets, would you?' He cocked his head to one side like an inquisitive puppy. 'Could you spare a bit of charity, it's almost the season for it.'

'Ask your mother, Calvin. She's got plenty.' Jess turned away and took a few steps before turning back. 'One last thing. Did you put any tracking software on my laptop when we were living in the flat?'

Calvin went a deep shade of red.

'Spyware... Why would I? Honestly, Jess. I would never do that.'

'Thanks for being so honest, Calvin. Just so you know though. I'm having the laptop cleaned up. So, the tracker won't be there for much longer and, if I find out you've been spying on me via my computer, you'll wish you'd never met me.'

Jess turned and stormed away, leaving Calvin standing, open mouthed, by the lychgate, his face, deathly pale.

Chapter 25

On Tuesday morning, Jess heard the sound of the council refuge lorry in the lane. Thirty seconds later, one of the bin men hammered a rat-a-tat on the door knocker.

'Morning, love, do the scarecrows go with us or do you want to keep them?'

'Take them away, please. They were someone's idea of a joke.'

'Ah, I wondered if your kids had made them. My little girl draws faces like that. She's six.'

'No, it was an adult, believe it or not. Art isn't his niche subject. Thanks for taking them.' Jess stepped back and began to close the door.

'They should go in the brown bin, really. But I won't tell if you don't.'

The man smiled, then looked over to his colleagues who were loading the mattress onto the lorry.

Jess looked quizzically at the orange-clad man, wondering why he was still on her doorstep.

'Is there a problem?' she asked.

'To be honest, there is. You only paid for the removal of four items. There are six items in your yard.'

'Yes, but two of the items are made of straw, and weren't there when I rang to book the collection.' She looked towards the lane where two other council workers were loading the old spring base of the bed, onto the lorry. 'Don't you have enough room for them on the truck?' She smiled at her little joke.

'You pay per item, and there are extra items.' The man stood his ground under Jess's withering look.

'Look, I'll remember you at Christmas, but I really don't expect to pay to remove what is, in essence, two, small piles of straw.'

The man looked disappointed and, turning away, he shook his head and walked back to the lorry with his thumbs pointed downwards. The three men climbed into the lorry and with a blaring siren, reversed onto the asphalt before pulling onto the lane, leaving the two miniature scarecrows propped up against the side of Jess's car.

Jess clicked the door shut and sighing a deep sigh, walked through to the kitchen where she opened Alice's memoir and turned to a clean page in her notebook.

November 1939

During September, Operation Pied Piper was put into action and over one and a half million children, and some mothers, were evacuated from London to save them from the enemy bombing that the government thought was about to begin.

Being so close to Gillingham, which evacuated many of its own children, our little town wasn't chosen as a major centre for the evacuees, but following an administrative cock up at the same time, the Gillingham evacuees were being transported to small towns and villages around Sandwich and Dover. A train from London, loaded with over a hundred children, arrived at our railway station. Amazingly, instead of just turning the train around and sending it to where it should have been heading, the authorities made a decision to keep the kids in our area and an appeal was sent out by the council leader, begging locals to 'do their bit' by taking them in for a short time while their futures were sorted out.

The kids were marched up the road to the church hall where they were made to sit on the floor with their bag of sandwiches, gas mask boxes and tiny suitcases. Hanging around their necks were name tag labels which hopefully matched up with the cases sitting at their feet.

To their credit, a lot of local residents took a stroll up to the church hall to select a child they thought they would be able live with, though some of them, thinking of the ten shillings a week they would be paid for looking after the children, had more mercenary instincts.

Living out in the sticks, I didn't get to hear about the call to arms until after all the children had been found places. I would have taken at least one, possibly two as I had a spare room at the farm. I had rented it out to one of Amy's friends for a couple of months earlier in the year, and I had hoped to use it as bait when attempting to snare a temporary worker for the farm until our own lads came back from the war. As it was, the remaining workers could easily manage the reduced workload during the winter months, but come spring, with only eight men remaining, I would be in desperate need of more hands.

In mid-November, I received a call from my old schoolteacher asking me if I could find the room for a couple of ten-year-old kids who, she said, had been placed in haste and were in urgent need of rehoming. She had been offered places for them but it would have meant splitting them up, and she was very concerned about that.

I shouted Miriam in from the kitchen and we had a ten second chat before agreeing to take them. The teacher said she'd drop them off that very afternoon.

Many of the children who turned up on that train had gone back home again because the expected bombing raids hadn't materialised, but these two kids had been unlucky. The same afternoon they arrived at Spinton their London home had been destroyed in a blast caused by a gas leak. Their parents, whilst unharmed, had to split up and live with relatives in a different part of the capital and there was, at the moment, no room for the children. The Council had told them they would be rehoused, but warned them that, because of the call up, the housing department had been left woefully short of manpower, and it might be months before a house in their area could be found.

The kids were called Stephen and Harriet. They arrived looking dishevelled, underfed and uncared for. They climbed out of the car at the front of the farm, each carrying a battered little case, looking frightened

and anxious. To say their clothes had seen better days
was a massive understatement. People used better
quality clothes to cut up for rags.

Mother Hen, Miriam, immediately took charge of
the situation and leaving me to sign their temporary
placement papers, she threw an arm around each of the
poor little mites and led them through the back door,
into the kitchen. By the time I got there, carrying two
tiny cases containing a change of clothes that were in an
even worse state than the ones they were currently
wearing, they were sitting in front of our big pot-bellied
stove, holding mugs of warm milk and hungrily eyeing
up the sandwiches that Miriam had prepared for them
earlier in the afternoon.

I took Martha out of her cot and sat her on my
knee, she was fascinated by the new arrivals who took
an almost equal interest in her.

'This is Stephen and this is Harriet,' I told her.

'Ste-un an 'arret,' Martha repeated.

I looked at her in amazement. For a toddler that
struggled, or stubbornly refused, to utter the word
Mama, their names fairly tripped off her tongue.

After they finished eating their sandwiches, Miriam
ran a hot bath and taking the pair by the hand, led them
through the parlour to the bathroom I'd had installed
the previous year. When they came out, wrapped in
fluffy, white towels, their faces pink and sweating,
blonde hair stuck to their heads, I sat them in front of
the pot-bellied stove, and as their thin little bodies dried
off, I brought out a book from under the stairs that my
father had bought me when I was about their age.
Sitting between them, so they could both see the
wonderful E. H. Shepard illustrations, I read them the
story of Winnie the Pooh and his friends from the
hundred-acre wood. I had always felt an affinity with
Pooh, as I lived on a one-hundred-acre farm, and in
summer, I used to sit in the copse of maples just below
Bessie's stable and pretend that Pooh, Piglet and Kanga,
were my friends, not Christopher Robin's.

At nine, I gave them both a hug and a kiss on the forehead, and Miriam took them up to the spare room. Martha, who should have been fast asleep by that time, but stubbornly refused to close her eyes, waved her hand to them as they went up. 'Ni-night,' she said.

The next day, we made what was to them, a wildly exciting trip into town in my rickety old truck, to buy new clothes from Woolworths. We also dropped into the thrift shop and picked up a couple of good quality, second hand dresses, a pair of knee length shorts, a few thick, winter jumpers and two pairs of wellingtons for them to wear when playing in the farm yard, which wasn't the cleanest of places at the best of times.

After lunch, I introduced them to the pigs and let them use the stiff yard brush to scratch the backs of my prize boars, Horace and Hector. Martha, who loved the boars as much as I did, giggled as they snorted and stuck their wet snouts through the bars of the pen.

That evening, Mr Starcher, who worked for the local council, dropped by to see how the children had settled in. They both hid under the table when they saw him walk into the kitchen. I coaxed them out with the promise of a slice of Miriam's famous jam sponge and the pair stood together holding hands, looking as though the bottom had just fallen out of their world.

'Don't let him take us away again, Auntie Alice,' said a sobbing Harriet.

I assured them that Mr Starcher wasn't about to do any such thing, and rubbing her eyes with her fist, she backed away towards Miriam, who swept them both up in her comforting arms.

Mr Starcher, it turned out, had reluctantly allowed a couple from Upper Middle Street to take the siblings home on the night that they had first arrived in the town.

'It was against my better judgement, Mrs Mollison, but they were a pair and no one wanted to take two of them on. The Ropers looked a bit rough, I'll admit, and I was sure it was the eighteen shillings and sixpence a week they'd be paid from the government that attracted them, rather than the moral desire to help children in need. But, as it was, they were the last kids in the church hall and the Ropers were they only prospective guardians, so I had to let them go. I said I'd look in on them once they'd had time to settle in but I got rather busy, what with all the new wartime regulations and what have you.'

Mr Starcher unbuttoned his thick overcoat and wiped beads of sweat from his forehead. It was always very warm in our kitchen.

'Anyway. I managed to find an hour yesterday and thought I'd nip over and see how they were getting along together. I had thought about them during the past six weeks, but there always seemed to be something more urgent to attend to.'

He looked down at his boots.

'The Ropers wouldn't let me in to begin with. When I finally threatened them with the police, Mrs Roper opened the kitchen door and allowed me to enter. The place was awash with empty beer bottles and old fish and chip wrappings. As I stepped inside, Mr Roper appeared from upstairs wearing just his vest and long johns. The kids, as I soon found out, were locked in a cupboard under the stairs.

'Mrs Roper bleated that they had to lock them in because they kept trying to run away.

'Mr Roper was far more concerned with losing the weekly allowance than losing the children. He wanted to know if he'd still be paid the week's money they were owed, as they had 'expenses' to consider. The kids didn't look like they'd been fed in days. They were wearing the clothes they'd arrived in, their hands and faces were filthy, they even had bits of cobweb hanging off them. They'd been in that cupboard a good while because they were blinking and holding their hands in front of their eyes when they came out.

'I got them away from there as fast as I could. We got their cases back but Mr Roper had sold their gas masks, so they will need to be issued with new ones. I telephoned Mrs Hopkins, the school head who had been with me the night the children arrived, and asked her if she knew of anyone trustworthy who might take the kids on for a short time while we found them a permanent placing. She said she'd ask you; she thought the farm would be the perfect place for them to get over their recent experiences.'

He tugged at the sleeve of his overcoat, not able to look me in the eye.

'I've spent the entire day phoning people I thought might be willing to help, but as yet, I've had no concrete offers. There have been a couple of maybes, and a possibly, but that's it. I'm sorry to have dumped them on you like this, but do you think you could keep them for another week or so? There's a lady in Gillingham that might be interested but, as Gillingham has had a lot of its own children evacuated, I don't think it's a viable option, really.'

I put my hand on his arm.

'Mr Starcher. I don't mind if the children stay with me until the day the war is over. They're very welcome here. They've enjoyed their first day with us and they seem very keen to learn about farm life. They want to help me feed the animals tomorrow. They have nice warm clothes and as I promised them last night, they will never, ever, feel hungry again, not while they are under my roof.'

A tear dropped down the council official's cheek. He sniffled as he wiped it away.

'I felt so guilty. The poor little things... I sent them there.'

I stepped forward and gave him a hug.

'It wasn't your fault. You had no choice.'

'I should have checked on them.'

'You were busy and... well, look at them. They're absolutely fine now. They didn't come to any real harm, distressing as their circumstances were.'

I pulled out a seat and Mr Starcher sat down. Looking across the kitchen, I held out my hand to the two seats opposite.

'Harriet, Stephen, sit down, please. It's going to be all right.'

Reluctantly, the children sat down at the table, looking at each other, me, Miriam, anywhere but at Mr Starcher. Miriam placed a reassuring hand on each of their shoulders and I poured the seemingly, ever-boiling kettle over fresh tea leaves.

'Now, Harriet, Stephen. There is a question I have to ask before I go.' Mr Starcher bit his lip and swallowed a huge lump in his throat. When he spoke again his voice was cracked and emotional. 'Firstly, I want to say how sorry I am for sending you to those people. I honestly didn't know that you'd be treated in that manner.' He looked down at the table before speaking again. 'However, Mrs Mollison has agreed to let you stay here while we try to find you a permanent home. What do you say? Would you like to stay at the farm?'

'We don't want to leave,' said Harriet.

'Can't we just stay here until it's safe to go home again?' Stephen looked at me, his face full of hope.

Miriam didn't give me a chance to say a word.

'You're going nowhere,' she said, presenting them with a kiss on the top of their heads. 'You're part of our family now.'

Stephen looked at me, I smiled and nodded encouragingly. He leapt off his seat and threw himself into my arms. Harriet, still uncertain, fixed Mr Starcher with a stern look.

'Is it true? You won't take us away again?'

Mr Starcher shook his head. 'No, this is your home now and I'm sure you'll be very happy here. Believe me, my child. No one... no one except your mum and dad, that is, will ever ask you to leave.'

He smiled at them in turn, then got to his feet.

'I'll drop the placement papers in during the week. I'll just post them through the letter box, I won't show my face again in case they think I've come to take them away.'

He walked to the door, stepped out onto the top step then turned back.

'Be happy,' he said.

Chapter 26

On Tuesday evening, Jess showered while a pan of Balsamic rice simmered on the hob. Her own recipe vegetarian chilli mix, had already been cooked and just needed a warm through before serving.

After choosing a green, mid-thigh length button through dress from her wardrobe, she slipped it on and stood in front of the dressing table mirror, turning this way and that, looking critically at the way the dress hung.

Finally satisfied, she brushed her hair and fastened one of Alice's long chain pendants around her neck. Not happy with the way it looked, she undid the top button of the dress to allow the enamel heart to hang over what she considered to be an acceptable amount of cleavage.

Back in the kitchen, Jess pulled on Alice's full front apron and checking the clock, took a bottle of Pinot Grigio from the fridge and sat it on the white linen tablecloth she had stretched across the big old table. She had just taken the lid from the steaming rice and lit the gas under the chilli, when she heard a knock at the door.

'I like a man who is punctual.' She kissed Bradley on the cheek and accepted the bottle of wine he held out to her. 'Ooh, prosecco. I love prosecco. I'm serving up Pinot Grig with dinner, shall we save this for afters?'

Jessica led Bradley through to the kitchen, offered him a seat at the table and slipped the wine into the fridge before giving the chilli a stir, and scooping the rice into two large bowls.

'I hope you're hungry, I made too much rice,' she said.

'I'm famished,' he replied, eyeing up the crusty roll on the side plate.

Jessica spooned the chilli onto the rice and placed the bowls on the table. 'Sponge pudding and custard for afters,' she said with a nervous smile. 'I hope this is all right.'

Bradley looked down at the steaming bowl. 'It looks delicious,' he said.

'There's no meat in it, I call it Chilli Sans Carne.'

Bradley laughed. 'Very clever,' he replied.

Jess took off her apron, folded it and laid it on top of one of the work surfaces, then sat down opposite Bradley.

'Tuck in,' she said.

Over dinner they discussed their plans for Christmas. Bradley would be spending it at home. 'It's a tradition. Mother would be horrified if I spent it anywhere else. When Dad was alive, he suggested we all go to warmer climes for a winter break, my mother didn't speak to him for a week. Christmas, to her, is cold damp, England, with the forlorn hope of a bit of snow, or at least frost to wake up to on Christmas morning.' He picked up a napkin and dabbed at his mouth. 'This really is delicious.'

Jessica grinned. 'Not too hot then?'

Bradley shook his head. 'The Pinot goes really well with it too,' he picked up his glass and took a sip.

'Surprisingly,' laughed Jess. 'I was torn whether to nip out and buy a bottle of Merlot, but I didn't have time in the end.'

'You can never go wrong with Pinot Grigio.' Bradley took another sip. 'So, what are you doing for Christmas?'

'Oh, not a lot. I spent the last three with Calvin. We used to stay with his mother on Boxing Day, but on Christmas Day morning I used to come here to see Nana, then nip over to see Mum, Grandma and Aunt Marjorie. Calvin used to stay at home. He didn't get on with anyone in my family, especially Nana.' She pulled a face at the memory. 'I don't know why Mum bothered. It was never a happy time for any of them. All they ever did was bicker.'

Bradley looked at her sympathetically. 'And, this year?'

'I'll go to see them again. I'll miss spending an hour or two with Nana, though. That was always the best bit of Christmas when I was growing up. There was never much in the way of... Never mind.'

'No, please, go on.'

'I was about to say, I didn't get much by way of presents at home. Dad used to blow the Christmas budget at the bookies, weeks before the big day, but Nana always made up for it. My parents would bring me over late morning and try to scrounge a few pounds off her. She always gave them a card with money inside, not a lot, but enough to keep them bringing me over every year. I loved it. They used to get out of here as soon as they had the Christmas cards and I'd sit in the front room with Nana and open my presents. I'd stay for a few days, then go back in time for school.' She sighed happily. 'It was always a magical time. Nana never, ever, let me down. I used to leave the more expensive presents here because if I took them home, Dad would sell them in the New Year.'

Bradley looked shocked. 'That's dreadful.'

'It was the way it was. I got used to it over the years.' Jess got to her feet and carried the empty bowls to the sink.

'Pudding will be ready in a couple of minutes. I just have to warm it up in the microwave. Do you want hot custard, or cold? I'm afraid it's out of a tin.'

After dinner, Bradley insisted on doing the washing up while Jess dried. When the plates and pans were stashed away, she put the empty wine bottle in the recycling bag that hung on the back door, opened the bottle that Bradley had brought with him, and picking up two fresh glasses she walked through to the lounge.

'You'll have to excuse the lumpy sofa. My new one is still being made.'

Bradley took off his jacket and laid it across the back of one of the armchairs, then sat down on the sofa and wriggled about until he was finally comfortable. Jess poured the wine, handed him a glass and sat down beside him.

'Do you fancy a film or a little music?'

'Is it still Simply Red for romantic dinners?' he asked with a fake look of horror on his face.

Jess laughed. 'Not in this house.' She switched on the Bluetooth speaker she had brought with her from the flat, then lifted the lid of her laptop and started her iTunes program. 'How about a bit of classical?' She flicked through her music collection until she found Vaughan Williams. 'This is nice for background music.'

They sipped wine and chatted the evening away, each revealing some of the lighter moments of their lives. Amidst the mixture of laughter and the wine, Jess realised that she felt happier and more carefree than she had for years. After one particularly hilarious tale from Bradleys Uni days, she threw herself back into the cushions and laughed until her stomach hurt. When she had recovered her composure, she tipped her head to one side and smiled softly. 'You're a very funny man, Bradley Wilson.'

'Oh, I bet you say that to all the boys,' he quipped.

Jess put her finger onto his lips and moved her face closer to his. 'I don't want any other boys.' Her face moved closer still, their lips met and Bradley put his arms around her, pulled her down onto the sofa and with one hand on the back of her head, he pulled away, look earnestly into her eyes, then moved back towards her, his hot tongue running over her neck, his fingers fumbling at the front of her dress.

Jess pushed his hand away and began to undo the buttons herself, then she arched her back to undo her bra. Bradley pushed the garment out of the way, exposing her breasts, then gently kissed each one in turn before lifting his head and kissing her lips again.

As the iTunes program paused before starting to play The Lark Ascending, and as Bradley's trousers reached ankle level, the blue camera light of the laptop lit up.

Chapter 27

Bradley lay on his back twisting his neck to look down at Jess who was lying with her head on his chest. He stroked her hair, then her naked shoulder before running a finger down the nape of her neck sending a shiver down her spine.

'How... No, it doesn't matter.'

Jess sighed, hoping against hope that Bradley wasn't about to ask her to rate his performance.

'Why the sigh?'

'Nothing.'

'Come on, you don't sigh like that for nothing.'

'Okay.' Jess rolled onto her side and propped herself up on her elbow. 'Finish your question.'

Bradley shrugged. 'I was just about to say, how did you manage to get Alice's hospital bed out. It was huge.'

'Oh... it went out easily enough in the end, they took a bit of paint off the doorframe but they managed to manoeuvre it into the hall.'

'You seem surprised. What did you think I was going to ask?'

Jess laid her head back on his chest.

'It doesn't matter, honestly.'

'Come on, Jess, what was that big sigh about?'

'All right, but promise you won't get angry.'

'I promise, come on, out with it.'

'It's just, well, I didn't want to bring Calvin's name up, but... look, whenever we had sex, he used to demand a rating. He always expected me to compare his performance with other boyfriends I'd had before he came on the scene.'

'What an idiot.' Bradley shook his head. 'It's probably the last thing I would have asked at a time like that.'

'He was, it just took me a long time to find out just how big an idiot.'

'Did he have low self-esteem?'

Jess snorted. 'That's the last thing he suffered from. He was a narcissist. He thought he was better than anyone else at just about everything. He just needed me to confirm it.'

Bradley shook his head again, then noticing the blue light on the frame of the laptop, he patted Jess on the shoulder.

'Do you know your laptop has the camera light on?'

'It does that at random, I think it has a fault.'

Bradley sat up, and easing Jess to the side, he stood up, pulled on his pants, walked across to the coffee table and pressed a button on the keyboard. The screensaver cleared and the iTunes playlist appeared on the screen. Bradley pressed a combination of keys and read the Task Manager's list of processes the computer was running.

'Hmm, there are a few routines here I've never seen before.' He turned back to Jess who was now sitting naked on the sofa.

'Oh God, don't tell me we've been recorded.'

The lawyer pulled a face. 'I don't think so, but I can't be sure.' He read the list again, selected a background process, and hit the button to close it down, when the blue light stayed on, he picked another process and closed that. The blue light went out.

Bradley walked back to the sofa and sat down next to Jess.

'I did an I.T. course at Uni. A few male students used to load spyware onto the girl's computers hoping to catch them at it after a party. I didn't see anything I recognised, but it doesn't mean your machine isn't infected.'

'I think Calvin might have put a tracker on my laptop and maybe my phone. He was a control freak and always wanted to know where I was. I doubt he'd go this far though. I never thought of being unfaithful to him and deep down, he knew that.'

'He really is an inadequate individual, isn't he?'

'He is,' agreed Jess.

Bradley pulled his shirt on and began to fasten it up.

'I'd get it checked out if I were you, just for your own peace of mind. There's a place in town that could sort it for you.'

'I've got an I.T. man, Wade, he set up my Wi-Fi and the new outdoor security camera software on my computer.'

'Do you trust him?'

'He's the one that pointed out that I had tracking software on my laptop. I gave Calvin a piece of my mind straight afterwards. He'll have deleted it from his computer now just in case I go to the police.'

'Well, it's up to you, Jess, but I'd get Wade to give your machine a good going over, just in case.'

'I'll ring him tomorrow,' Jess promised.

Bradley pulled on his trousers and reached for his shoes as Jess slipped on her dress and fastened a few of the buttons at the waist.

'I'd load spyware on your computer myself if it meant I could see you dressed like that now and again.' He reached out his hand and pulled the top of her dress apart.

Jess slapped his hand. 'Stop it,' she said, laughing.

Bradley stretched, then tucked his shirt into his trousers.

'I'd better be going. Thank you for a wonderful evening.'

Jess stepped towards him and put the palms of her hands on his chest. 'Do you have to go?' she pouted.

Bradley held her face in his hands. 'I don't have an appointment until ten...'

Jess took his hand and led him towards the stairs, flicking the light switch off as she stepped into the hall.

'I'll make sure you're up,' she said, huskily.

'I can't see that being a problem,' he replied with a wink.

Chapter 28

At seven o'clock on Wednesday morning, Marjorie surprised Martha by bringing a letter into her bedroom instead of the expected breakfast.

'What's this? I can't eat an envelope.'

'It's my letter, Martha, it came about six weeks ago.' Marjorie nervously turned the envelope over in her hands.

'I don't remember you getting a letter.' Martha looked puzzled.

'I hid it.'

'You hid it.' Martha shook her head. 'For pity's sake, Marjorie, you aren't five years old. Why did you hide it?'

'Because it's from the dentist and you know I'm frightened of the dentist. I hoped they'd just forget about me if I didn't turn up.'

Martha sighed. 'When are you supposed to turn up?'

'Today, at eleven. I don't want to go, but...'

'But what?' Martha looked exasperated.

'I've got a bit of a pain in my back tooth.'

'How long have you had the pain?'

'A couple of weeks. I took an aspirin when it got bad.'

'Marjorie!'

Her younger sister hopped from foot to foot. 'I'm sorry, Martha, I know I should have told you but you would have taken me to the dentist. I just hoped the pain would stop on its own, but it hasn't.'

'How bad is the pain?'

'Not too bad. I can bear it easily enough.'

Martha slipped out of bed and pulled on her dressing gown.

'You do realise how inconvenient this is, don't you, Marjorie? I was going to try to talk sense into Jessica today. She was supposed to pick me up... do you know what time she was meant to arrive?'

'Eleven?'

'Eleven,' Martha repeated. 'Well, that's out of the window now, isn't it?'

'I don't have to go, Martha, I can put up with it.'

'Listen, Marjorie. If you leave it, your tooth will decay, then it will turn black, the pain will be excruciating, and it might well spread to nearby teeth. You don't want them to fall out, do you? You've managed to keep them for seventy-six years. Do you really want a set of plastic dentures?'

Marjorie shook her head. 'No, Martha.'

'Then, you're going to keep your appointment.'

'Yes, Martha, will you come with me, I can't go in on my—'

'Look at yourself, shaking like you've got the palsy. I don't really have a choice, do I?'

Marjorie began to wring her hands. Her appointment reminder fell to the carpet.

'Thank you, Martha. Shall I get your breakfast now?'

'No, I've lost my appetite, just run my bath while I call Jessica. Maybe we can have our chat a little earlier than planned.'

Although she owned a mobile phone, Martha wasn't a fan and didn't really understand the technology at all. She only ever used hers to receive calls if she was out and about so, leaving her Samsung mobile on the table, she picked up her landline handset, and flicking through her little black book of important telephone numbers, picked out Jess's mobile number and tapped it out on the keypad. The phone rang but no one replied. Thinking she might have misdialled, Martha tried again with the same result. Frustrated, she slammed down the receiver and searched the black book for Nicola's number.

'Nicola? Good, now listen. I want you to pick me up and drive me over to the farm.'

'The farm? look, Mum, I—'

'Yes, Nicola, THE FARM, you know, the one I'd own if there was any justice?'

'Mum, I can't drive you, I'm at work. It's my early start today.'

'Can't you take a couple of hours off?'

'No, Mum, Mrs Kaur is going to the wholesaler. I have to watch the shop.'

'Damnation!' Martha slammed the receiver down again.

'Is something the matter, Martha?' Marjorie stepped into the kitchen drying her hands on a flannel.

Martha ignored her and searched the book for a local taxi firm. After being told her cab would be there in twenty minutes, Martha stormed past her sister and stomped her way up the stairs.

'Have your bath now, Marjorie, then get ready for the dentist. I'll be back at about ten-thirty.'

'But...'

'No buts, just do as you're told for once. I'm going to call in on my granddaughter and give her a piece of my mind. What use is all this modern technology if it doesn't work?'

The taxi driver was two minutes late and although Martha was dressed and ready to leave when he pulled up at the end of her drive, she still berated him for his tardiness as she climbed into the back seat of the cab and slammed the door shut.

'I'm sorry, love, but there's a fair bit of traffic around this morning.'

'Firstly, I'm not your love, and secondly, you should have known all about the traffic problems. Don't you listen to the local radio station reports?'

The driver tutted to himself and decided not to get into a discussion about how he did his job.

'Mollison's farm is it?'

'It is, I haven't changed my mind since I booked the cab.'

'We'll be there in five minutes.' He turned the radio up just as the traffic presenter gave out the latest bottlenecks. 'Would you listen to that,' he said. 'They know about it already.'

Martha had to climb out of the cab on the lane as there was no room for the driver to pull onto the asphalt. She paid him through his open window and made shooing motions with the back of her hand.
'Thank you,' said the driver sarcastically, but Martha had already turned away and was staring fixedly at the sleek, silver Mercedes that was parked next to Jess's little Toyota. She put her hand on the bonnet to see if the engine had been running recently, then tutting to herself, stepped up to the front door and rattled the knocker.

Chapter 29

'Do you want coffee or tea with your eggs?' Jess called up the stairs as Bradley stepped out of the shower room wearing her short, pink, fluffy dressing gown.

'Coffee, please.' He walked to the stairs fastening the belt around his waist.

'It suits you,' said Jess with a laugh. She looked down to her short blue PJ set. 'You could have borrowed these if you'd asked nicely.'

Before Bradly could reply, there was a loud rap on the door knocker.

Jessica looked puzzled and thinking it was the postman, opened the door about eighteen inches and stuck her head around it.

'Grandma? What...'

'I'm early, as you'd know if you ever answered your telephone.'

'Have you been ringing me? Sorry, Grandma, I switched it to vibrate-only last night and forgot to switch it back to the ringtone this morning.'

'Vibrate, ringtone? I have no idea what you're talking about. Well, are you going to leave me standing here all day?'

Jess looked over her shoulder and grimaced at Bradley. 'It's Grandma,' she mouthed.

Bradley stood frozen to the spot as Jess eased the door open to allow Martha to gain access.

He tugged at the pink belt to tighten it. 'Hello, Mrs Crew,' he spluttered.

Martha gave him a withering glare, then looked Jess up and down.

'Do you always answer the door half naked?'

'I am wearing PJs, Grandma.'

'You'd at least look decent if you wore that.' She pointed up at Bradley who turned around and hurried up the stairs to get dressed.

'Come through, Grandma,' said Jess, leading the way to the lounge. 'Would you like a coffee? I'm just making—'

Martha looked across the room to where Jess's underwear lay in an untidy heap on the carpet. 'It doesn't take a genius to see what's been going on here.'

'Oh, Grandma. I am entitled to a private life you know? I'm not married or anything.'

'In my day, you got married before you even thought about removing your underwear for a man, and even then, you did it in private, or under the bedclothes.'

Jess bit her tongue, just managing to stop herself reminding Martha that this wasn't 'her day'.

'Times have changed, Grandma. We have different standards now.'

'None of them are an improvement on what went before.' Martha looked back towards the stairs. 'It didn't take you long to find someone new to climb into bed with, did it? You've only been on your own for five minutes.'

'Look, I'm not going to argue with you, Grandma. What do you want? I thought I was picking you up at eleven.'

'Marjorie has a dentist appointment at eleven. The silly woman didn't tell me about it until this morning.'

'Can't she go on her own?'

'MARJORIE!' Martha looked incredulous. 'You couldn't trust her to find the place, let alone go inside, have the treatment and come home again. She's hopeless.'

'Maybe you should slacken the reins a bit,' suggested Jess. 'A little independence would do her good.'

'Don't tell me what she is, or isn't capable of, young lady. You can't imagine the chaos that would ensue if I left her to her own devices.'

Martha scowled as Bradley appeared at the lounge doorway.

'And you… you should be ashamed of yourself.'

Bradley looked genuinely puzzled. 'What have I done wrong?'

'You've taken advantage of my granddaughter who has only just broken up with her long-term partner. You're a professional man… allegedly… and she is your client.'

Bradley picked up his jacket, patted the pockets to find his car keys, then gave Jess a peck on the lips.

'I'll call you later.' Fixing Martha with a tight smile, he let himself out of the house.

As soon as the front door closed, Martha resumed her attack.

'I don't know, Jessica, what were you thinking?'

'I'm sorry to be such a disappointment, Grandma. But I have my own life to live and I'll live it as I see fit. Now, are we going to have our little chat?'

Martha looked at the big clock on the wall and shook her head. 'I'm not in the mood now. You can give me a lift back home; I'm not paying for another taxi.'

Jess sighed and turned towards the stairs.

'And make yourself look half decent at least.' Martha ordered. 'Most of your backside is hanging out of those shorts.'

Twenty minutes later, Jess had dropped Martha off at home and had returned to the farm. She showered and dressed in some comfortable old clothes for a day of research and notctaking on her computer. First, she sketched out a rough outline of the two articles she had been contracted to write and to which she intended to expand on that afternoon, but after lunch, as she was washing up, she gazed out over what used to be a busy farmyard and her thoughts turned back to Alice.

'I'm sure you wouldn't have had a go at me for having my backside hanging out of my shorts, Nana.'

She laughed to herself. Although Alice held some very old-fashioned values herself, her views on female sexuality, hadn't counted among them. Alice had been a sexually liberated female before the term had been invented. Martha would have been outraged at the thought of her mother seducing her lawyer in his own office, and if she thought Jess's shorts were indecent, what would she have made of Alice going out on a date without bothering to pull on her knickers?

Jess sat down at the table and opened up her laptop only to see the dreaded blue light come on as soon as she lifted the lid. She immediately thought back to her conversation of the night before, picked up her phone and called Wade.

'Hello, Jess.'

'Hi, Wade, I hope I haven't caught you at a bad time.'

'No, it's cool. How can I help you?'

'I've been thinking about the spyware that could be on my computer. You said you'd only need it for a day or so. Could I book you to have a look at it, please?'

'Of course, I could drop by tomorrow lunchtime. I can't do it tonight; I have a hot date.'

Jess almost clapped with relief. 'Well done! You see, you weren't doing anything wrong. You just had to meet the right girl at the right time.'

'She's a cracker too,' Wade boasted. 'I met her this morning at Costa, she works there.'

'Well, I hope you have a lovely night out. Where are you taking her?'

'The Computer Games Fair in Gillingham. She's a mad gamer too.'

'Fabulous, looks like you were made for each other. I'm hopeless at computer games.'

'We wouldn't have got on then,' said Wade, seriously. 'I'm a gamer first and a lover second.'

'Thank goodness we didn't click then,' replied Jess. 'One of us would have been very disappointed.'

Jess moved her mouse around the screen and found it hovering over the notes she had made from Alice's memoirs.

'I won't lose any work, will I? I have a lot of files on here that are really precious to me.'

'Back it up before I call. I'll do a secondary back-up of docs and pics before I start work. It should be fine though. I think we're talking basic tracker software here, not ransomware or anything like that.'

'Ransomware? I've read about that,' Jess replied. 'Pay up or lose the contents of your computer forever. Why do people want to do such things?'

'Greed. It's as simple as that.' He was silent for a moment. 'Right, I'll see you at lunchtime tomorrow.'

'Have a lovely gaming night,' said Jess, pressing the red button on her screen to end the call.

Returning her attention to her computer, Jess opened the folder containing the two article projects, created a new, blank document in her word processor and typed in a title. ARE THE TIMES REALLY CHANGING? She pressed the enter key then typed a subtitle. Society's Reaction To The Female Sexual Revolution. 1939-2019.

Satisfied with the working title, Jess saved the document and began to think about the opening line. Ten minutes later, with nothing more on the page, she closed the document, opened Alice's Memoir and turned to the last chapter in the 1939 notebook. She ran her hand over the page written in Alice's beautiful script, opened her own jotter, and made a new heading.

December 1939

The month started out rather mild, weather-wise, and we thought we were in for another in a run of warmish Decembers, but by the second week the temperature began to drop and we had heavy frosts and freezing fog at night. The fog hardly cleared during the daylight hours which meant the sort of work we could do on the farm was very restricted. When an eight mile stretch of the Thames froze over, people were, at first, relieved as they thought it would stop the Germans sailing up the river to attack London. We also breathed more easily knowing the fog would hamper the Luftwaffe's efforts to bomb us into submission.

The farm's finances were helped by only having eight farm workers to pay for being mostly idle. I deliberately left Miriam out of that statement because she didn't have a minute of the day in which to take a breather. The two new recruits to our family, Stephen and Harriet, had settled in well but with the weather as it was, their activities were limited and they were desperate for some outdoor time to enable them to burn off all that excess energy.

When I came in one morning from cleaning out the pigs, I was almost knocked over by Stephen as he ran laps of the kitchen pretending to be Godfrey Brown, the athlete who had won a gold medal for Britain in Hitler's 1936 Olympic Games.

Hearing the name Godfrey made me think of my Gangster Lawyer who I had seen nothing of since he departed for Chatham a few weeks before but, as if I had suddenly developed the ability to use telepathy, less than two minutes later the telephone rang.

'Alice?'

My heart swelled. 'Godfrey? I was just thinking about you. How are you? How is training going? Are they feeding you well? Have they made you a General yet?'

Godfrey laughed.

'They turned me down, Alice. For military service at least. I found out this morning. They noticed my limited fighting skills and decided that my efforts would be better suited to activities elsewhere.'

I jumped up and down in excitement. 'So, where are they sending you?'

'I am to liaise between The War Office, the Home Office, and local councils in the Kent area. Apparently, my ability to understand legalise, makes me indispensable in this field. Basically, I will have to explain government orders and regulations to local officials who will put them into practice. I'll basically be

doing my old job, but for much less money. I do get a
uniform to wear though, so I can pretend I'm doing my
bit.'

Godfrey sounded so disappointed. I hurried to
reassured hm.

'Of course you'll be doing your bit, and I'm so
relieved to have you carrying a fountain pen around
instead of a rifle. I honestly can't see you with a Lee
Enfield in your hands.'

'Nor could the army,' said Godfrey, 'especially when
I hit everything but the targets on the rifle range. The
instructor asked me if I was Hitler's secret weapon.'

I tried to hold back a laugh, but gave in.

'Oh, Godfrey. I know you think you missed out in
the last war, but honestly, at nearly forty, I think you
should really sit this one out too. Wasn't forty the upper
age limit?'

'Near enough. Forty-one, I think.'

I did my best to make light of it all. 'Well then,
they'd probably have invalided you out because of your
great age inside a year anyway.'

'Add in the fact that they wanted me to shoot at the
enemy, not the blokes around me.'

'Don't be disappointed, Godfrey, think of your
family, they'll be pleased to have you safe at home.'

'My son says he won't be able to face his friends at
school because most of their fathers are going to fight.'

'They won't be so happy when they can't sleep at
night, worrying about them,' I replied.

'Do you know, Alice, I rather get the impression
that you don't like the idea of this war.'

'You'd be right if you thought that, Godfrey. I
understand why we're doing it and I'll back our lads all
the way, but I don't have to like it. I'm so pleased you
were given a desk job. I can't tell you how pleased. I've
worried about you since the day you told me you were
joining up.'

Godfrey was silent for a while. When he spoke, his
voice was broken.

'I missed you terribly, Alice. I thought about you every night in the barracks and I will be honest, when they told me today that I wasn't needed at the front, my first thought was of you. Not my wife... You. Does that make me a bad person?'

My own voice suddenly broke up.

'No... it makes you Godfrey, my Gangster Lawyer. Will you be spending a lot of time in London? Will we still be able to meet now and then?'

'I will spend a fair bit of time in Westminster... but, I know a couple of very nice hotels nearby if you could find the odd free weekend.'

'Just name a date, I'll be there.' I had never been to London even though my only surviving, adult relative lived there.

'It'll be a bit hairy when the bombs start to fall,' he said.

'It will just add to the excitement,' I said, confidently.

'That's my girl.' Godfrey sounded a little happier. 'I'd, er, better go. I've got a lift on an army truck and it's leaving in ten minutes.'

I blew a kiss down the phone. 'Travel safely, Godfrey. I hope to see you before you set off for London.'

'Count on it,' he said.

By Christmas, the weather had taken an even bigger turn for the worst and we were suffering the lowest temperatures for forty-five years. I arranged to meet Godfrey, one freezing-cold Thursday afternoon, but our tryst was called off because the train he was supposed to catch was cancelled due to ice on the lines.

Our Christmas party was a very subdued affair. My remaining workers felt a sense of guilt for not at least offering to take up arms themselves, even though Barney and George were in their late fifties and the rest were over conscription age. They couldn't look the wives of our missing workers in the face, even though the ladies in question let them know from the start that they didn't think of them as lesser men. Emily Tomkiss, Benny's young, pregnant wife, had us all in tears when she announced that she knew Benny was well because, not only could she feel it in her own heart, the baby could feel it in its heart too. 'He's coming home to us, I know it,' she said, to a round of loud applause.

By eight o'clock, the temperature had dropped so low that the farmyard wasn't safe to walk on. Icy cow pats and splashes of pig mess, which we hadn't been able to wash away because the water from the hose froze almost as soon as it hit the floor, made our usual, farmyard-party impossible. So, instead of the roaring brazier outside, we spent our time crowded into the kitchen, huddled around our pot-bellied stove. We still sang our favourite Christmas carols and the kids caused havoc playing games of blind man's buff and pin the tail on the donkey (though instead of a tail and a donkey we had a newspaper cutting of old Adolph, and the idea was to pin his silly little moustache onto it). When the game was over, we ceremonially tossed his picture onto the stove and we all cheered as we watched it burn.

Chapter 30

Wade was as good as his word and at exactly one o'clock on Thursday lunchtime, he arrived at the farm to pick up Jess's laptop.

Jess unplugged it from the charging cable, saved her work and passed it to him.

'So, how was the big date?'

Wade grinned. 'We had a great time, thanks. We teamed up and played the new version of Black Ops Armageddon, it hasn't been released to the public yet.'

'Did you win?'

'Slaughtered all-comers. We made a great team.' Wade puffed out his chest to emphasise the point.

'Love at first fight then.' Jess grinned at her own joke.

Wade nodded seemingly missing the gag.

'So, when are you seeing her again?'

'We're hooking up remotely tonight to play Call of Duty, Modern Warfare.'

'Remotely?'

'Yeah, we want to get to know each other's tactics properly before we go any further.'

Jess frowned. 'Oh, right, well, good luck with your bourgeoning relationship. I wish you many hours of happy slaughter.'

Wade grinned again. 'Thanks. I think this might be fate lending a hand. I wondered why I couldn't pull, recently. This was meant to happen, I think.'

He carried the laptop out to his car, placed it in a padded bag in the foot well of the passenger side of the vehicle, then walked around to the driver's side.

'I'll get it back as soon as I can. I know you need it ASAP.'

'I'd really appreciate that, Wade. I have a couple of important articles to write up and there's a deadline looming.'

As Wade powered off up the lane to the ear-splitting noise of the drum and base, Jess closed the door and walked through to the lounge. She had been trying to psyche herself up all morning to make a second visit to the attic. She had finished reading the 1939 memoir and the 1940 notebook, along with the ones that covered the rest of the war, were in a tea chest in the far corner of the loft.

Jess found the room unnerving to say the least. She had heard so much nonsense about the attic from her family when she was growing up, that she found herself on edge even thinking about climbing the stairway that led up to it. She only went up last time because Alice had requested it and she often found the swaying figure she had seen in the cobweb-covered full-length mirror, haunting her dreams. Alice had said it was probably her best friend, Amy, checking up on her and she shouldn't be frightened, but Jess was still reluctant to find out whether the figure had been a trick of the light, or a message from beyond.

'I know, Nana, I'm just a wuss,' she said aloud.

She decided to build up to it in stages, and walked slowly up to the first-floor landing where she made her way to the window at the front of the house and looked out over the lane. Taking several deep breaths, she was just about to turn to embark on stage two of her mission, when a battered old car with a late-nineties number plate pulled up on the drive. Two men in their early thirties, wearing badly fitting suits, got out of the car and walked quickly to the front door. Jess, relieved at having the trip to the attic postponed, stepped briskly down the stairs.

She opened the door to find one of the men standing on the top step, the other stood at the bottom, looking nervously up and down the lane.

'Hello, love,' the man on the top step said, slipping his foot into the gap between the door and the frame.

Jess, thinking the pair were Jehovah's Witnesses, or a team working for an energy firm trying to get her to swap providers, smiled politely and waited for him to continue.

'Is your dad in? We'd like a word.' The man on the bottom step turned and fixed her with a thin smile.

'Why would he be in? He doesn't live here,' replied Jess.

'Well, in that case, we'd like a word with you,' said the taller of the two.

Jess began to feel very nervous. 'I'm all ears,' she replied, with more confidence than she was feeling.

'We represent... let's call it an insurance company.' The man closest to Jess pushed his hand into his pocket, Jess expected him to produce a business card but he didn't. Instead, he withdrew the hand, patted the pocket, then let it fall to his side. 'The company hasn't been paid the instalments on the life policy, so we,' he pushed his thumb towards the man behind, 'are here to collect.'

Jess closed the door an inch.

'I don't have life insurance,' she said, fighting to keep control of her voice.

'No, you don't, but your father does, and he told us last week, that you would pay the instalments he owes. We don't expect you to have the full amount in cash, obviously, so you have a choice. You can get the money by tomorrow, or you can just pick up your phone and transfer the money. Call this number when you're ready and you'll be given an account number to pay it into.'

The man put his hand into his pocket again and pulled out a folded piece of paper.

Jess suddenly felt anger stir inside her.

'And just how much are you asking me to pay?'

'Fifty thousand. I know it was forty, last week, but with the interest...'

'You have to be joking. I don't have anything like that kind of money, and I wouldn't give it to you if I had.' Jess tried to close the door but the man pushed his knee into the gap and leaned in closer.

'Well, you had better find a way of getting the money, love. The debt is now a joint one. One of you has to cough up, and since your father doesn't appear to be able to pay, the onus falls on to you.' He narrowed his eyes and stared into Jess's from about a foot away.

Jess lifted her shaking hand and pushed a stray hair out of her eyes.

'I told you, I can't just put my hands on that kind of money. I—'

'FIND A WAY!' The man glared at her, then his voice became as cold as ice.

'It will be best for both you and your father, if you pay up without any fuss because, when we find him, and we will find him, you could be forking out for a funeral, on top of the debt.'

Angry tears misted Jess's eyes. She rubbed them away with the back of her right hand.

'I'm not going to be blackmailed like this. I'll call the police.'

'I wouldn't if I were you,' the man on the bottom step joined in the conversation. 'Not if you know what's good for you.' He fixed her with a cold eye. 'These remote old houses can be scary places when you live alone like you do. I bet it would go up like matchwood.'

The taller of the two men dropped the piece of paper into the hall. 'You have until noon tomorrow. I think bank transfer would be easiest. Tell them you're investing in an insurance company.' He looked over Jess's shoulder into the hall. 'You might want to think about buying a policy for yourself, anyway. As my associate said. These old houses go up like tinder.' The man looked hard at Jess. 'We aren't the only ones looking for him, love. He can't hide for long in a town this size.'

Jess tried to hold the man's stare but looked away after only a few seconds, then a mobile phone rang and the man on the bottom step answered it.

'Yes... all right. We're on our way.' He pushed the phone back into his pocket and looked towards the taller man. 'They've got an address.'

'Did you hear that? They've got an address,' he snarled. 'I'd get on to the bank if I were you... and don't even think about handing that number to the cops. It won't be traced.'

Jess pulled back the door with her left hand and slammed it as hard as she could onto his knee. The man cursed and pulled his leg back, Jess quickly pushed the door shut, and turning to face the stairs, stood with her back against it as the man outside hurled threats at her.

After a minute or so, she heard a car engine start, she waited until it had pulled away before rushing through to the kitchen and blinking away the tears, she picked up her phone and dialled her father's number.

'Hello, Jess?' For a man whose life was in mortal danger, her father didn't sound too worried.

'I've just had two men here making threats.'

'Oh no! Jess, I did say they might find you. What did they say?'

'They wanted money of course. Fifty thousand pounds.'

'Fifty?' Bill sounded puzzled.

'The latest round of Interest is included.'

'Jess, please, don't mess with these people, just pay the money.'

'I'm not giving them a penny, Dad.'

'Jess, please. I don't want you to get hurt. You don't know what these people are like.'

'What are they like, Dad? Do you know this pair?'

'No, of course I don't. I'm just saying. I know their type; I know their boss. These people will have been sent up from London. They're with one of the East End gangs. I was warned about them.'

There was silence on the line, then Bill began to plead.

'Jess, I beg you. I don't want to die. I don't want you to die. You live alone down there. I worry about you. I couldn't get to you in time if there was a fire.'

'Oh, so you know about the threat of a fire?'

'No... no, it's just one of the things they do if they can't get people to pay up.'

Jess thought for a few moments.

'Do London gangsters always drive around in twenty-year-old bangers?'

'I don't know... they might have stolen it... Jess, please pay the money. Parents should never have to attend their children's funeral. It should be—'

'You're disgusting. Don't try to scare me like that. Your friends couldn't and nor will you.'

'Jess, they're not my friends, I don't know who they are. I'm just worried about you, honestly, love, I'm more concerned about your life than mine. It's my fault we're both in this mess, but there is a way out. Just do as they ask, darling.'

'Don't give me the darling bit. I saw through that when I was eight.'

'Jess... wait, there's a car pulling up outside. Oh God, Jess, please, let me tell them you're going to pay up... Look, your mum is here, I don't want her to get hurt.'

'YOU BASTARD!'

'Jess, please.'

'Dad, I saw through this scheme of yours as soon as you picked the phone up.'

'What do you mean, scheme. I don't—'

'Dad,' Jess spoke slowly and calmly. 'Here's how I worked it out... One! East End gangsters wouldn't be seen dead in cheap, Asda suits. Two! East End gangsters wouldn't be seen dead in a twenty-year-old car that sounds like it's about to conk out. Three! East End gangsters don't speak WITH A LOCAL ACCENT! I grew up with that accent, Dad. I know a Spinton accent when I hear one. I doubt if that pair have ever been out of town in their lives.'

'I don't know where they're from, Jess. They might be working for the local hoods.'

'Or they might be working for you.'

'Jess...'

'Dad. I'm not going to go to the police straight away. I'm going to give you one last chance. Now, go back to wherever it was you came from, get out of our lives for good. I'm coming over to Mum's on Saturday, and if you're still there, I'll call the police there and then.'

'You think you're so clever,' he sneered, 'but there are people in this town who would genuinely hurt you, and I really don't want that to happen.'

'Who, Dad? Who would think I'm worth killing? They'd never get the money if anything happened to me. If I die, the trust goes to a farm worker's charity.'

'They can still hurt you, Jess. The Duncan brothers are a bad lot. I'm still on their radar from five years ago. These people never forget, especially when money is concerned. Don't be surprised if they call again, one dark night.'

'I'm ending the call now, Dad. I meant what I said. I never want to see you again. Goodbye.'

Jess hit the red button to end the call, then sat down at the kitchen table and with her head in her hands, sobbed until there were no tears left.

At six-thirty, Jess was just about to cook herself dinner when there was a knock on the door. She tiptoed to the front window and opened a crack in the front curtains. To her relief, she saw Wade standing at the bottom of the steps.

'Hi, Wade, come in.' Jess stood aside as the technician stepped inside carrying her laptop.

'It only took twenty minutes to remove the spyware. It was an amateurish attempt really.'

'Calvin won't like being called an amateur,' said Jess with a little laugh. 'He thinks he's a tech guru.'

Wade put the laptop on the kitchen table and opened it up. 'There was a spyware tracking app on it, but that was all. This guy Calvin, or whoever it was that loaded it on, attempted to add a bit of extra code to the tracker. It's different with phones. Lots of people use the Apple, Find My Phone, app. Parents use it to keep an eye on their kids, spouses to keep an eye on unfaithful partners.' Wade pointed to Jess's iPhone. 'He'll have your Apple I.D. and password; just change that password and he won't be able to track you.'

Jess grinned. 'So, it's as easy as that. What about the blue camera light?'

'He tried to be a little too clever. I think he wanted to adapt the tracker code so the camera started up whenever he checked in on you. But it didn't quite work and all that happened was, the light came on at random intervals. You were never being recorded. As I said, amateurish.'

Jess almost gave him a hug, but managed to stop herself just in time. Wade tipped his head to the side and looked at her quizzically.

'Are you all right? You look like you've been crying?'

'Oh, don't worry, I've been watching an old movie on TV, this afternoon. They always make me emotional.'

Wade wasn't convinced.

'If you say so, but look, Jess, if you ever need someone to talk to, I'm always on the end of the line.'

Jess patted him on the arm. 'Unless you're up to your neck in dead zombies?'

Wade's eyes widened. He checked his watch then almost ran to the front door. 'Sorry, can't stay. I need to get my fingers warmed up for tonight. She'll be online in thirty minutes.'

'Good luck with the zombie slaughter,' Jess shouted after him.

After closing the door behind the technician, Jess went back to the kitchen and started up the security camera software. She clicked on the cloud link and opened up the first of twenty photographs that the device had taken that morning. On opening picture six, she found herself looking at a perfect, hi-res photograph of the two men that had visited her. Downloading a copy to her laptop, she printed it off and put it in the drawer of the coffee table.

'Gotcha,' she said with a fixed smile on her face.

Chapter 31

'What do you mean, she didn't fall for it? She looked frightened enough when we left her.' Paul Austen lit a cigarette, took a deep draw and slipped the packet of cigarettes and his lighter back into his pocket.

'She saw through it,' Bill sighed. 'She's a clever kid.'

'Saw through what? We should be offered a part in the Sopranos we were that good.'

'Well, for a start, there's the suits? Why didn't you just wear jeans and a hoodie? Casual stuff, the suits were well over the top.' Bill looked the pair up and down. 'Cheap Asda suits, she said, she wasn't wrong, was she?'

'Sod off! These are from Burton's sale, we got them for Uncle Tony's funeral.'

'What about the car? She said it was a right old banger.'

Paul's cousin, Neil, looked sheepish. 'It's all I can afford. We couldn't very well just go out and nick one, it was too short notice.'

Bill held up his hands in mock surrender.

'All right, all right... She picked up on your accents too, she grew up around here, she knows you're local.'

'Shit,' Paul looked for an ashtray, when he couldn't find one, he dropped the stub of his cigarette in the sink. 'Do you want us to pay her another visit?'

'Not yet, but we do need to ramp up the pressure. I'm her father, she won't go to the police, she told me that when she rang. She might be angry but she isn't going to see her old dad in jail.' Bill got up from the kitchen table. 'Right, here's part two of the plan. Her lawyer's name is Bradley Wilson. He controls the money via a trust. He might be persuaded to turn on the taps if enough pressure is applied. She might cave in if she sees other people being dragged into it.'

Neil shook his head. 'A lawyer? I don't like the sound of that. He'll know every copper in the area, and every copper in the area knows us.'

'If you're smart, he won't know who you are. Mask up, make it look like an attempted mugging or something.'

Paul scratched his head. 'But how will he know what we want if we just take his wallet and watch?'

Bill tapped his head, then pointed to his feet. 'Up here for thinking, down there for dancing.' He looked at each of them in turn. 'I was hoping that Jess would cave in straight away but she hasn't and as I said, she's clever, so, we need to box clever too. We'll put the squeeze on in stages. A nudge here, a hint there, let the pressure build up gradually. She's a woman, she'll back down if things look like getting nasty.'

Paul was still puzzled. 'So, how do we go about it?'

'Don't mention money, and for God's sake don't mention Jess. Don't leave any clue to your identity. It's one thing my daughter thinking you two are locals, but as far as she knows you could be working for the Duncan brothers. She has no idea who you are. Let's keep it that way.'

'So, ski masks, gloves, hoodies?'

'That's it, but as I said, be smart. Don't do it in broad daylight, and make sure your bloody car isn't in sight. There could well be CCTV on the premises.' Bill thought for a moment. 'It might be better to follow him home and grab him when he gets there. Whichever you think is safest. Just don't get bloody caught.'

Neil nodded. 'Erm, could you give us a bit of cash up front?' 'My Universal Credit doesn't come through until next week.'

Bill shook his head. 'You'll be very well looked after when she pays up, don't worry.'

Neil looked at Paul who shrugged. 'Okay then. We'll have a run out later. What time does his office close?'

'Google it,' suggested Bill. 'But be careful. He doesn't work there alone. There may well be others leaving at the same time.'

Chapter 32

Jess, still angry with her father's machinations, decided to channel the outrage she felt, telling herself that if she could stand up to two, bullying thugs, she could almost certainly garner enough strength to face a trip to the attic. Girding her loins, she stomped up the stairs and marched along the landing until, her nerve weakening, she reached the white painted door that stood between her and the final stair to the loft.

Closing her eyes and calling up every last bit of mental strength she could muster, she pulled the door open and slowly climbed the twisting, bare stair treads. At the top, she stopped at the final barrier; an unpainted, panelled door. Jess cocked her head to the side and listened for any noise emanating from the inside, then, giving herself a mental slap, she turned the key in the lock and took hold of the handle.

'Come on, you fool. What on earth do you think is lurking in there?'

Jess took a deep breath, twisted the handle and pushed the door open. The room was silent, the air hanging like a shroud. She stuck her head into the gap between the door and the jamb and looked into the roof space.

It was just as she remembered it. The room was lit by a dappled light that filtered in through a dirty, Dormer window. It was littered with old suitcases, tea chests, piles of old bedding and curtains. Further into the room were stacks of newspapers, tied into bundles with string. Leaning forwards so she could make sure nothing was lying in wait for her around the corner, she took another huge breath and stepped into the attic.

Trying to avoid looking into the shadows at the back of the room, she hurried past the crates that were laid out randomly, making her journey something of an obstacle course.

As she reached the Dormer, she glanced to the right where an ornate, full length mirror stood on its block-timber feet. The antique mirror was tarnished around the edges and silvered in places. It was covered, almost entirely by a film of dusty cobwebs which gave her reflection a surreal appearance. She blew out her cheeks with relief as she realised there was no shadowy figure, swaying from side to side behind the cobweb screen.

Jess focussed her thoughts on the chest in the left-hand corner of the attic where Alice's remaining memoirs were stored. Scraping her knee on the sharp, metal strip on the edge of a tea chest, she winced and keeping her eyes straight ahead, stepped around a large, bulging, cardboard box and limped her way to the wooden crate that contained Alice's old ledgers, seed catalogues and most precious of all, her hand-written notebooks.

She picked them up carefully, and taking a quick glance at each cover, made a small pile on the edge of a neighbouring tea chest.

'1940... 41... 42... 43... 44... 45... That should be the lot... No, hang on, what's this?'

Jess crouched, reached into the bottom of the crate and pulled out a leather-bound photograph album. Stacking it on top of the notebooks, she grabbed the dusty pile and turned back towards the door where a sliver of dim but welcoming daylight, spread itself across the bare floorboards at the entrance to the loft.

'Don't look at the mirror, don't look at the mirror,' Jess chanted as she began to pick a route through the crates and boxes.

As she reached the Dormer, she tried to concentrate on looking directly ahead, but a slight movement broke her will and she flicked her head to the left. To her astonishment, a few of the broken strands of cobweb had begun to float about, although there wasn't as much as an eddy of air current in the attic.

Jess stopped dead, the hairs on the back of her neck standing on end. She tried to concentrate on the block feet of the mirror and tried to force herself to keep walking towards the safety of the stairway, but a movement behind the matted, spidery silk grabbed her attention. She willed herself to turn away, to ignore the faint, swaying figures that were becoming more distinct by the second. The ghostly shapes were, at first, facing each other, a hand on the waist, the other around the partners back. As the shapes became clearer, Jess could make out two young females, their white, dresses floating around their calves as they danced. One of the girls was fair, the other had chestnut curls falling around her shoulders. As Jess caught her breath, the faces turned towards her.

'Nana,' Jess gasped. 'Is it really you... and... is that Amy? Oh, Nana, I wouldn't have been so afraid if I'd known you were up here waiting.'

As she took a step towards the mirror the vision began to fade, and she found herself looking at her own, murky reflection.

'No! Please don't go. Not yet.'

Jess took a step back, her mouth dropped open as the vision returned, then the dancing figures parted and the darker of the women turned to face her, full on. Her eyes were soft, her smile sad, then she mouthed something. Jess pricked up her ears but the only sound to be heard was that of her own, stifled breath. Narrowing her eyes, she concentrated on Alice's mouth to see if she could make out what she was saying. She appeared to be repeating the same word, over and over again. Then, suddenly, Jess heard her beloved Nana's voice in her head. Not the age-cracked voice she had grown accustomed to over the last few years, but the light, almost melodic voice of Alice's youth.

'Beware,' it said. 'Beware.'

The mirror suddenly cleared, leaving only her own hazy reflection standing in front of the Dormer.

'I'll be careful. Goodbye, Nana,' Jess whispered, then turning to her right, she walked briskly out of the room.

Chapter 33

Back in the kitchen, Jess placed her armful of notebooks on the table, then put the kettle on and made coffee. As she sipped it, she opened the leather-bound photo album and slowly worked her way through the pages.

The first few pictures were of Alice's mum and dad standing in front of the farmhouse and in the back yard near the pig pens. Above each photograph was a short description and a date. Alice herself appeared after the fifth page, at first as a baby, then a toddler. After that were a few school aged pictures, with one showing Alice and her best friend Amy, holding hands to the backdrop of the town's annual fair. There was also a photo of Alice and Amy in the Old Bull, looking slightly the worse for wear, standing in a group with two, tall, dark-haired men who had their arms draped around the girl's shoulders. At the top off the page was the tagline: The Long Arm of the Law. Bodkin and Ferris. Movie Night. Jan 1939. Interest piqued; Jess jotted down a quick note. *Check out the policemen in the photograph.*

Towards the back of the album were some grainy black and white photos of Alice with Martha and Marjorie. Right at the back, tucked into the cover, were half a dozen loose pictures of the farm workers and their families. The final two were of Alice and her Gangster Lawyer, Godfrey, standing arm in arm next to the very Alvis that Jess herself had been riding in only a few days before.

Smiling, Jess closed the album and ran her hand over the soft, leather cover.

'Lovely memories, Nana,' she said to herself.

Jess made a sandwich and poured a glass of milk, then opened her notebook and wrote 1940 on a clean page. Picking up the memoir from the top of the pile, she took a sip of milk, opened the jotter and began to read.

April 1940

There are no entries for January and February in this volume, mainly because there wasn't much to relate. The freezing cold weather that arrived during late December continued over the next eight weeks with very few days getting above freezing. It was recorded as being the coldest winter for 45 years.

Very little work was done on the farm. The lads turned up every morning, but after milking and feeding, they were generally sent home to sit by their coal fires for the rest of the day.

Rationing of basic foodstuffs had been introduced in January and it was a major shock to the majority of the population. We had it easier, living on a farm, and although, feeling guilty we cut back ourselves, we didn't have the same privations as the rest of the public as we produced milk and made our own cheese and butter. Despite offers from many quarters, we steadfastly refused to sell to the newly created black market, and let the government agencies have the bulk of our produce.

By mid-March the worst of it was over but the land was so wet we couldn't do a lot in the fields. The previous autumn, the government had decreed that farmers should plough up the pastures that were normally left fallow, but as the land had been frozen for all those weeks, we hadn't had a chance to do it.

In the second week of April, we led Bessie, our aging shire horse, out of her paddock, harnessed her up and began to plough one of the three fields that had been left to nature.

Bessie loved being out in the fields and she was spoiled rotten by the lads. Before the rationing came in, they would feed her sugar lumps, but now that sugar was in short supply, they fed her apples, and mint humbugs, ignoring my half-hearted warnings that she would get fat or her teeth would fall out.

We had discussed retiring her during the winter, but because we could only dream of buying a tractor and because trained shire horses were now priced at a premium, we decided that she was fit enough for at least one more year of farm work, though we would keep a sharp eye on her for any sign of weakness. Bessie had her own paddock and a double-stalled, stable. Through the summer months she would be brought out to help clear fallen trees and drag the sawn up trunks into the hedge bottoms to block up any gaps that would allow our sheep to get out onto the lane.

Bessie also made appearances at the country show held in our town every summer and had been the proud winner of a dozen rosettes over the years. The local kids always made a fuss over her whether at the show or whether walking with me or one of the lads around the country lanes during the warm summer evenings.

I had often wondered if she ever felt lonely, but Barney, who knew horses as well as anyone, said she was happy enough. During the summer of 1939 we put a young mare in with her while its owner went into hospital for a minor operation, but we had to separate them after a few hours because Bessie wouldn't stop biting her.

Barney suggested we try again with an unwanted foal, or invest in another shire horse when she finally retired.

'She might get bored when she's stuck in the paddock, week in, week out. We should have a chat about it in the autumn, Missis.'

As it turned out, she got company much sooner than that.

The next morning, Tinker Toby arrived at the farm with his donkey drawn cart. Toby was famous in the area. He was in his seventies, with a mass of unkempt, white hair sticking out at all angles from beneath his large-brimmed, floppy, felt hat. He lived in a ramshackle hut at the junction of Main Street and the Gillingham Road where he sorted and sold the piles of scrap metal, rags and other items the residents of the town couldn't find a use for. The place had been condemned twice and had been earmarked for demolition for over ten years, but when the contractors turned up to begin work, they found a crowd of angry locals waiting for them. A hasty meeting was arranged between the protesters and the council and it was agreed that the demolition work would be postponed until either Toby, or his residence, keeled over.

I was alerted to Toby's arrival by the sound of a braying donkey. Smiling to myself, I grabbed a couple of apples and a large carrot and made my way through the five barred gate and up the side of the house to the lane.

Toby was holding the reins of a young, tan coloured, donkey that was harnessed to his cart. The docile animal swished its tail and looked towards me as I approached.

'Toby! Where's the old girl? I'm sure I heard her.'

'She's at the back, Missis,' he said. 'She's too old to pull the cart nowadays, but she makes such a racket if I leave her behind that the neighbours complain.'

'Who is this then?' I patted the young donkey and scratched between its ears.

'That's Tan,' Toby replied. 'I've had her a few months now.'

I held out one of the apples, Tan took it from my hand, and as he crunched on it, I walked to the back of the fully loaded cart to find an old, grey donkey trying desperately to look around the side of the wagon.

I threw my arms around the donkey's neck and she rubbed her head against mine.

'Hello, my lovely,' I said. The animal was older than me and I had known it all my life. Toby had been a regular visitor to the farm over the years and he would always stay for a natter with my parents while Amy and I petted the beast. He had never given the animal its own, unique, name, he just called it Donkey.

Toby suddenly appeared at the other side of the cart.

'I've got a big problem, Missis,' he said.

I continued to fuss Donkey as she tried to fish the apple out of my pocket. I laughed, pulled it out and fed it to her.

'Anything I can help with?' I replied.

'I've been told to get rid of Donkey,' he said sadly. His face crumpled. 'She's too noisy. People complain about her all the time now. A man from the council came around last week and gave me ten days to take her to the knackers yard or they'd send out a vet to put her down.' He patted Donkey and ran his hand through her matted mane. 'That means a bullet. It's no way for a hard-working animal to die.'

I was outraged.

'What the... who is this councillor? I'll have a strong word with him.'

'There's nothing to be done, Missis.' Toby produced a screwed-up sheet of paper from his pocket that detailed Donkey's death sentence.

As if she'd just read the paper herself, Donkey threw back her head and brayed.

I stroked her ears to comfort her. 'Don't worry, lovely, it's not going to happen.'

'I was hoping you'd take her on,' said Toby. 'You live at the back of beyond, no one is going to complain about her out here, are they?'

'It's a farm, Toby, it's noisy from dawn 'til dusk. We have cockerels, cows, sheep and pigs, the noise can be deafening sometimes.'

'So, you'll take her? It would be a big weight off my mind, Missis.'

'Of course I'll take her. I'm not sure how she'll get on with our Bessie, but there are two stalls in the stable. We can partition the paddock if we have to. She'll have a happy retirement here.'

Toby wiped his grateful tears from his eyes and scratched Donkey's head. 'I've had her for twenty-eight years. She was younger than Tan when I first got her. She was with a travelling circus and I caught her owner whipping her because she wouldn't pull the wagon. She was a stubborn thing, even then. She brayed and brayed and flatly refused to even try to move it so much as an inch. The thing was so big and heavy it needed two full grown horses to pull it any distance. The man threatened to get his gun and put a bullet in her head, so I offered him five shillings for her and we've been together ever since.' He looked lovingly at the animal, then went on. 'Five bob was a lot of money just before the First World War and I hardly ate for the next two weeks, but I never regretted taking her.'

I nodded sympathetically. I had heard the story many times.

Toby untied the tether from the back of the cart and with tears streaming down his face, handed it to me.

'You can come to see her any time you feel like it, Toby, you know that. Bring Tan with you too.'

'They don't really get on, Missis. That's one of the problems.'

I led Donkey to the side of the road and Toby turned his cart around. Holding Tan by the harness, he waved to us.

'Goodbye, old girl, I'll come and see you soon,' he promised.

Donkey pulled her head back and brayed as the old man disappeared from view.

I thought she might play up as I pulled on the tether rope to lead her away, but after one lingering look back towards the lane, she allowed me to lead her down the side of the house and into the yard.

Barney, my foreman had been working in the cowshed. He came out as I was closing the gate.

'What's this? More livestock?' He ruffled Donkey's mane.

'It's us or the knacker's yard, Barney,' I replied. 'There was never a choice, really.'

'We were only just speaking about getting Bessie a bit of company.'

I nodded. 'I do hope they get on.'

Barney walked with me as I led Donkey to the fence of the paddock. 'We can easily partition a bit off for her,' he said. 'I'll do it myself; George can take over in the dairy.'

Bessie was chewing grass in the far corner of the paddock, so I tied Donkey to a fence pole and lifted the lasso rope that held the gate shut.

'We'll have to give her a name, we can't just call her, Donkey,' I said, pushing it open.

Donkey, spotting Bessie ambling towards us, began an ear-splitting volley of brays. I let go of the gate and put my hands over my ears.

'Good God, no wonder her neighbours were complaining.'

Bessie plodded up and hung her head over the fence. The two animals sniffed at each other, then rubbed their heads gently together. Donkey stopped braying immediately.

'I think we'll skip the partition,' I said. 'Though it might be best to keep them in separate stalls for tonight at least.'

I led Donkey into the paddock and removed her tether. Bessie tossed her head and began to walk back the way she had come. Donkey trotted after her until she caught up, then they walked side by side, towards Bessie's favourite part of the pasture.

'Maybe the mare we brought in for her was too young,' Barney said scratching his head. 'These two old gals will have a lot more in common.'

At nine o'clock that night, I was sitting in the kitchen reading to Stephen and Harriet from The House at Pooh Corner, when we heard Donkey braying nonstop for over ten minutes. Thinking she might have picked up a fox's scent, or was unable to settle into her new surroundings, I lit an oil lantern, grabbed my wellies, pulled my overcoat over my calf length nightie, rushed out of the back door and scurried down to the paddock with the children in hot pursuit.

I pushed open the gate, and with the lantern held in front of me, I hurried across to the stables.

Donkey redoubled her efforts as I opened the stable door and stepped inside. Holding up the lantern I took in the scene. Donkey was standing with her head over the stall gate while Bessie, usually so docile, lifted her head to join in with a series of neighs.

I got the message at once and opened Donkey's stall. She stopped the racket immediately and waited patiently while I opened the gate to Bessie's stall and moved aside so that she could enter. Donkey walked slowly up to our big old shire and once again, the pair rubbed heads. Bessie's stall was huge and there was plenty enough room for the two of them, even if they were sleeping lying down, so I pulled the stall door shut and wished them both a good night.

Out in the paddock, I ushered the giggling children towards the gate. The night was clear and a frost was beginning to form on the tips of the grass stalks. I pulled my collar up and shivered. It wasn't the sort of weather to be wearing a nightie outdoors, thick coat or not.

'We should give donkey a new name,' Harriet said. 'Donkey just doesn't seem right.'

'What do you suggest?' I asked, as I pulled the five barred gate shut and tied it off.

'We should call her Bray,' said Stephen. 'It's all she ever does.'

And so, it was decided. Donkey now had a proper name. On the way back to the house, I resolved to get her a leather harness, with her new name burned into it. Bessie had one, so it was only right that Bray should have one too.

Bray settled in well, and was rarely ever seen more than a couple of metres away from our big shire.

On Wednesday, the following week, Barney announced that the ground had dried out enough for us to plough up the bottom field. Being on a natural slope, all of our fallow fields drained well and that morning, he had walked the two remaining unploughed fields carrying a sharpened pole that he poked into the ground here and there to test how dry the top layer of soil was.

He harnessed Bessie and led her to the first pasture, which was in clear view of the paddock. Bray stood forlornly, her head hanging over the perimeter fence. Spotting Bessie in the neighbouring field waiting to have the plough attached, she lifted her head and roared her displeasure.

Barney tapped Bessie on the flank and took hold of her harness to begin the ploughing process. Bessie, usually so compliant, stood her ground and refused to move. Barney tried again, coaxing her with soothing words. Eventually he resorted to bribery and fed her one of the mint humbugs he kept in his pocket. Bessie happily ate it, but refused to budge. Meanwhile, our new lodger's plaintive calls, echoed around the farm.

After ten minutes of the standoff, Barney gave in and marched back up to the paddock. As he pulled the gate open, he was forced to leap aside as Bray hurtled past him, galloped across the open ground, burst through a small gap in the hedge and trotted up to Bessie's side. Barney hurried after her, worried that he might soon be involved in a game of chase around the farm. He needn't have worried.

As he walked into the field, Bessie, without waiting for a command, began to pull the plough. Bray, taking a cue from her big, lumbering partner, began to trot alongside. Barney hurried around Bessie's back and took hold of the harness on the left side of her head.

Bessie trod the fields all morning, up and down, up and down, the furrows so straight, the Romans could have built their roads along them. Bray trotted along happily at her side. At lunch, when Barney sat down on an old tree stump to eat a sandwich, the two new friends stood side by side, chewing grass until he got to his feet again, and the trio went back to their labours.

The farm now had a new celebrity, and word got around fast. On Saturday morning, half a dozen children walked the half mile down the lane and formed an orderly queue at the farm gate, their pockets stuffed with apples and carrots. After a few minutes, a cheer went up as the farm lads led Bessie, and a noisy Bray, up to the gate to be patted, fussed over and fed their treats.

During the last week of the month, Toby called, to see how his old friend had settled in. I led him down to the pasture where Bray spotted him instantly. Calling out a loud greeting, she trotted across the field to welcome him to her new home.

'Blimey, she's like a new animal,' said Toby with a huge grin. 'If I'd have known she could run like that I'd have entered her in the Donkey Derby at the Country Fair.'

The two greeted each other like the old friends they were, but after a few minutes, Bray began to back away, and after giving Toby one last, lingering look, trotted back to Bessie who was watching proceedings from her favourite corner of the paddock.

As she turned the final page of the chapter, Jess found a photograph, placed towards the top of the page, as though used as a book mark. The picture showed an aging, dappled, shire horse and a grey-haired donkey, standing side by side at the paddock gate, both baring their teeth as if grinning for the camera. On the back, in Alice's beautiful script were the words. The Inseparables. Bessie and Bray. April 1940.

Jess suddenly became very emotional. She had heard the story of Bessie and Bray from Alice's own lips when she was a child.

She got up from the table, opened the back door and walked between the old barn and the dirty concrete slab, that was all that remained of the milking parlour, and strolled into the meadow that once housed the old shire horse and her best friend. The stone slab was in what Alice had described as, 'Bessie's favourite corner of the pasture.' Jess crouched and pulled up a clump of grass that was growing over the memorial and using the tuft to brush away a layer of accumulated soil, she read out the words that had been lovingly carved into the stone. *Bessie and Bray. Together Forever.*

Chapter 34

At five forty-five, Jess's phone rang.

'Hello, Bradley. How are you?'

'I was better before I heard from the SRA a few minutes ago, honestly, Jess, I—'

'Hang on, what's the SRA when it's at home?'

'The Solicitor's Regulation Authority.'

'Okay, what did they want?'

'They want... to investigate my legal practice, especially my dealings with you and the trust.'

'The trust... Why? What's wrong with the trust?'

'Nothing is wrong with the trust, Jess. It's just that someone... Your grandmother, I assume, has put in a complaint, alleging malpractice.'

'Malpractice? What are you supposed to have done?'

'Well, according to your grandmother, I am using my position to take advantage of a client by forming an improper relationship. That client is, of course, you.' Jess could hear the anger in Bradley's voice.

'That's ridiculous.'

'Unfortunately, according to the regulations, she does have a point regarding an improper relationship. Fortunately, apart from handing over the annual allowance you are entitled to, we haven't made any joint decisions regarding the fund. So, she will have great difficulty proving her allegations. The one thing she can prove is that our relationship status broke the rules.'

'Do you mean I'm not allowed to have any sort of relationship with you outside of the office? That's hardly fair, and anyway, my friend's mother married the solicitor who worked on her behalf during her divorce. No one tried to stop them.'

Bradley sighed. 'It's a grey area, Jess, but your grandma has obviously done her research.' He paused, 'I've just read a few paragraphs from the SRA guidelines. My contact emailed me a copy so that I could familiarise myself with them.

'Basically, they state that while it isn't illegal for a solicitor to have a relationship with a client, the practice must put systems and controls in place, to assess whether the depth of that relationship might impair the solicitor's ability to act in the best interests of the client.'

Jess listened intently as Bradley continued.

'A Family Lawyer should not have sexual relationships with a client. Should such a relationship develop, the solicitor should immediately make it clear to the client that they can no longer act on their behalf.'

Bradley cleared his throat. 'So, you see, Jess, she has me over a barrel. I will have to stop acting for you, at least until the investigation into my practice is over. Fortunately, I spoke to Sarah, one of our partners and she is happy to take on the role of trustee on a temporary basis, which means we won't have to offload the trust onto another firm of solicitors.'

'Oh, Bradley, I'm so sorry. I thought you had called to say you were going to drop round. I was getting my hopes up.'

'I can't do that. Sadly, our personal relationship is over. I'm sorry, Jess, but I can't risk my career over...'

'Over what? A one-night stand, a fling that meant nothing?'

'Jess, you have to understand, I've worked so hard to get where I am, I can't just throw it away on... Look, I don't mean it to sound as bad as it did, but...'

'But it does mean what it sounded like. I'm not worth the risk to your career.'

'No... Jess, look, I like you, I really do. I wish to God that your grandmother hadn't turned up when she did, another half hour and I'd have been back at the office and she'd have been none the wiser.'

'And there was me thinking you were different to the other men I've had the bad luck to form relationships with, but you aren't, you're just the same. Your interests will always come first; you're only ever going to think of yourself. Christ, Bradley, you're as bad as Calvin.' Jess felt tears well up in her eyes.

'I'm nothing like him. Jess, listen. I don't want to fall out with you over this, let's wait until the inquiry is over. Let the dust settle. Maybe we could meet for a coffee and I can explain what I really meant to say, face to face.'

Jess's voice began to crack.

'I really liked you, Bradley. I thought my luck had changed.' She wiped at the tears running down her cheeks. 'It seems to me that you got what you wanted and now you're looking for a way out. Well, you don't have to look any longer. You're out.'

'Jess, please, let me explain properly.'

'Do you think I'm stupid or something, Bradley? You explained it all perfectly. You see me as a liability. Well, that's fine. You've just got rid of that problem. Now, if I need to sign anything agreeing to Sarah taking on the trust role, post it to me, I'll sign it and send it back. Actually, thinking about it, it might be best for her to take on the role permanently.'

'Oh, Jess, don't be—'

'Goodbye, Bradley.'

Jess hit the red button on the phone to end the call. Then she walked through to the front room, threw herself on the sofa and let the tears flow.

Chapter 35

At seven-thirty, with no tears left to cry, Jess got up from the sofa, picked up her car keys, grabbed her coat and walked out to the car. A frost was already beginning to form on the roof and bonnet of her Toyota. Jess looked up to a cloudless sky to see the universe open up before her eyes. The farm was well away from the light pollution of the town and she had a clear view of the ancient, blinking stars that had emitted their twinkles billions of years ago, arriving just in time for her to see them.

Still thinking about the vastness of the universe, she started up the car, switched on her lights and drove to the Tesco Direct store in town where she made her way to the wine aisle and picked up two, mid-priced bottles of Pinot Grigio from the chiller cabinet. On the way to the checkout, she suddenly thought of her mother and the alcohol problems blighting her life. Jess could remember her mum drowning her sorrows in a wine glass when she was growing up, and making a quick decision, turned around and placed one of the bottles back in the chiller.

At the counter, she produced her card to pay for the wine, then, seeing the glass cabinet behind the till operator, she ordered a packet of twenty cigarettes and a disposable lighter.

Back in the car, Jess switched on the radio just as the weather forecaster was speaking.

As temperatures plummet to minus five degrees overnight, residents of the area are being asked to keep an eye on their energy use as one of the region's power stations is shut down for maintenance.

Jess shivered at the thought even though her car heater was on. The farmhouse was centrally heated, Alice had installed a new boiler only three years previously, but the old place had many a draughty corner.

When she arrived home, she poured herself a generous glass of wine, picked up the cigarettes and lighter and closing the back door behind her to keep in the heat, she sat on the back doorstep and spent half an hour stargazing as she smoked cigarette after cigarette.

She had given them up, supposedly for good when she first met Calvin who hated the smell of tobacco smoke, but quitting had always felt more like a bereavement than an achievement. She had often thought about grabbing a packet as she stood at the supermarket checkout during a particularly difficult time in her relationship with him. She had always managed to overcome the urge, telling herself that it was stupid to take up the habit again after the horrendous time she'd had getting over her addiction. Tonight, felt different for some reason. Maybe it was the absence of Calvin's accusing look as he sniffed her clothes when she got back in from shopping, or a trip to the library. Maybe the stress of all that had happened over the past few weeks had finally got to her. Whatever the reason, she thoroughly enjoyed the three cigarettes she had smoked and stubbed out on the concrete floor.

Craving sated, she picked up her empty glass and stepped back into the kitchen where she took off her coat and hung it on the back of a chair before pouring herself another glass of wine. Carrying it through to the lounge, she placed it on Alice's old lion's foot coffee table and picked up her phone, intending to call her best friend, Sam. Noticing the black screen, Jess cursed and pressed the start button only for a charging bar to appear, showing her that her phone was almost completely dead.

'Damn,' she said as she plugged the USB cable into the mobile and sat it on Alice's writing bureau to charge.

Picking up her glass, she sat on the sofa and wriggled her bottom about until she became comfortable and picking up the remote control, she switched on the TV and flicked to Netflix.

Selecting an episode of The Crown that she had already seen. Jess leaned back into the cushions and thought about the ramifications of what Martha had done.

She decided that she would call in on her grandmother in the morning for the heart to heart she had allegedly been craving. She was just working out which approach would work best, when the power went off.

Chapter 36

Jess suddenly found herself in total darkness. Easing herself off the sofa, she took baby steps across the lounge until her knee made sharp contact with the corner of the coffee table. Cursing, she reached down and rubbed her leg, then placed her hand on the edge of the table as she worked her way around it. Trying to visualise the room that she had spent so many hours in with Alice, she edged sideways until she bumped into the wall, from there she felt her way along until she found the frame of the kitchen door. Trusting her judgment, she stepped through, turned slightly to the left and groped her way across the room until she found the big, oak table. She ran her hands over the surface carefully until she located her new lighter, then flicking it on, she crossed to the wall units and rummaged through what Alice called her 'bits and bobs' drawer, until she found one of the candles that Nana had kept for such emergencies.

The lighter was getting hot to the touch, so Jess quickly lit the wick of the candle and extinguished the lighter flame. Taking a saucer from the cupboard, she allowed a little of the melted wax to fall onto its smooth, white surface, then sat the candle in it. Placing the saucer on the table, Jess walked to the kitchen window and looked out. All of the lights were out across the entirety of the housing estate that had been built on the land that Alice had sold to the developers over the years. In the far distance, the street lights on the Gillingham road were still lit, telling her that a local substation must have gone down under pressure of demand. Suddenly, feeling an urgent need to pee, Jess picked up the saucer and carried it upstairs.

When she came out of the bathroom, she went through to the spare bedroom where she had stored Alice's old landline telephone. She plugged the RJ11 connector into the upstairs phone socket, picked up the cordless handset from the cradle and held it to her ear but there was no dial tone.

'You idiot, Jess,' she said to herself. 'These digital phones have to be plugged into the mains to work.'

Shoving the phone and cradle back into the cupboard, she held the candle in front of her and walked along the passage to her own bedroom where she had left her laptop. She placed the saucer carefully on the bedside table and opened up her computer. Finding no internet signal because of the power cut, she sat down on her bed and read back the twenty-paragraph article she had written the day before.

Half an hour later, satisfied with the work in progress, she snapped the laptop shut, stuck it under her arm and picking up the saucer again, she headed for the stairs.

Shielding the flame in case her movement caused it to go out, she walked along the landing, but as she reached the top of the stairs, a single flash of light exploded across the window that overlooked the front of the house. Puzzled as to who would be wandering along the remote lane in a blackout, Jess put her laptop on a side table, hurried to the front window and looked out just in time to see a figure carrying a torch, walk slowly past her car and disappear down the side of the house.

Thinking quickly, Jess assessed the situation. *Surely if it was someone she knew; they would come to the front door? Why would they go all the way around to the back?*

She pricked up her ears as she heard the click of the gate latch, then, panic struck as she realised that she hadn't locked the back door after going outside for a cigarette earlier in the evening.

Holding the saucer in front of her, Jess raced for the stairs but as she reached the top step, the candle flame flickered in the sudden rush of air, then died.

'Noooo.' Dropping the saucer, Jess reached out her hand and felt for the banister. Using it as a guide she hurried down the stairs, turned right into the hall and after stumbling twice, found the kitchen door just as the torch beam flashed across the back window. Taking advantage of the small amount of light that filtered into the kitchen, Jess fell to her hands and knees and crawled as quickly as she could across the wooden floor. Reaching up as she neared the door, she twisted the key in the lock, turned her back to the door and tucked her knees under her chin as the sound of the creaking gate, echoed across the yard.

Jess wrapped her hands around her knees, and scarcely daring to breathe, twisted her head to the right as the full torch beam was directed into the kitchen. The ray of light moved back and forth across the room, lighting up the table, then the cupboards and the door to the lounge. She put both hands over her mouth and closed her eyes tight as she heard footsteps approach the door.

Jess held her breath as the intruder tried the handle. Then she felt a shiver of terror run down her spine, as whoever was outside, put their shoulder against the door and tried to force it open.

Thirty of the longest seconds in Jess's life later, she heard the footsteps retreat towards the gate. Desperate to know what the interloper was about to do next, she got to her hands and knees, then moving to a crouched position, scurried through the darkness until her shoulder hit the doorframe leading to the lounge. Forcing down the yelp that tried to escape her mouth, she felt for the opening, then slid along the floor on her stomach until she found the coffee table. Lifting her hand, she groped about on the table top until it came into contact with her phone. Hoping against hope that it had received enough charge to enable her to make a call, she pulled it off the table, pressed the 'on' button and with her heart pounding in her chest, watched the screen as it loaded up the phone's operating system.

As the home screen appeared, Jess took a quick glance at the status bar, and seeing only a tiny amount of charge in the phone, decided it would be better to speed-dial Sam, than spend time she might not have, waiting in a queue for the police to answer.

'Please, pick up, please pick... Sam? It's Jess... Yes, listen, my power is off and someone is trying to—' Jess looked at her phone in horror as the in-call icon disappeared, to be replaced, once again, by a black screen. Tears of frustration filled her eyes.

'Damn,' she spat as she dropped the useless phone onto the floor.

As someone tried the handle of the front door, Jess lay flat to the floor, then she listened intently as footsteps crunched on the gravel path beneath the window. A second or two later, a broken beam of light broke through a small gap in the curtains and flickered onto the TV screen and along the back wall. Hardly daring to breathe, Jess waited until she heard the footsteps walk back along the gravel path before crawling down the hallway, one hand flailing ahead until it made contact with the heavy, front door. Sitting sideways on, she rested her ear against it and listened.

After a few minutes of silence, she heard a screeching of brakes as a car came to an abrupt halt on the asphalt drive, then all hell seemed to break loose as doors were opened and a man's voice began to shout. A few seconds later, she heard fists hammering on the front door, then the letterbox was lifted and a clearly worried female voice yelled through it.

'Jess, Jess... It's Sam. Are you all right? Come on, love, let me in.'

Jess opened the door and fell into Sam's arms as the sound of a scuffle ensued from the side of the house. A minute or so later, Sam's boyfriend, Jamie, half-marched, half-dragged a hooded figure through the gate and onto the asphalt.

'Caught him at the back of the house,' he said, keeping a careful hold on his captive's arm.

Jess peered around Sam to get a better look. 'What are you doing hanging around my house,' she stormed.

The man lifted his free arm, pushed back his hood and pulled down the woollen snood that covered the bottom half of his face.

'Dad! What the hell...'

'I was just checking that you were all right, Jess.'

'With your face covered like that? Pull the other one,' Sam spat.

'It's cold,' muttered Bill. 'Honestly, Jess, I was worried about you, what with those men hanging around the farm.'

'Men?' Sam gave Jess a puzzled look.

'Two blokes came around trying to put the frighteners on me, that's all,' said Jess, 'I was never in any danger then... but I tried to ring you when I thought they may have come back.'

She turned her attention to her father.

'If you were so concerned, why didn't you just knock on the door like any normal person? Why the flashlight through the windows, and why try the door handles?'

'I did tap on the door, but not very hard, I didn't want to scare you.'

'I didn't hear you knock, but I do know that you sneaked around the back and tried to force the door.'

'I thought someone might have broken in. I was just testing it.'

'Don't give me that, Dad. You were trying to scare me into handing over the money you need.'

'That's diabolical.' Sam took a couple of steps toward Bill and shoved her face into his. 'And you're a disgusting, creep. What type of father would do something like that?'

Bill struggled to break free from Jamie's grip. When he spoke, there was a note of desperation in his voice.

'I promise, Jess. I'm only dressed like this because it's so cold. I tried to ring, but when you didn't pick up, I thought I'd better walk down to make sure you were all right. That's all there is to it.'

'I'm calling the cops.' Sam pulled her phone from her pocket.

'No, please... don't bring the police into it, Sam.' Jess put her hand on her friend's arm. 'They won't be able to prove anything. There's been no damage done. They'd have to give him the benefit of the doubt.'

Sam looked from Bill to Jess and reluctantly returned her phone to her pocket.

'If you're sure...' She turned back to Bill. 'I don't care if she's your daughter or not, if I ever hear of you even getting as close as the end of the lane, I'll call the police and have you arrested for harassment.'

Jamie looked at Jess and shrugged. 'So, do I let him go?'

Jess nodded.

Once free of Jamie's grip, Bill straightened his jacket, pulled up his hood, and fixing Jamie with a glare, turned and walked onto the pavement that ran alongside the lane. As he reached the first of the bushes in the long hedgerow, he turned back and pointed a stumpy index finger at the tall, young man.

'You had better watch out for yourself.'

'Just clear off, Dad,' Jess called. 'I mean it too, go back to where you came from. Leave us alone, you're not wanted here.'

Bill waved her comment away with a flick of his arm, then turned and disappeared into the dark night.

Back in the house, Jess, guided by the flashlight on Sam's phone, relit the candle, then, using her lighter, lit all four burners and the two ovens of the gas cooker. Filling a saucepan with water, she put it on the hob and took three clean mugs from the hooks fixed to the closest of the wall units.

Before the water had even begun to simmer, the power came back on. Two minutes later it went off again, then five minutes after that, it came back on for good.

Jess plugged the charging cable back into her phone and loaded up the operating system. When the home screen slashed up, she checked her call log to find the only recent calls and texts she had received had been from Sam.

'Well, if there was any doubt, here's the proof. He didn't call.'

'I didn't think he had for a moment,' replied Sam who had known Jess's father for a few years. He had asked her to lend him money on more than one occasion when Jess was away at Uni.

'Ah, well, he won't come back now. I'll call the police myself if he does.' Jess pulled the photograph of the two men who had paid her a visit from the coffee table drawer and handed it to her friend. 'Any idea who these two muppets are? They're local that's for certain.'

Sam shook her head. 'No, but then, I wouldn't, living and working where I do.'

Jamie took a quick look and shook his head. 'I only moved in with Sam a few weeks ago. I'm from out of town.'

Sam put the photograph on the coffee table and wagged a finger at Jess. 'Report them. If they are local hoods, the cops will know them.'

'I will if I get any more trouble,' Jess promised. 'And thanks so much for coming over to rescue me.' She looked from Sam to Jamie and clapped her hands. 'Right, coffee or wine?'

'It had better be coffee for me if I'm driving,' said Jamie.

'You're not,' said Sam, firmly. 'At least not until the morning. You, my big, strong, knight in shining armour, are going to stand guard over us tonight. There's no way I'm leaving her alone after all that has happened.'

Jess walked to the fridge and pulled out the half bottle of wine she had bought from the store. 'Damn it. I actually picked two up but put one back, there's not enough left for me, let alone all of us.'

Sam looked directly at Jamie and raised her eyebrows. 'Sir Knight, your services are required. We have two damsels in distress, or at least they will be if their wine supplies aren't topped up.'

Jamie turned away holding his arm in the air.

'Sir Pinot de Grigio at your service,' he said, as he walked into the hall.

Jamie came back half an hour later with three bottles of wine. Placing them carefully onto the kitchen table, he went back out to the car and returned carrying three huge, pizza boxes.

'One Hawaiian, one meat lovers and one of those pointless veggie and cheese things,' he announced.

'You bugger, you know I've been on a diet these past three weeks.' Sam lifted the lids on all three boxes, took out a slice of Hawaiian, bit into it, then closed her eyes in ecstasy. 'Oh pizza, how I have missed thee.'

Jess rubbed her hands together, 'Ooh pizza, what a treat.' She put two of the wine bottles into the fridge, and placed three wine glasses on the table. 'In here or on the lumpy sofa?'

'Sofa,' said Sam and Jamie together.

The three friends ate, drank and laughed away the evening. At eleven o'clock, Sam yawned, stretched and announced that she was going to bed as she had to be up early for work. Jess stood up unsteadily and gave her a hug.

'Thanks again for looking after me.'

'That's what friends are for, my darling.' Sam returned the hug.

'You two go up. I'll sleep on the sofa tonight.'

'Not a chance,' replied Sam. 'The fates decree that I will, once again, be sharing your bed, my dear.' She turned to Jamie. 'Don't get any wild ideas if you hear the sound of bed springs, boinging away. We won't be having kinky sex. One of us will just be turning over.'

Jess laughed. 'I've got a new bed now, so he won't have a clue what we're up to.' She winked at Jamie.

'Well, if you find you need a man to assist you in your nocturnal endeavours, just give a shout out.'

Sam kissed him on the lips and pointed to the back door.

'Know your place, Sir Keeper of the Watch.'

'I'm so sorry about the state of the sofa,' said Jess, pulling a sad face. 'I'll get you a duvet and some pillows.'

When Jess got up at seven-thirty the next morning, she found that both her visitors had gone. When she walked through to the kitchen, she found a note on the table.

Any more nonsense, call the cops. Sam xxxx

As the kettle boiled, Jess tidied up the wine glasses and pizza boxes, then sat on the sofa to watch the morning news, but the only topic on offer was the upcoming General Election. Jess had got into politics during her Uni days and had been a bit of a radical, but over the last few years her opinions had mellowed. Recently, the rancour and the constant bickering in the House of Commons, with vote after endless vote on the Brexit Bill, had pretty much turned her off politics. She would vote, but she hadn't yet made up her mind which way.

After a bowl of muesli, she nipped around with the vacuum before showering. By the time she was dressed and ready to face the day, it was almost nine o'clock.

Jess was still determined to have it out with Martha, and picked up her phone to dial her grandmother's number, only to slip it into her bag without making the call.

Why should I warn her that I'm on my way? She just turned up here without a by your leave.

Jess pulled on her thick, winter jacket, grabbed her keys and bag, and walked out to the car. Still angry about Martha sticking her nose into her affairs, she started up her Toyota and fixing the road ahead with a stern look, she set off up the lane.

Ten minutes later, Jess arrived at the house that Martha shared with her younger sister, Marjorie. She parked up in the drive and walked slowly to the door, knowing that her grandmother had seen her arrive.

'Hello, Jessica, this is a nice surprise,' Marjorie gushed as she let Jess in.

'How's the tooth?' asked Jess.

'It's much better now, thank you. Martha sat with me while the dentist filled it.'

Jess stood on the door mat looking over her great aunt's shoulder towards the lounge.

'Is Grandma in?' she asked after a twenty-second silence.

'Oh, yes, she's in the drawing room. Do go in. I've just made tea, would you like a cup?'

Jess stepped into the lounge to find Martha sitting in an armchair, watching a house renovation program on TV.

'I had plans for that farmhouse, and the land around it,' she said, stiffly.

'Ah well, never mind, Grandma. I'll tell you what. Jot your ideas down on a bit of paper and I'll have a look. See if anything appeals to me.'

'Don't be facetious, Jessica, it doesn't become you.'

Jess dropped her bag and sat down in the armchair opposite Martha. The old woman looked up from the TV and studied her.

'What brings you here?' she asked with a look of suspicion on her face.

'Can't a granddaughter just drop by to see her relatives?' asked Jess, innocently.

Martha bridled. 'We both know why you're here, Jess. Now, stop beating about the bush and get to the point.'

'All right, Grandma, let's do it your way.' Jess's face hardened. 'I have one simple question and it's this. 'What do you think gives you the right to continually stick that big nose of yours into the affairs of others?'

Martha snorted.

'Affair is the right word for it. Don't you know he's a married man?'

'Was, married, Grandma... was.' Jess's hard stare matched her grandmother's. To her surprise, it was Martha who looked away first.

'I was doing what any caring relative would do. I was looking after your interests.'

'Looking after your own, more like.'

'I can assure you, Jessica, I did what I did because I love you and don't want to see you hurt.'

'Oh, what a wonderfully, caring family I have,' Jess replied with a steely look. 'My father was saying something similar only last night.'

'Your father wouldn't know how to do the right thing if there was a sign in front of his face, saying, this is the right thing to do,' Martha snarled.

'I agree, Grandma, but you and he are made from the same mould. The only difference between the pair of you, is that you are more subtle with it.'

Martha got to her feet and looked at Jess with narrowed eyes.

'Your, MARRIED, solicitor, hasn't followed the guidelines laid down by his own legal association. I know, I've looked into the matter at the library.' Martha began to pace the room. 'He is breaking their rules by having a sexual relationship with a client.' Martha stopped and leaned over Jessica. 'It is frowned upon even more, if the solicitor is making decisions that affect the client's financial situation. You would be classed as vulnerable under the rules of the professional organisation he belongs to. I couldn't just leave him to take advantage of you like that. I had to act. It was in your best interests.'

Jess reached over the side of the chair and picked up her bag.

'The only interests you have ever looked out for, are your own, Grandma. It's never been any different. You were so confident that you would be made the main beneficiary in Nana's will, even after treating her so abominably over all those years. You were her daughter but you behaved as though she was your arch enemy.'

'Don't you dare talk to me like this,' Martha stood, open mouthed as Jess continued.

'You never had a good word for her when I was growing up, you accused her of being a witch, of casting spells on you, of mistreating you as a child. You tried to extort money from her, you told lies about her to anyone that would listen. Is there any wonder she decided to cut you adrift?' Jess looked around the large, well-furnished room. 'You have enough to live comfortably, but you always want more. It's not your concern for my welfare that made you do what you did. It was pure, selfish, greed.'

Jess wiped an angry tear from her eye, but then her voice softened. 'I really liked Bradley, Grandma. He made me laugh, we got on really well together, he was everything that Calvin wasn't, and you... you, went and ruined it.'

Without waiting for a reply, Jess stormed past her grandmother and headed for the door.

'Jessica!'

'Jessica turned to fire off another volley at the old woman, but her attention was drawn to the TV where the mid-morning, local news program had just begun. On the screen was a female reporter, standing in the car park of the Wilson-Beanney Solicitor's office.

'Jessica I really must—'

'SHHH.' Jess pointed at the screen where the reporter was describing what she referred to, as a *'serious assault.'*

'The solicitor, Mr Bradley Wilson, was taken to St Margaret's Hospital where he was treated for facial cuts and bruising. He was allowed to go home after treatment and a period of observation.' The camera panned across to the office, then back to the reporter.

'The attack took place at five minutes past six, yesterday evening. If anyone has any information regarding the attack, or might recognise the description of the two men who assaulted Mr Wilson, they are asked to contact Crimestoppers, or their local police. Now, back to the studio.'

Jess looked from the screen to Martha's shocked face.

'I had nothing to do with that,' she said.

Jess gave her one last withering look, and turning on her heel, rushed out of the house.

Chapter 38

Jess rushed to her car and had started the engine and pulled away before she realised that she didn't know exactly where she was going.

She wracked her brains to try to remember what Bradley had told her about his living arrangements the day they had lunched together at the Café Blanc, but because of her heightened stress levels she couldn't remember where the flat was. Pulling up at the side of the road, Jess switched off the engine, grabbed her phone and did a quick LinkedIn search. He was listed but merely in his capacity as a solicitor, so only his office address was supplied.

Maybe I could access the electoral roll at the council offices? she thought, then quickly discounted the option. In this day of data protection, she would almost certainly need a better reason than she had for wanting to know his address. She then thought about accessing the census records through her Ancestry UK account, but again, there would only be limited information available.

There has to be a way... Jess suddenly had an idea, and pulling his business card from her bag she looked for his email address. Seeing that it ended with btinternet.com, she googled her phone for the BT online phone book, typed in his forename, surname and the area in which he lived and pressed search.

'GOTCHA!' she cried as his name appeared on a short list of Wilsons. She checked the address the listing showed and realised it was only a couple of miles out of town, just off the main Gillingham road.

Jess left the screen open on the search page, started the engine again and set off for Atwood Park apartments.

Knowing the area well, she turned off the main road on her grandmother's estate and drove along a narrow B-road until she hit the dual carriageway. A mile and a half further along, she pulled off onto a private track that led to a newly tarmacked area with enough room for a couple of dozen cars. Jess parked in front of a row of young Cypress trees, got out of the car, checked her phone again for the apartment number, then walked along a shrub lined path and up a set of wide steps that led to the huge, tinted glass doors that fronted the apartment block.

Built into the brickwork at the side of the doors was an electronic calling system. Jess pressed the button for flat two and waited. A few seconds later a familiar voice answered.

'Yes.'

'Bradley, it's Jess.'

'Jess? What the... I'll be right out, give me a minute.'

Jess waited patiently, looking through the doors into a wide entrance lobby. A minute or so later, Bradley appeared from a corridor at the top right-hand side of the foyer. He shuffled towards her, his face badly bruised, one eye almost closed and his right arm in a sling. Jess's face fell.

Bradley pressed a button on the right-hand side of the entrance and the glass doors slid open.

'Oh, Bradley, I'm so, so, sorry,' she said.

Bradley pulled his head back and winced in pain as Jess leaned forward to give him a peck on the cheek. He forced a thin smile, then looked nervously over her shoulder, into the car park.

'You had better come in,' he said.

She followed him in silence across the foyer and along a wide corridor until they reached a thick wooden door. Bradley pushed it open, then stood aside to allow Jess to walk in.

The apartment was expensively furnished with two, white-leather sofas, a black, leather recliner and an antique coffee table set in the middle of the room. The walls were hung with family photographs and a series of what looked to be, original water colours.

Bradley waved to one of the sofas and waited until she sat down before sitting on the sofa opposite.

Jess smiled softly and put her bag on the seat at her side.

'Bradley, I'm... oh, I've already said that.' She reached towards him. 'How are you feeling now?'

'Sore,' he said abruptly.

'I bet. You look it.' Jess withdrew her hand and clasped them on her lap. 'What happened, Bradley? I saw the report on the news this morning, I was so shocked, I had to come straight over to see how you were.'

He touched his face and winced again.

'Two men in hoodies were waiting for me when I came out of the office last night. I didn't notice them as I locked up. They took my watch and my wallet, but thankfully left my briefcase. It was just an opportunist mugging according to the police...' he hesitated. 'I think they're probably right; I don't have any enemies that I know of... apart from your grandmother that is, and I doubt that even she would go as far as to hire a couple of thugs.'

Bradley leaned back on the sofa.

'What were they like, these men? Did they say anything when they attacked you?'

'Not a word, they just set about me. I thought it odd that they didn't take my phone, but maybe they thought they'd got enough with my wallet and watch. I only had about fifty quid in my wallet so they'll be disappointed with that when they open it. I rang the bank and cancelled the cards as soon as I could stand up.' He paused. 'It's the watch I'm most upset about. My father bought it for me a few weeks before he died.'

'Oh, Bradley. I'm so sorry.'

'Don't be, Jess, It's hardly your fault.'

Jess bit her lip. 'What were they like?' she repeated her question.

'Oh, I don't know, just men, not teenagers, but young-ish. They had ski masks and hoodies on, both wore Nike trainers and track suit bottoms.'

'And they said nothing at all? So, you don't know if they were local or not?'

'Oh, I'm sure they were local. Why would anyone travel from a distance, on the off chance of meeting me as I came out of the office?'

'True, I suppose. It's just that… Well, two men came to the farm the other day, they demanded I pay fifty thousand pounds into a bank account. They gave me a phone number to call and said I'd be given the account number to transfer the money to.'

Bradley straightened, listening intently.

'And?'

'And nothing. I didn't do anything. I can't anyway without your agreement.'

'But how would these men know you had money, Jess? I don't understand.'

Jess sighed.

'I believe it's all to do with my father's gambling debts.' She held up a hand to silence Bradley. 'He owes money all over the place and not to the sort of people who are willing to allow him to set up a debt repayment plan. He owes money to people in London, bad people, and he's owed money to a couple of local gangsters, called the Duncans, for years. Now, I don't know if the two that called on me were sent by my father, trying to scare the wits out of me, or whether they're in the pay of the Duncans.' Jess looked down at her hands, then continued. 'I really don't know if the two who called on me were the same men that attacked you, that's why I asked if you thought they were local. It could still have been a random mugging, even after what happened to me.'

Bradley was quiet for a while. When he spoke, it was through gritted teeth.

'Why the hell didn't you warn me?'

'How was I to know they'd go looking for you? I had no idea what they know or who they know. As I said, Bradley, this could still just be an awful coincidence.'

'I don't believe in coincidences,' Bradley hissed.

Jess wrung her hands.

'Bradley, if the two events are connected, I—'

'Of course they're connected! Why in God's name didn't you go to the police?'

'Because... because... I thought my father might be behind it and he wouldn't have let them hurt me. I thought it was just a scare tactic... Even now I'm not sure he was involved, other than letting the Duncans think I was about to pay his debts for him.'

Bradley struggled to his feet.

'You and your bloody family. I wish to God I'd never met any of you.'

'Bradley, don't, it's not my fault. I didn't ask for any of this. I just turned up to hear what Nana had left in her will.'

'She's the instigator of all this. Why the hell couldn't the old... why couldn't she have just left a normal will like anyone else? Just keep everyone happy.... Do you know how many wills and estates I've dealt with in my working life? Hundreds, and not one of them brought anything other than a letter from another solicitor, contesting the will.'

Bradley eased himself around the coffee table.

'Your grandmother was a shrewd old woman who knew exactly the sort of people she had in her family. You thought she loved you, but she just left it to you to deal with the eruption of ugliness she knew would follow. Did she love you, Jess? or was she just having the last laugh on all of you?'

'Don't... don't.' Jess got to her feet and grabbed her bag. Her eyes glistened as she stared Bradley down. 'Nana was my best friend, the person I cared for more than anyone else on this earth, don't you DARE sully her memory like this.'

Bradley took a step back.

'Look, Jess, I'm sorry, I didn't mean to—'

'No, Bradley, you never mean to, do you? Like the phone call the other night. You say so many things you don't mean, I'm finding it difficult to believe anything you have said to me.'

Bradley held up his good hand.

'Jess, I'm truly sorry. It's just… he looked down at his sling, then pointed to his face with his good hand. 'I don't deserve this. I was only following Alice's instructions.'

'No, you don't deserve that, Bradley, I wouldn't wish it on anyone, but I've seen another side of you recently, and to be honest, I don't like it. I don't like it at all.'

Clutching her bag, Jess walked quickly down the hall and out into the foyer, leaving his apartment door open behind her. At the entrance she pressed the security button at the side of the glass doors, then head down, she hurried along the shrub-lined path to the car park.

As she reached her car, Jess took a deep breath, then opening her bag, she fumbled for her keys. Realising they were in her coat pocket; she held the bag strap in her left hand and fished for them. She was just about to open the central locking when she heard a voice. She turned to see an olive-skinned woman in her late twenties, standing behind the open boot of a VW Golf. Inside the boot were bags of shopping that bore the Waitrose brand.

'You're Jessica Griffiths, aren't you?'

Jess nodded.

'I'm sorry but I don't know you, do I?'

'No, you don't,' replied the woman, pushing strands of chocolate-brown hair out of her eyes. 'I'm Leonora Wilson, Bradley's wife.'

Chapter 39

Jess blinked.

'His wife? I thought...'

The woman smiled softly, then closed the boot of her car and held a hand out to Jess. 'Come, sit with me a while. I think it's time we had a chat.'

Jess clicked the locking button on her key fob and followed Leonora out of the car park to a paved, seated area to the right of the shrubbery. She sat down on a wrought-iron chair at a stone-topped table and gestured for Jess to sit opposite.

'How do you know me?' Jess asked. 'I've never seen you before.'

'Oh, I make sure I know who my husband is seeing behind my back,' Leonora replied. 'I know all about you, Jessica.'

Jess put her hands together on the table top. 'He told me he was single.'

'No, he didn't. He told you we were still friends. He never mentioned a divorce.'

Jess looked at her quizzically. 'How do you know all this?'

'Because he told me, you silly girl.' Leonora lifted the skirt of her dress and crossed her elegant legs. 'He tells me everything.'

'So... let me get this right. You and Bradley still live together?'

Leonora laughed. 'No, no, but we do see a lot of each other. We talk, we laugh, we are still the best of friends even though we live separately.'

She took a packet of cigarettes from her bag and lit one with a silver lighter before tilting her head to one side, blowing out the smoke as she studied Jess.

'You're very beautiful, I can see why he chose you.'

Jess blushed and tucked her dark hair behind her ears.

'He *chose* me?'

'Pursued you then, does that sound better?'

'Not really, no. I thought... well, it doesn't matter now anyway.'

'Don't be sad. He really likes you. I've never seen him like this with anyone before.'

'You mean he does this regularly?'

'Not regularly, but there have been one or two over the last few years.'

Jess shook her head, her mind reeling at the revelations.

'None of them got him worked up like you, Jessica. He was really excited when he met you. He spoke of nothing else for days.'

Jess shrugged. 'Am I supposed to be impressed by that?'

Leonora leaned forward and patted Jess's hand. 'No, I think it would take a little bit more than that.' She flicked the ash from the end of her cigarette, took a final draw, and stubbed it out on the stone table top. 'I was impressed with you, the moment I saw you. I even admit to being a little jealous as I could see in his eyes that he was really interested in you.'

'See in his eyes?'

Leonora laughed. 'At the little restaurant by the river. I sat in my car while you ate. I stood on the bridge as you talked to the swans.'

'That's a little over the top isn't it? Especially as you don't actually live together.'

'You might think so, my dear, but I have to look after my interests.'

Jess pulled her hand away; she was sick to death of hearing that word.

'Don't be angry,' Leonora said, soothingly. 'Anger makes us do things we wouldn't normally do.'

'Jess's mouth dropped open. 'Don't tell me you had something to do with the attack on him?'

'Now you're being ridiculous.' Leonora shook her head. 'I did damage his car when the two of you were canoodling inside your farmhouse though.' She tipped her head and studied Jess again. 'Canoodling... that's such a lovely word, isn't it?'

'Does Bradley know you did that? I blamed my ex for it.'

'No, I doubt Bradley would ever forgive me for damaging his mother's pride and joy. Are you going to tell him?'

'No, that should be something you do.'

Leonora got to her feet and picked up her bag. 'My conscience is clear. I think he deserved it.'

'But you said you were separated.'

'We are, but as I said earlier, we still... how shall I put it... comfort each other in times of need. If you see what I mean.'

Jess and Leonora walked side by side along the shrubbery path to the car park. When they reached Leonora's Golf, she stopped and held out her elegant hand.

'It's been an absolute pleasure to meet you, Jessica.'

'Likewise.'

Jess turned away and walked back to her Toyota. As she flicked the fob to unlock it, Leonora spoke again. Holding the key in her hand, she turned to face her.

'There is no future in your relationship with Bradley. We're married, we both come from good Catholic stock. Families like ours don't believe in divorce. His mother wouldn't allow it even if we wanted to, neither would mine, actually.' She pulled two bags of shopping, placed them on the floor, then slammed the boot shut. 'Having said all that, you do concern me, Jessica Griffiths. I'll be keeping a wary eye on you.'

Jess watched as Leonora picked up her shopping and walked through the gap in the Cypress trees before disappearing from view. Turning the key over in her hand, Jess unlocked her car and climbed in, then looked back towards the apartment block.

'Don't waste your time on me. He's all yours,' she said, firmly.

Chapter 40

'The stupid buggers, what did they think they were doing?'

Bill slammed his hand down on the table as he watched the local news.

Nicola placed a cup of coffee in front of him and looked over to the TV.

'Oh, Bill, you didn't have anything to do with that, did you?'

'Why would you even think that? Don't be ridiculous.'

'I just wondered. You did go out in the power cut last night.'

'Spying on me now, are you?'

'I just happened to be looking across the road from the shop window. I saw you go out.'

'Look, you stupid bitch. This attack happened at about six o'clock and if you saw me go out, you'll know it was much later than that. The lights were still on at six.'

'Where did you go then, Bill?'

'What I do and where I go is no business of yours, but, if you must know, I went to see if our Jessica was all right, what with the power going off an' everything.'

'That was thoughtful of you, Bill.'

'She's my daughter for Christ's sake. I worry about her living on her own in that big old house.'

'Was she all right?'

'Her friends were with her, that trollop, Samantha and some bloke.' He hesitated. 'There was a bit of a misunderstanding.'

'What do you mean misunderstanding? Bill, what have you done?'

Bill swept his hand across the table, knocking the coffee over.

'I've done nothing. I was just making sure she was all right. They jumped to the wrong conclusion, that's all.'

'I'll ask her when I see her next.'

He got to his feet and got hold of Nicola's arm.

'Bill, you're hurting me, let go.'

'I'll bloody hurt you all right if you don't keep your nose out of my affairs.' He picked the empty coffee cup up and stuffed it into her hand. 'Now, go and make another one.'

Nicola walked back to the kitchen rubbing her arm.

'I mean it, woman. Don't you dare go talking to Jessica behind my back.'

Before Nicola had the chance to boil the kettle, someone hammered on the front door.

'Nicola! Get that. If it's that bloody Kaur woman, tell her to sod off.'

Still rubbing her sore arm, Nicola opened the front door about a foot, then found herself pushed back against the wall as a broad, dark-haired man forced his way into the house. Spotting Bill cowering behind the table, he clapped his hands together and a huge smile appeared on his face.

'Hello, Owen… Oh, I'm sorry, It's Bill now, isn't it?'

'Dougie, I—'

'It's Mister Duncan to you, you snivelling little turd.'

'Sorry, Mister Duncan.'

Duncan pursed his lips. 'Now then… Bill. I've been looking forward to this little chat for about five years. Five, long years, Bill.'

'I'm sorry, I went away to try to get you your money back but—'

'Five years without a word, five years without you even attempting to make contact.' Dougie pulled a sad face. 'Do you know, at one time I thought you were dead. You won't believe how pleased I am to find out that you're alive and well.'

'Get out of my house,' Nicola called from the doorway.

Dougie didn't bother turning around, his eyes never left Bill.

'In a moment, love. Bill and I need to have a chat first. Isn't that right, Bill?'

Bill nodded dumbly.

'Would you like to know how I found you, Bill?'

Bill shook his head. 'You have your methods, Mr Duncan.'

'I'll tell you anyway, shall I? It was the two pathetic individuals you sent to beat up that lawyer.'

'That wasn't him, he had nothing to do with it,' Nicola shouted. 'Tell him, Bill.'

Dougie ignored her.

'I wouldn't have been any the wiser about your whereabouts, but with the police knocking on my door asking if I knew anything about the attack, well, I had to make my own inquiries.' He shook his head. 'Those two soft bastards gave you up in seconds, Bill. They gave you up, they gave up your get rich quick plans and they gave up working for you. They've left town for a while.'

'Doug... Mister Duncan, the only reason I came back was to make it right with you, honestly. I just want to make it right.'

'That's very nice of you, Bill. Just tell me, how are you going to go about it?'

'My daughter, Mister Doug... My daughter, she's inherited a fortune from her grandmother. She'll give you the money I owe; I promise.'

'But I don't want the money from her, Bill, I want it from you.' He turned around towards Nicola. 'As you see, I don't hurt women and I don't threaten them. Only cowards do that, hey, Bill?'

Bill nodded. 'If you say so.'

'Oh, I do, Bill. You see, my mother had a hell of a time with my dad when he was around. She protected us from the worst of it, and I always respected her for that. He was a coward, Bill, just like you.'

'I'll get the money... Five thousand, I'll get it as soon as I can. I just need to talk to her, she'll understand.' He looked towards Nicola. 'Won't she, love?'

Dougie took two steps forwards, grabbed hold of Bill by the neck and forced his head down onto the table.

'It was five thousand five years ago.' He lifted a fist and brought it down onto Bill's temple. 'But, with interest and inflation... I'd say that amount has risen somewhat.' He brought his fist down again. 'So, let's call it a nice, round, twenty thousand, shall we?'

'I'll get it... Let me up, I'll go find her. She'll pay, she—'

'You've got until the banks open in the morning,' Dougie let go of Bill, turned away and nodding towards Nicola, walked out of the house.

As Nicola slammed the door behind him, Bill stood up groggily and held his hand to his ear.

'Thanks for the help,' he spat.

'What could I do?' Nicola stepped towards him. 'I'll see if I've got something to put on that cut.'

'Never mind the sodding cut,' Bill raged. 'Just ring that bloody useless daughter of yours. Tell her to get round here this minute.'

Chapter 41

Jessica had just pulled out of the car park and onto the rough track when her phone rang. She took a quick look down, then stopped and picked it up.

'Hello, Mum?'

'Jess, could you come over please?'

'Is he still there? I'm not coming if he is.'

'Please, Jess, we need you... I need you, please come as quickly as you can.'

'What's wrong, Mum? is it him? What's he done now?'

'Please, Jess... for me.'

The call was cut off.

Jess sighed, then putting her car into gear, drove up the dirt track, waited for a lorry to cross in front of her, then pulled out behind it and headed for her mother's house.

As she climbed out of the car on Burnett Street, she noticed Mrs Kaur, waving frantically from the door of her shop. She opened it as Jess approached.

'I'm worried about your mother, Jessica. I saw a brute of a man go in about half an hour ago, he's gone now, but there was a lot of noise while he was there.'

'Thanks for your concern, Mrs, Kaur, but I think she's okay. At least she was a few minutes ago when she rang me.'

'I'm pleased to hear it, dear. He looked a nasty piece of work.' She paused, then spoke again as Jess turned her back to leave.

'I know she thinks I'm a bit of a tyrant, but I have her best interests at heart. I'd have sacked anyone else, months ago.'

Jess smiled at her. 'I know she has her problems Mrs Kaur, and I do appreciate you keeping her on. Going to work regularly will be the way out of the mess she's in, she just has to realise it.'

Jess crossed the road to her mother's house. the door opened as she was about to knock.

'Jess, thank goodness.' Nicola ushered her inside, took a quick look up and down the street, then closed it behind her.

Bill was sitting at the table, an ice pack held to his ear. 'Don't ask how I am, Jess.'

'I wasn't going to, Dad. I'm sure it was well deserved.'

Bill jumped to his feet. 'Don't take that tone with me, young lady. You're not too old to be put over my knee.'

'I'd like to see you try.' Jess glared at her father.

His demeanour quickly changed.

'Let's not fight all the time, Jess. Just for once, let's have a civilised conversation.'

Jess looked at her mother's tearful, frightened face, then giving her father another glare, sat down at the table and put her bag in front of her.

'Would you like tea, love?'

'No, thank you, Mum, I'll get one when I get home.' She turned to her father who had moved to the opposite side of the table. 'Well?'

'This,' Bill pointed to his bleeding ear. 'Was a gift from Dougie Duncan.'

'As I said, Dad...'

Bill took a deep breath as he tried to control his temper.

'He, erm, reminded me that I still owe him the money I borrowed before I went away.'

'I didn't think he'd come round to wish you a Happy Christmas,' replied Jess.

'This is just a taste of what he'll do if I don't pay him back when the banks open tomorrow.'

Jess shrugged. 'Do you even have a bank, Dad?'

'Jess, I'm serious. The man will kill me.'

'For five thousand pounds? I doubt it. It's not worth getting caught for.'

'It's twenty thousand, he added interest and inflation on.'

Jess burst out laughing. 'He's intelligent enough to work that out, is he?'

'Look, love...'

'Don't you 'look, love' me. Not after all you've done. Not after scaring the living daylights out of me last night.'

'Bill, you said it was a misunderstanding?' Nicola walked across the room and stood next to Jessica.

'It was, she heard me trying the door handle. I only went to see if she was all right. She scares easily.'

'I wouldn't have been scared if you'd knocked on the bloody door,' Jessica snarled. 'Instead, you crept around the place wearing a face mask and a hoodie.'

'Bill!'

'Shut up, you.' Bill's face turned to thunder. 'Now, Jessica... Jess... are you going to help me or not? I'm not just asking, love, I'm begging.'

'The answer is no, Dad. Stand up to him, or do a runner like you normally do when you get yourself into trouble. I'm not going to bail you out.'

Jess got to her feet, picked up her bag and walked around the table, heading for the door.

'Get your coat, Mum, you can stay with me until it's safe to come back to get your things.'

'She's going nowhere.' Bill pushed Nicola out of his way and squared up to Jess. Nicola crashed into the ironing board, knocking it over, the iron crashed to the floor.

'Mum,' Jess stepped across and held out a hand to help her up.

Nicola shook her head to clear it and reached out, but Bill had already taken hold of Jessica's shoulders and spun her around.

'Selfish bitch,' he spat, and hit her across the face with the back of his hand.

Jess staggered, tripped over her mother's legs and ended up on the floor on top of the broken ironing board. She looked back as Bill unfastened his thick leather belt and pulled it from the loops of his trousers.

'You need a lesson in manners,' he snarled.

Jess crawled for the door and yelped as the heavy belt buckle came down into her back. She looked up through tear-soaked eyes, as he raised his arm again.

'Dad, please...'

Before the second blow could land, Nicola threw herself onto Bill's back, digging her nails into his face. Bill dropped the belt, and flailed his arms while spinning around, trying to shake her off.

'Run, Jess, get out,' Nicola shouted.

Jess got unsteadily to her feet, her back stinging where the belt had landed. She eyed up the distance to the door and decided she could make it, but then changed her mind and turned back to face her father.

'I'm not going without you, Mum.'

Bill suddenly pushed himself backwards with all his force, crushing Nicola against the wall, knocking all the air from her lungs. Her grip slackened and she slid onto the floor. Mustering what strength she had left, she lifted her arm and pointed to the door.

'Go,' she gasped.

Jess took a step towards her helpless mother, then twisted away as Bill caught hold of her shoulder.

'I'll get help,' she screamed, then twisting, and dropping her shoulder in one movement, she dragged herself away from her father's grasp, and throwing herself forwards, placed a foot on the sofa and threw herself over the back. She landed awkwardly and felt a flash of pain shoot through her ankle as she straightened up. Bill bent over, grabbed his belt and came for her again, but by the time he got around the sofa, Jess had opened the door and was limping out into the street. She had only struggled three painful paces when he came out after her.

'Leave her alone,' Mrs Kaur stepped out from the doorway of her shop and hurried towards Jessica.

Wrapping an arm around her shoulder she helped Jess limp across the narrow street.

Bill stopped dead, then waving the belt at them, he swore, turned around, and went back inside, leaving the door, wide open.

'Mum,' Jess tried to get to her feet, but her ankle gave way underneath her. Sitting on the pavement, she opened her bag, grabbed her phone and dialled 999. To her utter relief, a voice came on the line almost immediately.

'Caller, which service do you require?'

'Police... and an ambulance... It's my father, he's gone mad, my mother is still inside, please hurry.'

'Where is the emergency? Where is the residence located?'

'Spinton, Burnett Street, number 47. Please hurry. He's gone mad.'

'The police are on their way, caller. Please stay on the line, I have some questions for you.'

Jess struggled to her feet and with the help of Mrs Kaur, half walked, half hopped back across the road.

As she got to the opposite pavement, she heard her father's angry voice inside the house.

'You stupid bitch. You ruined everything.'

Jess lifted her phone towards her mouth. The emergency call centre officer was still talking to her.

'Please, hurry, please hurry,' she whispered.

As she pulled the phone away from her mouth, she heard the distant sound of a police siren.

Chapter 42

As he walked back into the house, Bill fixed his eyes on Nicola who was just getting to her feet.

'You broke my iron, Bill,' she said, pointing at the appliance on the floor.

'Sod your iron.' Bill walked slowly towards her, still carrying his belt. 'I'm screwed, and it's your fault.'

'How is it my fault? You gambled all our money away, then borrowed more.'

'She would have given in.'

'I'm not going to stand by while you beat my daughter.' Nicola stuck out her chin belligerently.

'Then you can have the beating instead.' Bill lifted his belt in the air.

'I'm used to it. You've done it often enough in the past.'

'Because you didn't do as you were told.' He took a step forward and brought the belt down on her shoulder. 'You'll learn one day.'

Nicola held her arms in front of her face as the next blow landed.

'Go on, Owen… do you worst. I'm not frightened of you anymore. Jess was right, you're pathetic.'

He snarled as he brought down the belt again and again. Nicola sank to the floor and curled into a ball as Bill, gasping for breath, threw the belt to the side, fell on top of her, pulled her hands from her face and began to use his fists.

Nicola lifted her right hand and dug her nails into his cheek. He screamed in pain and the blows suddenly stopped raining down on her. Instead, she felt two strong hands around her throat.

'You've crossed me for the last time,' he growled, pressing his thumbs onto her windpipe as his thick fingers applied pressure to her neck.

Nicola gasped for air, her hands on top of his, scratching, trying to pry them away from her throat.

Bill squeezed harder. When Nicola's eyes flickered and her struggles became weaker, he leaned up slightly and straightened his arms to apply the extra pressure that would finish her off.

Nicola, feeling the blackness coming, stretched out her arms in desperation, her fingers grasping at the carpet. Then her hand came into contact with the iron, and using every last bit of strength she could summon, closed her fingers around the handle and swung it, catching him cleanly on the temple. The pressure on her throat eased and as Nicola smashed the iron onto his head a second time. His body jerked once, then he collapsed on top of her, his lifeless eyes staring into her face.

Chapter 43

Jess, hearing her mother's screams coming from the front room, eased herself away from the supporting arms of Mrs Kaur, and standing in the doorway, she propped herself up on the doorframe and looked at the carnage in the living room.

The furniture was scattered, dining chairs lying on their backs, at the far side of the room, close to the broken ironing board, lay two, motionless, bloodied figures. As the sound of police sirens got louder, Jess dropped to her knees and crawled across the room.

'Mum, Mum. Oh God, Mum.'

'Don't touch anything,' commanded a voice from the door.

Jess wasn't listening, she eased herself across the dirty carpet until she was next to her mother, then she reached out and stroked the blood-soaked fringe of her hair.

'Miss, please... the paramedics are here, come on, love, let them do their work.'

Jess looked back towards the door as the policeman moved to the side to allow two, green clad paramedics into the room. They hurried to the prone bodies and as one of them eased Jess away from her mother, the other, checked for her father's pulse.

He looked back to the policeman, shook his head, then placed his fingers on Nicola's neck to check her carotid artery pulse point.

'This one is still with us,' he called and pulling Bill's lifeless body to the side, he began to work on Nicola.

As a policewoman came into the room, the second paramedic sat Jess on the sofa and held her face in his hands. 'How are you, miss? Do you need assistance?'

Jess shook her head. 'It's just my ankle, I think I sprained it. Please, just see to my mum.'

The paramedic looked to the policewoman and flicked his head towards Jess, then moving back to his colleague, he pulled a pen torch out of his pocket, lifted Nicola's eyelid and shone the beam into her eye.

The policewoman crouched in front of Jess. 'I'm Tracey. What's your name, love?'

'Jess... Jessica... Griffiths.'

'All right, Jessica. These men are professionals, they know what they're doing, let's just let them get on with their jobs, eh?'

Twenty minutes later, Nicola was loaded onto a stretcher and carried carefully out to the waiting ambulance. Jess tried to get to her feet but the policewoman shook her head.

'I want to go with my mum,' said Jess, attempting to squeeze past the officer.

'In a minute, Jess. They'll wait for you, don't worry.'

A few minutes later another paramedic came in pushing a wheelchair. He helped Jess onto the seat, then pushed her outside towards a second ambulance. She struggled to get out of the chair, but gave up when the first ambulance pulled away, its lights flashing, its siren blaring.

'They need to work on her in the ambulance, love. You'd just be in the way.'

Jess gave in and allowed herself to be pushed into the ambulance. The medic locked the chair down to stop it moving about, then, after a nod from one of the plain clothed policemen attending the incident, he jumped down from the back of the vehicle and walked around to the cab as the detective took his place.

'Are you all right... Jessica, isn't it?'

Jess nodded, 'Just my ankle, is Mum going to be all right?'

'She's in good hands,' replied the policeman, non-committedly.

Jess ran her hand over her brow. 'Dad went mad, he...' she paused. 'He's dead, isn't he? He looked dead.'

'I'm afraid he is, Jessica.' He sat on the bed next to her wheelchair. 'What can you tell me about this? You don't have to go into everything at this stage, we'll take a full statement at the station, later.' He pulled out a notebook and a stubby, bookmaker's pen. 'How did it all start?'

Jess took him through the incident from the moment she had arrived at the house. 'I didn't see them fighting at the end, but I heard the commotion. I was outside with Mrs Kaur from the shop over the road.'

'So, it was more than just the usual domestic row. Even at the beginning?'

'Dad's been putting pressure on me to give him money for a while now. The family fortune was left to me and everyone has been demanding a share. It wasn't just Dad, they're all at it.'

'So, you feel like you're the piggy in the middle? Was your mum sticking up for you? is that how it started?'

Jess nodded. 'I'm sick of it. I wish I'd never seen the money.'

'Let me just jot down some personal details and we'll get that ankle sorted out for you.'

Five minutes later, the policeman shut his notebook, slipped it back into his pocket and got to his feet.

'All right, Jessica. I'd like you to come down to the police station in the morning. Any time between ten and twelve. If you can't physically get there yourself, we'll send a car for you.'

He jumped down from the ambulance, stuck his head around the side of the vehicle and whistled. A few seconds later, Tracey climbed in, followed closely by a paramedic who closed the back doors and banged twice on the side of the van. A few seconds later, Jess watched the row of parked police cars fade into the distance as the ambulance drove steadily away from the scene of the horror.

At the hospital, Jess's ankle was examined by a young, tired-looking doctor, who diagnosed ligament damage and booked her in for an X-ray. After queuing for an hour to get the procedure done, her ankle was bandaged, then she was given a pain killer and left to wait in a corridor for the doctor to give her the nod to go home. Tracey brought her coffee and chatted to her about her parents as she took notes. After a further twenty minutes and after listening to Jess's continuous nagging, asking her to check on the condition of her mother, she finally relented and walked over to a separate area of the A&E department where Nicola was being cared for in a single room. She returned ten minutes later with a smile on her face.

'She's going to be fine, Jess. They'll move her onto a ward later tonight.'

'Can I see her, please? I just want to see her.'

'She's been sedated, Jess, so there would be little point. Wait until she's been cleaned up a bit. You really don't want to see her as she is.'

'I do… Only for a minute, please?'

Tracey shook her head. 'I'm sorry, Jessica. It's not possible. We need to question her before she's allowed any visitors.' She patted Jess's hand. 'I'm sure you'll be able to see her tomorrow… the day after for sure. I know it's difficult for you, but honestly, don't worry, she'll make a full recovery.'

'Jessica Griffiths?'

Jess's head snapped up as her name was called out, hoping that the authorities had changed their minds and they were going to allow her to see her mother after all, but it was just the young doctor, giving her permission to go home.

'Shall I organise a taxi?' Tracey asked.

Jess shook her head. 'No, it's all right, my friend will pick me up.'

Jess pulled her phone from her pocket and tapped Sam's name on her contact list. She arrived ten minutes later and walked worriedly alongside, as Jess, now equipped with an underarm crutch, hopped her way down the corridor to the A&E entrance.

Chapter 44

The next morning, after phoning the hospital and receiving a positive update on her mother, Jess drove with Sam to the police station where she gave a formal statement, detailing everything she knew about the events leading up to her father's death. After signing the statement, she was told that she would be allowed to visit her mother on the following day.

'We'll be talking to her this afternoon,' the officer told her. 'When she's released from hospital, hopefully in a day or so, we'll take a formal statement, here at the station.'

'Will you... is she... are you going to charge her with an offence? She was only defending herself,' Jess asked.

'The Crown Prosecution Service will make that decision after we present them with all the evidence,' the officer replied. 'We're still waiting for the Post Mortem report. We should have the forensic report in the next few days.'

'You mean she could be facing a murder charge? That's insane. She was defending herself.'

The officer looked sympathetic.

'I can't promise anything, Jessica. It's unlikely that she would be charged with murder, given the circumstances, but, when you look at it, the only person who really knows what happened, is your mother.'

'It was self-defence,' said Jess, firmly. 'You don't need forensic evidence to see that.'

The detective held up her hands.

'We'll just have to wait and see what comes out this week.' She leaned across the table towards her. 'Look, Jessica. Don't worry about it yet. I know that's easier said than done, but just hang in there. Until we speak to your mum, we won't be able to make any sort of decision.'

The officer leaned back in her chair. 'Does she have a solicitor? We can arrange one for her if not?'

'Will the solicitor have to be present when she's questioned?'

'Not this afternoon. She'll be seeing our Domestic Abuse Support Officer, but when we question her formally, she will need one.'

'I'll organise that,' said Jess, 'I know… I'll find someone.'

The detective scooped up the papers from the desk and tapped them into a pile. Then she stood up and opened the door of the interview room. As Jess limped out on her crutch, Sam waved to her from a bench near the entrance.

'Are we going to the hospital?' she asked.

'No. They won't let me see her until tomorrow. They want to question her first.'

'Bugger.' She held the door open to allow Jess to hop out, then, after getting her settled in the car, she drove her home.

'Are you sure you don't want me to stay, Jess. You shouldn't really be alone after what's happened.'

'I'll be fine, Sam. I really do need to spend a bit of time on my own to process all this.'

'I'm not so sure. I honestly think you need a shoulder.'

'I'll call you if I do, Sam.' She gave her best friend a hug. 'Promise.'

'I'll come back in the morning; I'll give you a lift to the hospital.'

'What about work?'

Sam shrugged. 'Let me worry about that.'

'That's kind of you, thanks, Sam.'

She started to get up from the sofa, but Sam pushed her back down. 'I'll see myself out, love. You just rest up.'

When Sam had gone, Jess went through to the kitchen and made coffee, then sitting at Alice's old table, she sighed, then put her head in her hands.

'How has it come to this, Nana?' she whispered.

Sliding Alice's old notebook towards her, she ran her fingers lightly over the cover and opened it to a short chapter she had bookmarked.

August 1940

It became a regular event to look up from our labours to see squadrons of German bombers fly in from the coast on their way to bomb London and other industrial targets along the Medway and Thames. On the fifteenth I was having a strip wash in the kitchen after feeding the pigs, when Stephen came running in from the yard.

'Auntie Alice,' he cried. He pointed upwards; his eyes wide.

Quickly fastening my shirt, I followed him out to the yard where Harriet and Miriam were standing with a group of the lads, staring intently at the sky. I looked up and my heart sank. The sky was black with bombers. I had never seen so many at one time. Since July we had become used to seeing waves of them pass overhead, but nothing like on this scale.

Stephen began to cry. 'There are so many, how can we stop them?'

I put my arm around his shoulders and tried to shush his fears away, although I was thinking the same thing myself.

Then, as though God had summoned his angels, our Hurricanes and Spitfires dropped out of the clouds and began to attack them, flying in and out of the German formations, forcing them to break up, buzzing around them like angry wasps.

After a time, they were joined by the enemy fighters and we watched impotently, as the Luftwaffe and the scarily smaller number of RAF planes, danced across the skies in a deadly aerial ballet.

All day long the enemy planes came in wave after seemingly endless, wave of attack, and each time they were met by our brave pilots from Biggin Hill, Gravesend and the other RAF stations around the South

East. We cheered as each enemy plane either exploded in a ball of flames or spiralled down to the sea, a plume of smoke in its wake.

At dusk, as the last of our planes left the sky and returned to their bases around the estuary. We knew we had witnessed an historic day.

On the twentieth. Winston Churchill made a speech in the House of Commons, praising the brave young men who had fought like demons to protect us all. As he wound up his speech with the words, 'Never in the field of human conflict, was so much owed by so many, to so few,' the tears began to fall and we hugged each other and prayed to whichever deity might be listening, to keep our boys safe.

As Jess read the short, but emotional few paragraphs, her mood became darker. Although she knew that eventually, the war had ended and life had slowly returned to normal, she began to understand a little more of the circumstances that had moulded Alice into the strong-willed, determined, woman she had become. She doubted that she, herself would have had the resolve and strength of character to have survived those times.

She leaned on her elbows and stared across the table to where Alice would have sat after serving up dinner to her when she was a child, and thought about how her life had been turned upside down since her grandmother had died.

I wish I still had the magic wand you gave me for my seventh birthday, Nana, I'd wave it in the air and things would be back to how they were a few short months ago. Life was normal then. You were my rock, my inspiration. I had my job; my mum had her problems but nothing like the ones she has now. Dad was out of our lives, even Grandma was just her grumpy old self, not the greedy, self-serving creature your death seems to have turned her into. I even had a relationship, of sorts. All right, it wasn't perfect, Calvin was Calvin after all, but at least he was there at the end of a long day. At least he pretended to listen before turning the conversation around to himself. I know what he did, I know what he was, but... I miss him, Nana. I'd give anything to go back to how things were. I don't want this; I can't handle the responsibility. I'm not as strong as you. I thought I could read people but the idea of money changes them, and I don't know who they are anymore.

What did you think of Bradley, Nana? Did you see through him? I bet you did. Men, eh? We have always been attracted to the wrong type. Why is that? We're both intelligent, independent women, yet we fall for the worst sorts of men. Are we really that easily fooled? Do we secretly want to be made to suffer, or is it just the element of danger we can smell in these people?

I'm dreading the next few days, Nana... please, if you have any influence at all, if you know Mum's Guardian Angel, put in a word for her. None of this is her fault. I know you had your issues with her, but they were pretty much all caused by Dad. She could have had a much better life without his controlling influence, but she loved him so much. I hope she can get over this. It could quite easily destroy her.

Did you foresee any of this, Nana? I can't believe you would have left me alone to face it all on my own. I feel so alone. Even your presence seems to have vanished. I can't feel you around me anymore. Please come back and help me find a way through. I don't think I can go on like this.

The room was dark by the time Jess got up from the table. Reaching for her crutch, she limped into the front room where she switched on the light and slumped down on the sofa. A few seconds later her phone rang. Without looking at the caller's name, she hit the answer button and held the device to her ear.

'Hello, Jess... It's Bradley. Do you think we could meet?'

The End

If you enjoyed The Legacy, you might also enjoy the first book in the series.

Unspoken

A heart-warming, dramatic family saga. Unspoken is a tale of secrets, love, betrayal and revenge.
Unspoken means something that cannot be uttered aloud.
Unspoken is the dark secret a woman must keep, for life.
Alice is fast approaching her one hundredth birthday and she is dying. Her strange, graphic dreams of ghostly figures trying to pull her into a tunnel of blinding light are becoming more and more vivid and terrifying. Alice knows she only has a short time left and is desperate to unburden herself of a dark secret, one she has lived with for eighty years.
Jessica, a journalist, is her great granddaughter and a mirror image of a young Alice. They share dreadful luck in the types of men that come into their lives.
Alice decides to share her terrible secret with Jessica and sends her to the attic to retrieve a set of handwritten notebooks detailing her young life during the late 1930s. Following the death of her invalid mother and her father's decline into depression and alcoholism, she is forced, at 18 to take control of the farm. On her birthday, she meets Frank, a man with a drink problem and a violent temper.
When Frank's abusive behaviour steps up a level. Alice seeks solace in the arms of her smooth, 'gangster lawyer' Godfrey, and when Frank discovers the couple together, he vows to get his revenge.
Unspoken. A tale that spans two eras and binds two women, born eighty years apart.

'The characters in the book have been created so well, they are strong, believable and memorable people. I particularly loved Alice for her strength and her best friend Amy. She is a woman everyone needs for a friend.'
Beyond the Books.

'Unspoken' is superbly written. I was blown away by the story, the characters and the author's writing style. The author certainly knows how to grab your attention and draw you into the story without you realising it.'
The Ginger Book Geek

'If family saga's and dual time novels are your thing, you'd be hard pushed to find a more enjoyable one than Unspoken. It's got drama, love, intrigue, revenge and secrets - so basically everything you need for a captivating read and that's exactly what I thought it was. I've also heard on the grapevine that there will be a sequel. I really hope that this is the case, but failing that, another book from this talented author would make me very happy!'
Neats